THE THORN AND THE SPIRE

KATHERINE MCINTYRE

Cover typography by: Cormar Covers

Illustration by: Linda Noeran

Editing: SJ Buckley

Printed in the United States of America

To the rebels with a cause, the people who know how to form community and when to stand up and fight, this one is for you.

ACKNOWLEDGEMENT

This series has been brewing in the back of my head for a long time now in various incarnations. And while I got my start in fantasy and paranormal romance, it's been a long while since I've been in that sphere, so I've been nervous about the return. However, it also felt a bit like coming home too.

For The Thorn and the Spire, I owe the biggest thanks to Molly, Lydia, and Rob for beta reading this book and making sure Beau and Cillian's story was the Beauty and Beast vibes I needed it to be. Also, thank you to Lydia, Rob, Molly, KC, Charlie, and Alethea for listening to me panic about hopping over into a different subgenre and still encouraging me regardless. Y'all are amazing.

I also owe a large shout out to my reader group for sharing their love for the Whipped crew with me. Your enthusiasm keeps me excited about this universe! A huge thanks as well to Yoly from Cormar Covers for the typography and Linda Noeran for the art illustration, both of which I adore, and to SJ Buckley for her sharp editorial skills.

I'm so grateful to my wonderful readers. Every review, every message, every comment helps encourage me to keep writing, to keep creating stories, and I appreciate you all so much.

And as always, a thank you to my caring friends and family for the support and encouragement—I wouldn't be able to do any of this without you.

CONTENT WARNINGS

This book includes on-page violence, including a murder, knotting, CNC, bondage, rough play, and edging.

CONTENTS

CHAPTER 1

No one went to Haven without a reason.

The reason might be refuge. It might be camaraderie. It might even be a desperate shot in the dark. However, Haven wasn't the sort of place one just wandered into.

The arrival was intentional.

And tonight, I was clutching onto a shot in the dark with all my might.

The neon lights illuminated the sign from the classic chrome exterior, Haven Diner in the bright yellows and greens. Haven sat at the end of the block, an iconic spot in Peregrine City. Whether you were vamp or human, witch or demon, it didn't matter here. Haven was protected. The spells in place leveled the playing field, providing a no man's land in a city full of chaos.

Sweat prickled my palms as I approached. What the hell was a nobody like me doing here? This was way outside my pay grade. I was equipped to handle patrons' questions and categorize stacks of books, not to engage in illicit meetings at Haven. Yet this was my only option.

Dad had been missing for days now.

I ran my hand through my hair, but that mussed up the strands, and my footsteps echoed with a *boom*, *boom*, *boom*, like the tolling of a bell. Maybe I was a little too sheltered. This shouldn't be such a nerve-inducing thing. Just a meeting at Haven. *The* Haven.

Granted, growing up in the suburbs of Peregrine City, the mesh of monsters and humans wasn't as common as it was here. When Dad had first moved us to the city five years ago, I'd gawked at all the different types of monsters and magic users that walked along the crowded streets. I'd been thrilled. I'd read stories of monsters and fantastical creatures for years, only ever getting an occasional glimpse.

The air held a hint of decay, but whether from the denizens of the streets or the leaves underfoot was a mystery. I tugged at the strap of my messenger bag, which was laden with a handful of books I was working through. Not that I needed them for this meeting, but I'd brought them anyway as emotional support.

I walked up the path to Haven Diner, the burnt-sugar smell that lingered in certain spaces of the city heavy with magic users tickling my nose. The chrome exterior gleamed under the surrounding street-lights, and the sense of danger the night brought put me even more on edge. My hand settled on the cool handle of the door, and I summoned my nerve.

I needed answers, and this was the place to get them.

When I stepped inside, the cozy interior struck me first. Despite some neon glow accents, the lights were a soft yellow and hung interspersed throughout the different booths, all dark-green vinyl with purple stripes. The floor was a checkerboard black and white, and the beige walls were like parchment paper, which fit perfectly with the purple velvet curtains.

A short woman stood at the host stand, her brunette hair pulled back into a neat plait. She had a guarded air to her rather than a welcoming one, but that fit my expectations of the place.

"By yourself?" she asked, grabbing a menu.

I licked my lips. I was early, so I knew my contact hadn't arrived yet. "I'm meeting someone, so I'll snag us a seat now."

"Sounds good," she said as she grabbed another menu. "Follow me."

Her footsteps didn't make a sound as we headed over to an open booth in the back, and curiosity filtered through me. Something about her broadcast danger and alertness, and I had the feeling she wasn't a garden-variety human like me. Humanoid didn't mean human, which was something I'd learned at an early age when my best friend in grade school started spurting flames. His family had moved from the burbs shortly after that, heading to the city.

I settled into the vinyl booth, which was surprisingly comfortable. The scent of spice lingered in the air—cinnamon and nutmeg, like bottled fall.

"What can I get you to drink?" she asked, her hand on her hip.

I licked my lips. Right, I needed to order something instead of just looking sketchy. "Coffee, please. If you've got a strong one, that's my preference."

"Got you covered," she said. "First time visiting here?"

"How could you tell?" I wrinkled my nose. Apparently I was as subtle as a sledgehammer.

"The whole doe-eyed look." She smirked. "I'll be right back with that coffee."

I withheld my groan and instead took the time to look around. As much as I interacted with all walks of life now at the library, there was a higher cluster of supernaturals in Haven due to the nature of the place. A horned satyr sat with a human in the other booth, engaged in an in-depth chat over pancakes, and a few down from them was a cecaelia, their purple tentacles spilling out of the side of the booth as they flipped through the menu.

Dad had left me a number to call in case I needed help. Sure, he hadn't explained who the guy was, just that his name was Maury and he was a catch-all when it came to information. Considering Dad worked as an accountant, I wasn't sure why he'd need a contact like that, but I guess it was good he had one because I was utilizing it now.

The server swung over with a piping hot mug, the steam wafting from the top. "Here you go. Let me know if you need me." The look she shot me implied that she thought the help would be necessary. I wasn't sure if it was a promise or pity, but I appreciated it either way.

I took a sip from the steaming liquid, enjoying the way it slid down my throat, even if my nerves simmered. Maybe I could pull out one of my emotional support novels and pretend I was sitting here reading a book and grabbing coffee, not waiting for a random contact to show.

Before I could take my book out, the door swung open again, drawing my attention. An older creature strode in, at least half my height and humanoid despite the forked tail and claws. An imp. He had the wizened, bushy eyebrows you'd expect on a grandfather, as well as wrinkles lining his features. His dark gaze landed on me, and his lips slid into a smile.

A shiver raced through me, a reminder of how out of my depth I was. To my surprise, after briefly conferring with the server, he headed in my direction. Was this Maury? I'd assumed he'd be human, but maybe that was an oversight on my part. Not that my father was a

Human First guy by any means, but he still didn't have friends who were anything but.

The imp stopped in front of my table, and he scanned me over a second time before arching a brow. "You're Hank's son?"

"Maury?" I asked, my voice shockingly steady. The coffee must've helped.

His eyes crinkled as his grin revealed fangs. "Yeah, kid. That's me." He slid into the seat across from me with ease. I didn't trust him per se, but not because of the imp thing. No, it was the familiar way he strode into the situation, as if he were used to dealing with desperate people, that rang my warning bells.

But we were in neutral territory, and if anyone might have a lead on my dad's whereabouts, it'd be him.

"My dad said if anyone has information about the goings-on in this city, it's you."

"You're aware information's not free, right?" he said, arching a wizened brow.

My throat bobbed with my gulp. I should've anticipated that, right? However, a librarian's salary wasn't the sort that lent itself to dropping cash with ease. "I've got a little on me, but I wasn't exactly prepared."

"I don't deal in money," he said, those dark eyes shifting to the door and back. "And you're protected here. If you're not interested in the trade, then we'll go our separate ways, no harm, no foul."

And why didn't that soothe me in the slightest?

"What do you deal in?" I asked, even though my nerves simmered on full boil.

"Favors and other sundry things," he responded.

Right. Of course. I'd read countless stories about making deals with creatures and how that could go terribly wrong. I took a sip of my coffee again, letting the heat coil through me. I might have been desperate enough to call Maury, but the idea of owing him a favor...a shiver ran down my spine.

However, I had one thing I could work with.

"You aren't the only one who deals in information," I responded. "A librarian's biggest asset is research, and I have access to Peregrine City's archives."

Maury's brows lifted. "Well, now. That's an interesting offer." His dark, gimlet eyes studied me, and I shifted in my seat. Far too quickly I was realizing that I sat across from a very dangerous individual. The one safety net I clung to was that he couldn't harm me here in Haven. "A trade, then. One piece of information now for one piece of information in the future."

That, I could work with. "Shake on it?"

"No need," he said, tapping the side of his head with one of his sharp claws. "I never forget a deal."

Well, bully for me.

The server swung by again, all sharp angles and caution. "You're back, Maury? You're aware this isn't your personal office, right?"

"This how you treat one of your best customers?" he joked, spreading his arms out on the back of the booth. Clearly, he was in his element here, and based on the softening of the server's features, he wasn't unwelcome either.

"Our best customers order more food," she said with an arched brow. "Speaking of, you getting the burger special of the day?"

"What's the meat today?" he asked.

"Your favorite. Goat," she said with a hint of a grin.

"Sold." He settled back in his seat.

"Food for you?" she asked, though the arch of her brow never wavered.

Given the state of my stomach, due to this whole meeting, I didn't think I could manage. "The coffee's fine for me, thanks." As if to prove the fact, I took another sip. So helpful. I was a master negotiator at the ripe old age of twenty-five.

"No problem," she said, slipping away just as fast.

"Gretel's been a mainstay here for a while. She's Sofia's partner," Maury explained. "I'll give you that for free."

"Sofia, as in Sofia Calderon?" I asked. "The witch who owns this place?"

"No, Sofia the leprechaun who's been chatting me up every time I go to the newsstand," Maury drawled.

I shot him a look. Right, so Maury apparently moonlit as a stand-up too.

"Okay, we're serious," he said, lifting his hands in defense. "I get it."

Too serious had been a character flaw of mine for a long while, at least when it came to interactions. It had cost me friends and boyfriends before. I swallowed down the sting, along with another sip of coffee.

"So, what's your question, then?" he asked. "What information are you seeking?"

Resolve settled inside me. "My dad's missing. He hasn't returned to his apartment, and I don't know where to even start my search."

Hope twisted inside me like a wet rag. If Maury didn't have answers, I wasn't sure what I'd do. I'd have to scour his apartment again for clues or at this point involve the police.

He shook his head, that easy smile still on his lips. "That's a simple one, I'm afraid."

My stomach plummeted. Somehow, I didn't figure this would be good news.

"You know the casino on the outside of town?"

I bobbed my head, that unease building, building, building. Everyone knew of the Spires, the set of buildings that rose to pierce the sky like cragged castles, owned by cutthroat businessman Cillian Ashmore. People didn't go to the Spires for casual gambling. They went to lose their souls.

"Your father was last seen outside the Spires."

Oh, fuck.

CHAPTER 2

I t took all my resolve to make it through my shift at the library today.

I pushed the cart over to the children's book stacks and started my work reshelving. The section was massive and always active, but the repetitive movement helped keep me from running out of this place screaming, which I'd been tempted to do quite a few times today. Peregrine City Library was a marvel, a building I could spend years in and never tire of, and my dream of being surrounded by books was a simple one I'd chased from childhood onward. When the bullies at school had become loud, I'd run off and escaped with a book. When the loneliness had corroded me, I'd also escaped with a book.

They'd been a refuge for me from an early age.

Despite the higher volume of people in Peregrine City, the move hadn't brought me more friends either. I liked my coworkers, and we got along, but I was shit at putting myself out there. They made plans with each other, lived in these bubbles of sociability that I could never penetrate, no matter how hard I tried. The words that had marked me from youth lingered, and no matter how I tried to scrub them off, they wouldn't leave.

I slipped a few books onto the shelf, taking a moment to make sure they lined up. Haphazard or sloppy books were the worst.

Tonight, I'd be going to the Spires.

If I'd thought approaching Haven was bad, it paled in comparison to this.

However, Maury had given me a direction to go in, and I had to chase the lead. My dad was the only family I had left.

"Beau, someone's here to see you," Laura called from the circulation desk. She was a peppy and ponytailed brunette, and she greeted every patron with a smile.

I froze in the middle of shoving a book back on the shelf. Dad never visited me at work, but he'd also never gone missing before either. Once in a blue moon, he had a business appointment that took him out of town, but he usually gave me advance notice. I'd only moved out a few years ago, and we still tried to have dinner on a weekly basis. When I glanced to circulation, though, the sight there socked me in the gut.

No Dad.

Instead, Damian stood at the front desk next to Laura, and his stare bored into me. He wasn't an unattractive guy, and the girls at work told me I was insane for not dating him simply on looks alone. The swoop of his black hair, the chiseled chin, the muscular chest—yeah, he was built like a fitness model, but he was also insufferable. Damian was one of those guys who loved to hear himself speak and hated to listen.

He also reminded me far too much of the bullies from my grade school days. Instant pass from me.

I sucked in a sharp breath and plastered a fake grin onto my face. I was at work. I couldn't break down here.

No, I reserved that for when I returned to my apartment on my own.

"Hey," Damian said, striding toward me upon my approach. He must've swung by straight from his job, as he still wore his button-down and tailored suit, all neat lines. He had this permanent swagger some might find attractive, but it set off my warning bells. I'd spent so long being glossed over or ignored that if I chose to date, I'd want a guy who saw *me*, not just what they wanted from me.

"Come to pick out a book?" I asked, even though I knew the answer. Damian wasn't a reader, which he liked to avidly proclaim. He just showed up here to bother me.

He let out a hearty laugh, loud enough that a few patrons glanced our way, and I drew on every withering ounce of patience I could.

"You weren't home until late yesterday," he said, his hands on his hips. "I wanted to make sure you were okay."

The downside of living in the same apartment complex as Damian was that I didn't feel like I could escape him—apart from moving to a new place. He found every excuse to "run into me," which annoyed the ever-loving hell out of me. But the rent was the right price, and a librarian's salary didn't leave me flush with cash.

"You know, I bet a dozen other people would love this level of attention," I started.

"Except it's all going to you," he said, a smug grin on his face. "Guess that makes you lucky."

"Mm," I responded, edging closer to the stacks of books as though they might leap off the shelves and attack him. He did seem allergic to education. "Lucky isn't the word I'd use. You've clearly seen that I'm fine. Is there something else you need?"

"Would you go to dinner with me tonight?" he asked, leaning against the shelf and blocking my way. I heaved a sigh, irritation percolating through my veins. Better to focus on that than the rising fear from the thought of what I'd face when I approached the Spires tonight.

"No," I responded, a word he'd gotten from me dozens of times by now. "I'm not interested in dating."

"I'll change your mind." He flashed me a smarmy grin, and my shoulders tightened. While I wasn't waifish, and I did have some muscle to me, he could probably still best me in a fight. And that attitude was goddamn dangerous.

"My mind is made up," I responded cooly, even though my temper simmered. "I think Amanda in the apartment a few down is interested, though."

"Amanda's not my type," he said. "She's a four, and I'm a ten."

"Charming," I responded, holding back my disdain by a thread.

"You should understand," he said. "Someone as gorgeous as you wouldn't date anyone ugly, would you?"

"Looks aren't what draws me to a guy," I responded, my hackles up. "There are so many other factors to consider."

Qualities Damian didn't have—kindness, empathy, and intellect.

"I think you'll eventually understand," he said. "Though I won't be waiting forever."

"Well, that's good," I responded, unable to restrain the bite in my tone.

"I'll see you around, Beau," Damian said, ignoring my comment, and irritation roiled in me right now, so I offered only a nod in return. Not like he listened when I spoke anyway. Then he sauntered out of the library as quickly as he'd showed up, and Laura sidled over, her ponytail swinging.

"So, are you guys going out?" she asked, waggling her eyebrows. Laura was a sweetheart, truly, but her taste in men was horrific. Case in point, she thought Damian was a catch.

"The answer continues to be no," I said as she walked with me over to the cart I'd abandoned in the children's section, where I continued reshelving the books.

"You have impossible standards," she said. "When's the last time you went on a date?"

"A while ago." My chest shriveled a little. Was kindness too much to ask for? I hated the emptiness of my apartment, but I used to go on more dates before the whole process just wearied me. Dating someone who made me feel worthless or small didn't seem worthwhile, and the guys on Prowlr were only interested in hooking up. I needed...more.

My fantasies weren't filthy, but they required one element a hookup didn't have—trust.

"That's my whole point, though. Would it hurt to give Damian a chance? He's made it clear he's interested in you, and he's gorgeous," Laura cajoled.

"You can have him," I said, gesturing toward the door he'd swept out of. This library was stunning, with its detailed crown molding and vaulted ceilings, and I adored the place so much. The thousands of stories contained throughout the stacks made me giddy on a normal day. "I've got books in the meanwhile."

Laura's eyes crinkled. "Did you read the latest Grimaldi?"

"Yes, and I adored it," I shared, finishing up with my cart. We strode toward the circulation desk, since someone now waited there. "I hope she keeps writing forever."

"She's a demon, and they are known for having a longer life, so at least we'll get her stories for a while." Laura slipped behind the circulation desk and faced the patron. "What can I do for you?"

I tuned out the chatter as I got the next cart of returned books in order, getting them ready for reshelving.

Would I even come back to this? Foreboding thumped through my veins. Sure, I was visiting the Spires, but I couldn't shake the unease that had taken root in me ever since my conversation with Maury. Everything I'd looked up about Cillian Ashmore cemented my concern. The demon was commonly referred to as "The Beast," due to the way he savaged other businesses. No one would dare steal from him or try to swindle him because the repercussions were deadly.

And he'd become more reclusive over the years, taking on fewer meetings, walking the casino floors less often, even though he lived in the upper levels of the Spires like a living wraith.

How I'd get ahold of him was a mystery. My ideas stalled apart from marching up and demanding an audience, but I had to try.

I stared at the cover of one of the books on my stack—a dark, forbidding castle with a strike of lightning in the background. Well, that was on the nose. I couldn't shake the feeling it was the same atmosphere I'd be walking into.

Yet, I had to try.

Dad was still missing, and it had always been us against the world.

I glanced up at Laura, who was deep in conversation with a patron, and then I soaked in the stacks stretched out in every direction, the musty smell in the air, and the antiquated flickering lighting that had led to the joke of there being a ghost in the library.

I could only hope that after tonight, my life would remain the same.

That I'd find my dad and return here for my shift tomorrow.

The alternative was unfathomable.

But as anyone in Peregrine City understood intimately, life could take a drastic turn in mere moments.

CHAPTER 3

The subway rattled and hissed as it came to a stop at the station. Casino Alley was what folks casually called this stop, but Strathmore Station was the official name. Peregrine City had been one of the first cities established after the Awakening, when the glamours keeping humankind unaware of the supernatural dropped, and the fissures between dimensions allowed monsters to cross into this world. A century had passed, and so little had changed on this continent, societally at least. While I'd grown up in the suburbs, a little town called Alder, this city was fascinating, teeming with history and haunts. The station itself smelled like rot, though, and I tried to ignore the sludge marks in the corners, which were questionable at best.

After all, many never returned from the Spires.

I patted down my slacks for the thousandth time, as if I'd actually find something there. Maybe I should be...well, carrying a weapon would feel a little ridiculous as I was completely untrained. Hunters might roam around packed to the gills with weapons, but they were schooled in their use from an early age. Books might impart knowledge, but they wouldn't hold up against claws or fangs or guns. As I stepped out of the station and into the night, the sight of the Spires struck me speechless.

The casino was situated in an actual castle, built over the remains of a skyscraper that had been torn down. The forbidding structure created an even darker black stain against the black sky, only lit up in small sections by spotlights. Unlike other casinos along the way that were all neons and glitz with their flashing lights and sparkling exteriors, the Spires needed none. The structure attracted people like moths to a flame, and its reputation was as well known as the building itself.

And I planned on walking through those gates and demanding an audience with its owner, Cillian Ashmore.

Maybe I could inquire after my father with the staff. Get the information I needed without attracting the attention of anyone dangerous. However, the pit in my stomach didn't dissolve as I wandered closer. The cold air chapped my cheeks and ruffled my hair, sending leaves skittering on the asphalt around me, and passersby rushed in every direction, the streets full in this district at night. Streetlights cast hazy lemon beams, but they didn't penetrate through enough of the shadows that threatened to consume around here.

Every creak, every shuffle, every clatter startled me.

Maybe I should've spent more time investing in friends, not books, as beyond the casual workplace friendships I had, the only person who'd be looking for me if I vanished was the one who'd disappeared. Dad had been there for me my whole life, the only stable presence I'd had after my mom passed away. I needed him to be okay.

The slap of my boots against the pavement echoed, and I tugged my peacoat a little tighter as I wound down the streets in the direction of the Spires, following so many others through those open gates. Instead of flashing neons like so many other casinos on this stretch, the Spires featured massive spotlights that spanned back and forth, illuminating the way.

My stomach twisted as I followed the cobblestone path that led to those open gates.

God, this was such a terrible idea.

So many people passed by me without even a cool glance in my direction, as if I were invisible, reminding me how much the loneliness ached sometimes.

A reminder of why I was here in the first place.

I shrugged the peacoat tighter, my stride quickening, as if I could race inside the Spire and it might not swallow me whole. The gaping blackened windows and the dark entrance looked unsettling, like a maw.

The scents of decay and rotten leaves quickly transformed into something cleaner the closer I got. The streets grew lighter, and the lamps multiplied to illuminate the path to the entrance with a steady glow. Grumbles, mutters, laughs, and shouts sounded around me, people jostling by on either side. Everyone headed in to gamble, whether for their first time or because they were a regular.

Maybe there was some subtler way to find my father, but I hadn't grasped it yet.

I wasn't sure I'd grasp it before I stepped through the main door either.

As I neared the glass doors, my heart beat so loudly I could swear it was audible to everyone around me.

My hand landed on the cool twisted metal of the handle, and I pulled.

Stepping inside the Spires, I witnessed the transformation. Outside was a cold, craggy building made of gray stone, formidable and withstanding time and age, an indomitable fortress. Inside lay the modern wonders one would expect of a casino, albeit with more class than some of the flashier, cheaper places in Casino Alley. The place was decked out in blacks, yellows, and purples, from the banners hanging above attached at the rafters, to the vibrant yellow and purple carpeting, and the black accents along the stone walls.

The electronic chirping and rings from the slot machines echoed my way, amplifying the farther in I wandered. The main floor was enormous, covered in gambling machines where people sat pulling levers, eyes glazed, along with tables for every type of game imaginable. I wasn't the gambling sort, but here I was putting everything on the line.

Massive glass and silver chandeliers dangled from the ceilings, and swords of every shape and variety were displayed on the walls like they'd been plucked from museums. Opulence and intimidation oozed from every corner of the place. Lavender and vanilla floated my way in the lobby, which surprised me due to the sheer volume of people rolling through. Individuals from every walk of life stumbled in here, rich and poor, human and monster alike, though the elite bypassed the slot machines for private rooms. The sights and sounds drew me in so much I almost stopped midstride, but I continued on, veering toward the left.

The information desk sprawled out in that direction, stone-topped with black facades, and columns in the background gave glimpses of farther beyond, where dealers worked tables with neat efficiency. Dozens of workers bustled behind the desk, some seated, some standing, some mid-motion.

I balled my hands into fists. This was insanity. Lunacy.

Yet my feet carried me forward anyway.

One of the men behind the desk ducked his head as he squinted at something glaring on the computer screen. Unlike some of the others, who appeared high-strung from the way they snipped on the phone, he seemed a bit more chill, so I veered in his direction.

My legs trembled as I came to a stop in front of him, even though I kept my face neutral.

"I'm looking for Hank Taylor."

The guy blinked at me several times. So many people traveled through here that of course he wouldn't know who I referred to.

"He was last seen here, but he's missing," I said, sweat starting to prick on my palms. "Look, I'm not even asking you to call for your boss...if you could just search the security footage?"

He opened his mouth, clearly coming in with a no.

An older woman with silver streaks through her chestnut hair and a tight bun swept in beside him. "Hank Taylor?"

"Yes." My lips were dry, and I licked them automatically. The hope felt paltry at this point. Knowing she recognized my father's name didn't encourage me, rather it increased the dread that had been circulating through my veins for days now.

"Wait here," she said, striding away. The click of her heels echoed in these towering ceilings, and I wrung my hands together behind my back, just to release some of the pent-up energy swirling inside me that was growing, growing, growing.

"Amelia will be right back," the guy behind the computer said, continuing to type away. "She's just making a quick call." Well, she wasn't handling hotel bookings, since this was one of the few casinos that didn't operate as a hotel as well. Instead, Cillian Ashmore lived in the entire upper part of the castle, which was blocked off from the public.

Would she be bringing my father to the desk, or something far worse?

Somehow, I didn't think I'd be lucky enough for the former.

Fuck. I took a few steps back, not sure even where I'd run if I was escorted out...or worse. Sweat prickled across my back as I glanced in the direction Amelia had disappeared in, and a few of the workers behind the desk glanced my way, their wide and worried expressions not setting me at ease. What the hell had I launched into motion?

Minutes passed by with no sign of her, and I shifted side to side.

Maybe I could leave. Pretend I'd never cracked open this box. Just slip out the way I came in.

My gaze slid over to the elevator on my right, the one cordoned off with velvet rope. The light on it flashed, the sound of the descent echoing off the polished floors and into the rafters. It wasn't until I realized all the workers had paused and were also staring at the elevator that my internal alarm bells started ringing.

Ding.

Ding.

Ding.

The doors of the elevator slid open, and an audible gasp echoed around the room, whether from one person or a dozen, I couldn't tell.

The moment a figure emerged from it, I understood why.

Massive didn't begin to describe him. From his towering frame to his bright red skin to the curled black horns on his head, it was evident a demon had arrived. He wore a crisp charcoal suit—clearly tailored, from its sheer size and delicate designs on the lapels—that clung to his body like it belonged there. Even beneath the suit, he was clearly muscular, his neck thick and corded, his shoulders the broadest I'd ever seen.

His black hair devoured the light with a shadow's inkiness, and his cleft chin, his strong nose, and his sharp jawline conveyed a hard, unforgiving face, if not a bit arrogant. Those thick brows formed wicked arches, and his lips pressed into a firm frown, at home with the rest of his features.

When his gaze landed on me, I flinched. The glacial chill in those golden eyes made me want to run on sight alone.

And I'd seen this man before. Never in person, but in the research I'd done.

This was the reclusive Cillian Ashmore.

The wealthy businessman who not only owned the Spires but crushed enemies with little care.

The man who'd be able to tell me what happened to my father.

And he'd come down here.

I didn't believe in coincidence.

His broad steps trembled the floor he strode upon, and the impulse to run rose fast and fierce. Except my feet were frozen in place. He closed the distance between us, each thunderous step bringing him closer and closer. I couldn't stop staring, even as he stopped a few feet away, looming well above my height. This close, the scent of brimstone rolled off him as if he'd emerged from the depths of hell.

"When Amelia mentioned the innocent little thing asking around for Hank Taylor, I had to come." His voice held the force of a semi rumbling down the highway, its echo reverberating off the polished tiles. The hushed silence that had fallen didn't help either. My whole body trembled to attention at the massive predator who had just entered the room.

Because that was what Cillian Ashmore was. Even the refined suit couldn't hide the feral gleam in his eyes or the long fangs on display with his lazy grin. I shivered, suddenly feeling like prey who'd been marked.

"I'm not innocent," I blurted out. Of all the things I could have responded to, I wasn't sure why that struck me first. However, now I'd set the tone, and I couldn't back down. I lifted my chin, squared my shoulders, and stared him in the eye. Except those eyes were stripping me down right in the middle of the casino, as if no one else existed but the two of us.

Cillian's grin widened, showcasing even more of the wicked arch of his brows. "Well, you've got some backbone, I'll give you that. Not sure if it'll help you, though."

"I'm not a fool," I said, even though I felt wholly like one. "If he went missing here, there must be a reason. I'm not here to storm down the gates, simply to talk."

And hopefully barter, though with what? This man had unimaginable wealth and people fawning over him left and right. This wasn't a simple meeting in a diner with my dad's information guy.

No, this was a meeting with one of the most powerful people in Peregrine City.

He could crush me with his reputation alone and bury me in an undisclosed location where I'd simply vanish.

"Interesting," he said, scanning me over with a deliberateness that made me want to back away a few paces. His silences communicated more, the sheer power simmering through the room enough that the strike of a match would light it all up.

"Mr. Ashmore, do you want a private room?" Amelia approached, even though she was the only one. "I can prepare one down here."

"No, we can arrange a meeting upstairs."

Amelia's face paled, and my determination faltered. For this calm, cool woman to blanch, it signified everything.

I wouldn't be leaving the Spires alive.

Self-preservation demanded I run, just bolt toward the doors of this building at top speed, but I hadn't looked away from Cillian Ashmore. There was a cruel glint in his eyes, as if he'd hunt me down himself—and enjoy it.

A shiver rolled down my spine, darker impulses that would never see the light of day.

"Right," Amelia said, the lines on her features a bit starker. Clearly reassuring. "Please follow me, Mister…"

"Beau," I rasped out, my throat dry. "Beau Taylor."

Her eyes widened, and then if possible, her lips pressed tighter.

"Let's go," Cillian said, turning his attention away from me as if I were a mere bug underfoot he was waiting to crush.

Yet the magnetism in his voice somehow tugged me forward, my feet moving of their own volition. I ran my fingers through my curls, the dread growing stronger with every step toward the elevator. I chanced a glance at the information desk behind us, and everyone stared, deadly quiet. Many of them watched as if it was their first glimpse of the man who owned this casino, unlike Amelia, who was clearly seasoned at working by his side.

"Come along," Amelia said, giving a light tap to my elbow. "Mr. Ashmore doesn't like to be kept waiting."

I hadn't even realized I'd paused, but when I looked back, Cillian stood by the elevator he'd arrived in, his broad arms crossed, his elegant chin thrust out in pure arrogance. Men like him thought they owned everything—everyone—and loathing bubbled up inside me. That he could toy with lives and continue along unconcerned was despicable.

Yet here I was, another desperate soul ready to make a deal with a devil.

CHAPTER 4

This was the most uncomfortable elevator ride I'd ever experienced.

Amelia was the human buffer here, but she was not on my side.

Cillian's presence was consuming, overpowering, and if it had been bad down in the casino, it increased a thousandfold crammed into the confines of this elevator, threatening to suffocate me.

I'd wedged myself into a corner and stared hard at the numbers lighting up with each floor we passed, zooming upward. Better than acknowledging the weight of Cillian's stare as it settled over me like lacquer.

Still, I'd gotten myself into this mess, and I would see it through. Based on Cillian and Amelia's comments, I could at least gauge that they knew where my father was, and with any luck, they were taking me to see him.

Granted, I hadn't been doing great in the luck department lately.

"How did you hear about Hank Taylor?" Amelia asked, her voice light, as if she wasn't fishing.

Yeah, no way would I give her that information.

"Around," I responded. "Word travels."

She gave me a disapproving glance, but what had she expected with a blatant question like that?

The elevator let out another ding, and the doors opened.

Cillian pushed through without waiting for either of us. Already, he struck me as an entitled asshole, someone used to getting his way, the exact sort of person I loathed. Not the type who'd be forgiving or understand that they'd ripped my father away from me.

"This way," Amelia said, casting me a look marginally less frigid—almost concerned, and I liked that even less.

The dimly lit corridor stretched ahead, bluish lighting and black walls guiding the way like a landing strip. Cillian's heavy footsteps echoed throughout the whole area, drowning out Amelia's and my own. Despite working in Peregrine City Library, I hadn't been around a ton of demons, and the sheer size of him intimidated me.

I wiped my palms on my slacks, an odd calm settling over me. I'd reached this far, which was farther than I'd originally believed I could.

Whatever awaited me, I'd face.

By myself.

Loneliness stabbed me in the chest yet again, that the only person I would've contacted for help was the one I'd set out to save.

The crisp scent of the hallway made my nose tingle, but for the life of me I couldn't figure out what it was. A few shut doors lined the length, and at the end of the inky black hall, another corridor intersected it. Who knew what lurked there. The elongated shadows crept under my skin, unsettling me. This area was nothing like the flash and glitz of the casino below, more akin to the forbidding silhouette the Spires cut against the night sky.

My avenues of escape were either the elevator behind me—which I could guarantee was either spelled or required identification—or the unknown.

"In here," Cillian rumbled, and he pushed open a big door to the right with a mighty creak.

"He just wants to talk," Amelia said, which wasn't a reassurance. "With any luck, you'll be on your way soon."

"That'd be ideal," I responded, unable to keep the sarcasm from my voice.

Cillian flicked the lights on, and we followed him into the room. It reminded me of a mix between a conference room and a dining room, with a massive table in the center. This one was black with legs like twisted tree trunks. The tabletop was glossy like the surface of a lake, and the chairs were made of the same twisted, blackened wood.

"The décor feels a bit gothic revivalist," I commented, approaching the seats.

Cillian had already settled at the head of table, because of course he did. A wealthy demon like him wouldn't be able to stand anything else without a tantrum.

"Works well to set the scene for my business meetings," Cillian said, the slightest curl of a grin on his lips. Amelia took one side, and so I settled into the seat on the other.

Well, damn. This chair was like sitting on a rock. "Couldn't spring for more comfortable furniture?"

He full-on smirked. "No, I like my visitors uncomfortable. It encourages them to leave."

"Right, then this should be fast," I responded, shifting on the seat.

"Hank Taylor," Amelia started, folding her hands in front of her. "He's made some poor decisions."

My stomach plummeted. "He's alive?"

That, I needed to know before all else.

"He is," Cillian said, though his golden eyes flashed with malevolence. "Though he'll soon wish he wasn't."

I rose from my seat, hands balled. "What are you doing to him?"

"Who are you to him?" Cillian asked, a predatory glimmer in his eyes that I didn't like.

I closed my mouth, probably something I should've done far earlier.

"His son," Amelia said, her gaze glued to her phone. "It wasn't a difficult search."

I sucked in a sharp breath and settled back in my seat, even though my thighs and calves tensed as if I might sprint away at any moment.

"Your father owed us a substantial debt due to a...problem." Cillian remained as cool and calm as ever, the pale light from the sconces making his curled black horns gleam. "He's been sentenced to the Pits to work it off."

Ice rushed through me in a fierce and fast torrent. The Pits were talked about in whispers, part of the thriving underworld in Peregrine City. The entrances were scattered throughout, but they all connected beneath the city proper into a true underground establishment. That was where the seediest gamblers went, anyone looking to chase their darker proclivities. Any sort of vice was for sale there, and many of the people who entered never emerged into the light again.

"How long is his sentence?" I asked, my heart in my throat.

"A decade," Cillian said. The calmness sparked ire in me. This bastard crushed innocent people under his thumb. My father had probably made one small mistake, and now he would suffer for the next ten years because of it. And given his age—fuck, would he even last down there? My chest tightened as resolve settled over me.

There was no other choice.

"I'll do it."

Cillian's brow furrowed. "Take his sentence?"

My stomach churned, and nausea rushed through me, but I wouldn't back down. "Yes."

Cillian sucked in a long, slow breath, drawing out my torture. Would he accept the offer? Or was he determined to punish my father?

And what sort of debt could my father have owed in the first place? What problem was Cillian referring to?

"I'll accept a trade," he said, slowly scanning me over. Cillian's gaze was that of a predator, as if he'd chew me up and spit out the bones. A shiver ran down my spine, and I clutched the arms of the chair with white knuckles. This was it. I was selling my soul to a demon, and I'd never see the surface again.

Someone like me wouldn't last long in the Pits.

"Hmm," he said, his low rumble like the purr of a jungle cat. His gaze hadn't left me, and I felt pinned by it, unable to move under his scrutiny. "Except you're not the right fit for the Pits. I've been looking for a personal assistant to replace the last one. As long as you're somewhat competent with files, then you'll serve your sentence up here."

With him.

Relief rushed through me that I wouldn't be sent to the Pits, but hot on its tail came the nausea again. Because I'd still be a prisoner for the next decade. Trapped in the Spires with this demon, whose despicable reputation preceded him.

I wasn't sure whether my chances of survival were any better.

"Cillian—" Amelia started, and then stopped when his golden gaze sliced her way.

"Do you have a concern with it?" he challenged, the low deadliness in his voice a giveaway that he would brook no argument on this.

"If you think it's in your best interest," she said delicately, though I didn't miss the stubborn glint in her own gaze. Amelia either had more backbone than I'd expected or she was more than just a lackey.

"I accept," I responded, my throat dry. "But please, let me see my father at least, one more time."

"Fine," Cillian said, his imperious gaze rankling me in the worst way. "He'll be going free anyway."

I swallowed hard. Freedom. Which I wouldn't have for a long, long while. What would my coworkers at the library think? That I'd been abducted? That I'd flat-out quit? Honestly, I'd probably fade from their memories far too fast. Fuck, I was going to vomit.

"I'll send him up," Amelia said, pushing from her seat and striding out of the room.

Which left me in here with Cillian Ashmore.

Fuck.

He rose from his seat and strode over to a cabinet. It opened with a creak, and he tugged out a bottle of amber liquid that looked like whisky or scotch, though who knew what demonkind drank. Cillian poured a finger or two into one of the glasses sitting there and then sauntered back over. Considering this man would be my new employer, he was treating me as if I were a gnat to be crushed. I supposed casual conversation would be beneath him.

He sipped at his drink, and the silence settled over us with a thick tension, like a barrel of gunpowder ready to ignite.

"I'm a librarian," I stated, cutting through the quiet. "So if you need help with files, that's within my expertise."

He arched a wicked brow at me. "Noted."

My temper flared at his dismissiveness. If he wasn't interested in my qualifications, what the hell did he want me here for? A dark thought flashed through my brain, but I squashed it before I could fully process.

I'd find a way out, no matter how long it took. Surely, sometime during my ten-year imprisonment I could muster a solution.

"Will I be confined to a room?" I asked, not sure whether I wanted the answer.

"There will be parameters," he stated.

Clear as mud.

Amelia stepped into view again, and behind her stood my father, who was handcuffed. A big burly redhead strode up behind him, filling the doorway to make sure he didn't bolt.

The sight of Dad offered a combination of relief and dread. He was alive, but I'd sold my freedom for his. His blond curls were matted against his forehead, streaks of dirt marring his skin. He looked worse for wear, his clothes wrinkled and stained, and his demeanor wasn't sturdy but bowed.

I swallowed hard and rushed toward him, and as Amelia stepped to the side, I threw my arms around him. He stank, like he hadn't showered in days, but I caught a faint hint of the overpowering cologne he always wore—the bay rum one. It reminded me of home, of him, and tears prickled in my eyes.

"You're alive." I hugged him even tighter. This might be the only chance I'd get in a long, long while. He sagged into me as if he'd been through horrors, and relief cascaded over me stronger than ever. I soaked up every ounce of it, from the heavy weight pressed against me to his ragged breaths. Gods, what would I even look like when I emerged from the Spires? If I emerged?

"What are you doing here, Beau?" he asked, his voice raspy, like it was unused.

"You're free, Dad," I said. "They can't hold you anymore."

He stilled against me. "What did you do?"

"Don't worry," I said, trying to shove the tremble out of my voice. "I'll be fine."

"No," he stated, his voice harsh. The desperation there coiled around my own. "No, they can't. I'll go to the Pits. This is my burden to carry."

My eyes stung, and his words alone reminded me this had been the right decision. "No, Dad. You won't survive the Pits. I'll be okay, I promise."

"Come on," the big burly guy said. "It's time to go."

Abruptly, my dad's weight vanished. His deep hazel eyes widened as they met mine, and his mouth was tight with a frown, those wrinkles more pronounced than ever.

"No," he said, trying to surge toward me again. "No, send me." His head whipped toward Cillian. "Take me, not him. He didn't do a damn thing."

"Get rid of him," Cillian said, the cool, cruel tone seeping into my bones. Dread settled in its wake.

The sight of my father being yanked away would be emblazoned in my mind for a long time to come—his deep-set eyes wide, his jaw dropped, his whole body surging as if he could somehow find a way to protect me. But he'd been protecting me my whole life, and it was time I stood on my own.

It was time I protected him.

My heart beat out of control as I froze in place, unable to chase after him, unable to do anything but watch as he was yanked out of the room. Amelia followed hot on their heels, leaving me alone with

Cillian once more. The silence now echoed louder, as if the chaos and intensity of mere moments before lingered in the room.

No doubt the Spires were filled with thousands of ghosts like this.

"No sense in waiting around here," Cillian said, cutting smooth strides toward the door. "I'll show you to your chambers."

Just like that. His calmness unsettled me and made me rage at the same time. That he could be so unfeeling at tearing a family apart. That he could send my father away so easily, hold people captive and treat them like hell. Bubbling anger scorched through me, the kind that wouldn't cool any time soon.

"Right, my chambers," I muttered as I followed him out the door.

More like my prison.

CHAPTER 5

I didn't know why I'd expected a tour.

Cillian clearly wasn't the welcoming sort, and after a quick gruff "here," he swept out of the room, closing the door behind him.

The click of the door echoed through the room like the lock of a prison cell, and I strode up to the knob and twisted it, just to check I hadn't been locked in. Open. I sucked in a shaky breath. The reality of what had occurred hadn't settled in yet, even though I had absorbed the facts of our meeting. My hands still trembled from the adrenaline. The lingering scent of Dad's cologne remained, but I wasn't sure if it was a phantom memory or an actuality.

I sagged against the door and viewed my surroundings. My cage was a gilded one, though that shouldn't be a surprise. I surmised that anything in this part of the Spires would be decorated to the same degree as the rooms I'd seen so far. The goth-chic motif continued here, a purple comforter looking like a splash of bright color against the black bedframe, and the massive dresser and armoire the same obsidian shade. The walls were a deep gray with pale-gray accents, and a large mirror faced the bed on the opposite side.

I slipped my phone out of my pocket, half expecting I'd be shut off from Wi-Fi access.

Curious, I clicked through a few webpages, and everything seemed to be in working order. The urge to type out a message to my dad, to hit up my coworkers, rose in a real way, but I had the sinking suspicion that was too easy. No wealthy casino owner would be negligent with the man he'd pressed into servitude for the next decade.

He'd given me no parameters, no inclination of what to expect from my new role, my new home, my new life.

Anxiety rushed through me like I'd stepped into a tub of menthol.

I dragged myself across the room and plunked down onto the bed, sinking into the mattress. My mind whirled, and I curled my fingers into the plush comforter, but no amount of luxury could eliminate the fact my life had gone through such a major upheaval in a mere hour. All I owned was the clothes on my back and what filled my messenger bag.

What made it even sadder was that I hadn't left behind anything of consequence.

My reflection stared back at me in the mirror, as hopeless and helpless as I expected. I'd inherited my father's blond curls, and I'd had to buy fitted clothes since I landed more in the slender category and liked my clothes snug. Yet I didn't look put-together. No, the man who stared back had looked ruin in the eye and welcomed it in.

If I stayed in this room, I'd lose my mind far too quickly. However, if I wandered around, would I invoke Cillian's ire? I stood from my spot on the bed, needing to roam. He hadn't stated I was confined to my room, so I'd err on the side of ignorance if caught. Anything was better than sitting in this box and letting my reality melt into place.

I slid my phone into my pocket and dropped my messenger bag on the ground, as if the motion would somehow make this room feel more like mine. Tall order. Pressure rose inside me, like a balloon ready to pop, and I bolted for the door. A few steps down the hallway and I could breathe again. If I could keep moving, maybe I could ignore the fact I was actually confined.

The hallway looked as dim and dark as before, but I didn't have Cillian's oppressive presence around at least, congesting the corridor even more. I drank in the crispness of the shadows and crept forward, making sure to keep quiet. How far did this upper area stretch out? If it was half as large as the casino below, guaranteed it'd be sprawling. I snapped a quick photo of the corridor, particularly the location of my new bedroom, and then continued on.

When I reached the end of the hall, I turned right, heading down a similar stretch of muted lights and dark, ominous doors. Truthfully, at this point, Cillian was coming across a bit edgelord or drama queen with the amount of black splashed around the place. A hysterical laugh bubbled up my throat, and I slapped my hand over my mouth to keep it from escaping. A bit farther down this corridor, light spilled out into the hallway from an open door.

My curiosity drove me forward. I'd tried to beat the trait into submission years ago, but then I'd chosen the career of librarian, which had allowed it to grow and blossom.

A jaunty whistle came from the open door, and I drew closer, slowing my pace.

Moving kept me from breaking down, though, so I'd keep going. That had been my strategy through life, and while it hadn't always served me the best, I'd survived. More than I could say for many in Peregrine City.

When I reached the edge of the door, I paused. Who else resided up here? I was utterly in the dark, and not just due to Cillian's dismal décor choices.

I sucked in a breath and peered around the corner. The room looked to be another meeting suite similar to the one he'd taken me to—honestly, what did one demon need with this many rooms?—and a tall figure was wiping a cloth over the table, his back to me. The song he whistled tickled at my memory, not because it was a sweeping classic, but I could swear it was some pop hit the radio had played on repeat ten years ago.

I rapped against the doorframe so I wasn't just gawking in like a creeper, and he whirled around.

The man was exceedingly tall, dressed in casual jeans and a T-shirt, a far stretch from Cillian and Amelia's formal attire. His glossy dark brown hair swept across his forehead, and when he caught sight of me, a broad grin split his lips.

"Well, well, we've got a visitor here?"

"More like a new resident," I said, leaning against the doorframe to keep myself up at this point.

The man lifted a brow as well as his cleaning rag. "Lia never mentioned anyone new coming on board."

"Just happened," I said, my throat far too dry with nerves. "I'm Cillian's new personal assistant."

He dropped the rag. He quickly collected both the rag and his jaw from the floor, then he strode toward me. "I wasn't informed of this development yet, but I'm Charles. I've been working for the bossman for a long time."

"What do you do for him?" I asked, even though one of the answers was clear from the rag in his hand.

"I'm his cleaner," Charles said, but based on the shift of his tone and his pointed look, that wasn't all his role was comprised of. However, his features relaxed, and his smooth grin placed me at ease.

"Don't suppose you'd know what he expects of his personal assistants?" I asked. Charles seemed to be the first friendly person I'd met in this casino, and I'd grasp onto anything right now. My feet were a little unsteady, so I leaned harder against the doorframe.

"Well, that's a question I have as well," he said, striding closer. "I'm assuming he dropped you off and rushed away? The peak of social skills, that one."

I snorted, and relief flushed through me for a moment. A single friendly face was enough to latch onto. "Does he not often employ personal assistants?"

"Not for the past seven years he hasn't," Charles said. "Do you have a special skillset?"

For the life of me, I hadn't been able to figure out why he didn't just send me to the Pits like he'd planned to do with my father.

"Considering he didn't grill me on that, I'm not sure. I'm a librarian by trade," I offered, crossing my arms to keep them from trembling.

Charles flashed me a grin. "Well, I'd say that's a useful trade to be in. Have you eaten yet? Why don't we find you something and hunt down Amelia. Surely she'll have answers. She always does."

My stomach grumbled as if on cue. I'd eaten earlier, but with the ball of fear and worry gnawing at my gut, I hadn't been able to stomach much. Not like the anxiety had disappeared, but given my fate was sealed, and my mind hadn't fully processed the bomb dropped on my life, the prospect of any sort of meal appealed to me. Well, anything but apples. Hated the fuckers.

"Thank you," I said, the slight rasp in my voice betraying how much the simple kindness meant. My insides were still fuzzy, numb from everything that had occurred, but I wasn't ready to face reality yet either.

"Follow me," he said, slipping past me and heading to the right, deeper down the corridor. He cut a quick pace with those long legs, and I hastened to keep up, our footsteps echoing through this cavernous place. How did one person need this many rooms? While I could admit after growing up with the bare minimum that the occasional bit of opulence enticed, this seemed ridiculous, even for a larger-than-average demon.

Especially since he didn't seem to entertain very often.

"Does he sleep in a different bedroom every night?" I wondered aloud. My shoulders tightened. Fuck, I'd gotten too comfortable. This was Charles's boss I was talking about.

A bark of laughter exploded from Charles. "Oh god, that's fantastic. The size of the place is a bit much, yeah? A hotel's worth of rooms lying there empty. Trust me, they don't remain so."

Curiosity flared through me yet again. I knew so little about Cillian Ashmore, only the highlights I'd read about online, which were either superficial or swirling with rumors. Yet I'd be living in his home for the next ten years, working with him in close quarters.

"Okay, here." Charles slowed in front of stainless-steel double doors, the porthole windows revealing the lights on inside.

The industrial-sized kitchen spread out farther than I was prepared for, with shockingly white walls, stainless-steel backsplashes, and gray-tiled flooring. Between the multiple stovetops, ovens, and stainless-steel fridges, it was obviously meant to be used to cook for the masses—as if this place were a restaurant—not just for a single man. Confusion percolated inside me yet again at how this eccentric demon lived.

"Theo made cassoulet for dinner tonight, and it was perfection," Charles said, sweeping over to the nearest fridge. His movements were all wild and akimbo, his body long and slender. He ducked into the fridge and emerged with a massive container.

"Can I help somehow? Grab a bowl?" I asked, heading over to the paste-white cabinets.

"Far right one," Charles said as he rummaged around to grab a ladle and a spoon as well. I snagged a basic black bowl from the stack, somewhat surprised these weren't ostentatious as well. After I passed it over to him, Charles ladled some of the soup out and popped it into a microwave.

"Mind if I ask what brought you here in the first place?" His eyes were inquisitive but not cruel.

"Offered myself in place of my father," I said lightly, as if the truth wouldn't knock me from my feet. "You know, the usual."

Charles snorted, and the microwave beeped. He drew out the soup, which was steaming hot, and the delicious scents of herbs, vegetables, and meat wafted my way. I supposed one benefit to my revised sentence was that the food would be infinitely better than fighting for scraps in the Pits. Charles plunked the spoon in and slid the bowl over to me. "Amelia's on her way over to brief you."

"Makes my new position sound very confidential," I joked, surprising myself that out of everything my dry humor hadn't quit.

"Clearly, this is a secret agency, and you'll get your training once Lia arrives." Charles hopped up on one of the stainless-steel counters, his long legs dangling from the edge. "Except it's terminally understaffed. The only people Cillian has employed up here are me, Amelia, and Theo."

"Theo is the chef?" I asked, dipping my spoon into the bean stew. I took a tentative bite, and the flavors exploded in my mouth. I bit back my moan.

"Among other things," Charles said, a softer note in his voice. I arched a brow, curiosity rising in me again. He grinned. "We're also together."

"So it's not all ominous doom and gloom in this place?" I asked, my heart thudding a little harder.

"Cillian gave you that impression, didn't he?" Charles teased. "He's quite dramatic."

After seeing the fear he'd inspired in so many down below at the casino, Charles's casual way of speaking about him soothed some of my raw nerves. While I couldn't imagine he'd be an easy boss, and I'd seen firsthand the way he could control people's fates, if there was a way to survive, I'd find it.

If there was a way to escape, I'd find that too.

I inhaled more of the soup, the decadent flavors melding together in my haste to fill my stomach, as Charles swung his legs back and forth, seemingly full of bubbling energy.

The double doors swung open.

"You're here." Amelia's voice announced her as she strode into the room. "I wasn't sure where Cillian had spirited you away to."

"I can see how someone could easily get lost," I commented. "Maybe I should leave a breadcrumb trail next time."

"Please don't," Charles said. "That'd be annoying as fuck to clean up."

A realization hit me. "Are all his staff humans?"

"Mmm, witch," Amelia said. "And Theo's a werewolf. Charles here is our only human. And now you."

Shame heated my cheeks at the assumption. "That was rude of me." Even though I'd been living here for a while, some of my small-town preconceptions had followed me. It wasn't that monsters didn't exist out in Alder...more that they stayed in separate towns, separate territories. I'd been told the nursery rhymes of the bogeys, taught the symbols to ward off demons. The only thing that had saved me from their small-mindedness was the amount I'd read. It had opened my mind like nothing else.

Amelia shrugged. "As long as you're not a bigot, we'll get along just fine. I'm not thin-skinned."

I stole the final remaining spoonfuls of the cassoulet, my stomach full at this point, even though that didn't entirely relax me. Not when I was residing in unfamiliar territory and surrounded by unfamiliar people.

"I suppose you're wanting some parameters?" she asked. "Of course, Cillian left that to me."

"If you're launching into a rules talk, I'm out," Charles said, hopping from his seat. "Nice meeting you, Beau. Try not to fall asleep during Lia's droning on."

She rolled her eyes as Charles strode out, and seeing their casual interplay offered a different view of the woman from the cold and formal individual I'd first met.

"Do you want to go somewhere you can sit?" she asked. "Or would you prefer to discuss things here?"

I leaned against the stainless-steel counter, letting the coolness of the metal seep into my lower back. "Here's fine. Hit me with it."

Amelia adjusted herself into a straight-backed stance, her legs evenly situated. "Cillian hasn't had a personal assistant in a long while, so I'm not quite sure what he expects to do with one now. My assumption is note-taking during meetings, as his last one did, and sorting the files in his databases, with limited permissions of course."

"My phone works," I stated, waiting for her to fill in the blanks.

"We're not barbaric, are we?" she said, a light smile tugging on her lips. "But we do have surveillance on what you send out, so don't act stupidly. Try to send SOS messages, and we can just as easily shut your phone access off. Besides, you'll be signing a legally binding contract for your employment, so you definitely wouldn't want to be in breach of that."

"Servitude," I shot back, unable to help myself.

Amelia crooked a brow. "You made the choice yourself."

I swallowed hard, my throat tight. She wasn't wrong. "And I'm allowed free reign up here? What about down below in the casino?"

Amelia let out a sigh. "Up here, you can explore most of the area. Just avoid the West Wing. I'll email you a layout so you've got a clearer picture. As for the casino, you'll only be able to go there with an escort. The elevators require an identification pass."

Which I wouldn't receive because at the end of the day, I was a prisoner.

"*If* those parameters shift over time, though, I will inform you," she said, a hint in her tone that implied certain freedoms might be earned. If I was a good pet. Amelia passed me over a business card. "And this is my business line, with my private number written on the back. If you have any questions, need anything, please contact me."

That was a dismissal if anything was. I took the card. "Thanks."

"Do you need help finding your way back?" she asked.

"Nah, I've got it," I murmured, even though the dread started to creep back in.

With that, Amelia turned and exited the room, the double doors swinging in her wake. I watched the shift of them, and my heart thudded hard.

The fluorescent lights beamed down on me, the stainless-steel fixtures and backsplashes gray and cold, and a chill settled inside me, spreading with rapidity.

While I might've clung to the brief notion for a few moments that my time here wouldn't be intolerable, the truth was, I remained confined. I remained a prisoner.

And the culprit, at the end of the day, was Cillian Ashmore.

CHAPTER 6

The days bled together after I arrived, and yet Cillian didn't summon me for tasks, for meetings, for damn well anything. If I were working for him, doing some tasks at least, I could distract myself from my current reality. This inertia was worse. A week had passed since I'd ended up here, and I'd expected far more work. Instead, I'd pored through books on my phone to escape, and Amelia had delivered an entire new wardrobe of clothing that was surprisingly close to my style as well as other toiletries I didn't have. So I wasn't without comforts.

Yet I was still confined.

I'd emailed the library my resignation, saying I'd taken a private position elsewhere, but I loathed that my favorite job had been stolen from me.

And I'd emailed my father, who at least checked in on me. A small relief I clutched onto.

Amelia had given me a layout of the areas within the Spires, including the higher floors I could access by staircase. The elevator was off-limits to me, a reality that made me angrier by the day, yet my rage melded with a numbness that threatened to consume me. I'd been trying to find anywhere with a balcony and a breeze here, and while stepping out to look over Peregrine City offered a transitory sense of freedom, the second I stepped back inside, my reality settled back in again.

I nudged the book at the base of my bed with my foot. It had appeared on my nightstand a few days ago—*Songs of Whimsy and Witchery*—and the read had been fascinating. Old poetry collated from all different time periods about witches. The flip between what we knew pre-Awakening and the poetry from after offered a beautiful contrast. Certainly nothing I ever would've read in my hometown.

Oddly enough, once the veil was undone, the whimsy faded from the poems, leaving the stark, bitter reality of the struggles in their history. I'd been reading the mysterious book in chunks, savoring the passages.

A knock sounded on my door.

I peeled myself off the bed.

Amelia waited in the doorway. "Your presence has been requested for dinner tonight."

I lifted an eyebrow and crossed my arms. "Is this in an official capacity?" If he'd wanted me to work, fine. But dine with him? Fuck that guy.

Amelia's mouth twitched. "Well, I could tell him you declined, but I wouldn't recommend it."

"Oh, is he going to call his thug over to drag me out of the room?" I shot back. Apparently my sass was the one thing that hadn't been stolen from me.

"We could, if that's what you'd like," Amelia responded coolly.

I swallowed hard. She wasn't the enemy here, not really. Cillian was responsible for my captivity. "When is this dinner?"

"It'll be starting in thirty minutes, down in the dining hall," she said. "We'll all be there as well."

Her answer settled it for me, as I was going out of my mind in isolation. If Cillian wanted to force me into interacting, he could deal with my salty self. "Fine." I huffed out a breath and strode over to the wardrobe, not bothering to wait for Amelia to leave. She'd vanish on her own, the same way she usually did when she needed to update me or deliver something.

I slid on a pair of brown trousers, nice black shoes, and a tan button-up shirt. My hair was a mess, my curls unkempt, so I went to the bathroom and sprayed some product in, taming them until they were ringlets again. I didn't know why I put in the effort—maybe because I was getting to at least be around people again—but the oppositional tug to show up in the same clothes I'd been wearing and looking unkempt also rose in me.

I sucked in a sharp breath and slid my phone into my pocket, a reflex more than anything. I felt so distanced from anyone on the outside at this point that the connection my phone offered didn't feel genuine. I craved face-to-face interaction. Shocking for an introvert, but at the library I'd been used to the interspersion of helping patrons find their next reads even if I wasn't too social in my daily life beyond that.

Time to go face down this new employer of mine.

When I stepped out of my room this time, purpose seized my feet, offering the renewed burst of energy I'd been craving. My aimlessness was what had eaten at me the most over the past few days. Now even something as simple as a dinner invite gave me direction.

I'd memorized the layout at this point, even if I hadn't come close to exploring the upper reaches of the Spires. The West Wing had been marked off, a small portion of it, but of course that drove my curiosity to distraction. My footsteps echoed through the corridor, and I turned left at the end, in the direction of the dining hall I'd already poked around in. Despite our habit of getting takeout together regularly, which my dad and I formed once I'd moved out, we hadn't been the formal dinner type growing up. We usually just shoveled food into our mouths before he was off to work or I was off to school, and then he'd leave me meals to warm up when he worked late. Despite being a single parent after mom passed away, he'd done the best he could for me.

Farther down, the doors to the dining hall lay open, cool white light spilling into the corridor. When I stepped into view, the enormity of the room smacked me in the gut. Honestly, I should be desensitized by now, but the sheer volume of this space Cillian owned was startling as well as ridiculous. I'd expected one huge table, but instead, the layout was more like a larger scale dining hall with many long mahogany tables stationed evenly around the room. Massive metal chandeliers hung overhead, polished and gleaming with pale white lights that cast dappled patterns on the ground. Blue, purple, and white stained glass decorated the windows on the far wall, creating a far too opulent space for a simple meal.

It wasn't hard to spot where everyone dined, given they'd clustered around a single table.

Cillian cut the starkest figure, far larger than the rest, and of course at the head of the table. He clearly needed the extra room for his ego. The others were all familiar—Amelia, Charles, and the big ginger bruiser who'd hauled my father away. Their ties to Cillian seemed to go way back, which made me feel like even more of an outsider. I hesitated midstride, tempted to turn around and head back to my room.

"Come join us," Cillian stated, his voice about as welcoming as the first time I'd met him—which was not in the slightest. He was in more relaxed officewear than the first time I'd seen him, but I hadn't even caught a glimpse of him since then. The white button-down created a stark contrast to his bright red skin, and the sheer size and heft of him threatened to burst the fabric at the seams. How he didn't break the seats was beyond me, but they also seemed to be larger than normal, which fit for a demon-owned place. His sleeves were even rolled up to the elbow, which I assumed was the most casual he got. The man had massive, ropy forearms, bulging with muscle.

All of which signaled how deadly he could be.

His steady golden gaze hadn't left me, so I forced my feet forward, even though it felt like entering hostile territory.

"Come eat," Charles said with a friendly grin. He clapped a hand on the back of the big ginger. "Theo here made beef bourguignon, and it's a delight."

"We haven't met formally yet," Theo rumbled, offering me an up-nod. "Welcome."

Well, already he was friendlier than Amelia and Cillian, yet I couldn't quite erase the image imprinted in my mind of him dragging my father away. A chef, but he clearly held other positions. What sort of operation did Cillian have here?

I took the open seat beside Amelia, even though she wasn't one of my favorite people on the planet right now either. Better than sitting opposite Cillian, though. A bowl of beef bourguignon lay in front of me with steam wafting up from it, and the rich scent made my stomach rumble, even though my appetite had been decreasing by the day. The more I languished in my room, the harder it was to find the willpower to eat, to do much more than sleep or stare at the wall.

"How's the new position working out?" Charles asked.

I arched a brow and met Cillian's gaze. "Of prisoner? Well, it's less than a delight. As far as being a personal assistant, I haven't been assigned any work yet."

Cillian let out a low rumble, but I couldn't give a fuck. I was trapped here, and though I might be here physically, he didn't own my mind. I hadn't sworn obedience.

I forced myself to take a mouthful of the soup. The flavors burst on my tongue but melted like ash, the same way everything else did. It had only been the first week, but if the rest of the next ten years were to involve this level of monotony, I was in for a different sort of hell than I'd anticipated.

"We can get you started on Monday," Amelia offered. "Cillian has a meeting first thing, and you can take notes."

"Is he even trained?" Cillian asked.

Rude. No matter how you dressed him up in power and prestige, he was downright rude.

"I'm right here." I spoke up, my voice even and low. "And I'd have whatever training was needed if you'd even bothered this past week. However, clearly you couldn't even deign to make an appearance."

A week ago, I'd been quaking in my boots talking to this man, but the fear had drained out of me, replaced by numbness instead.

"New guy's got sass," Theo said, a slow smile rising to his lips.

Cillian fucking Ashmore, on the other hand, looked less than pleased. "Make no mistake," he responded, his voice quiet and deadly. His fangs protruded slightly. "You're here to assist *me*. That's on my timeline, not yours. If I don't call for you for a week, it's because I've got no use for you."

Those words slammed into me like a sledgehammer. To him, I was nothing but an annoyance—a means to an end. My temper flared again, and I didn't bother restraining it. Not like I'd be able to eat anything anyway after the way this meal had gone.

I pushed up from my seat, which made a loud squeal. "Looks like I'm not hungry after all."

With that, I turned on my heel and exited the room. My footsteps echoed through the massive room, and I could feel the pressure of their gazes on me.

Fuck him. Fuck him and his arrogance.

"You didn't have to be such a dick." Charles's voice traveled from the table as I left the room.

Maybe I should take some small solace in the fact he'd called Cillian out, but my heart thumped hard, my whole body burning a little hotter. I couldn't return to my room like this. Instead of turning in the direction I'd come, I continued on, farther down the corridor. I had no idea where any of his staff even slept, or Cillian himself, though considering the West Wing was off limits, he most likely brooded and scowled there.

The absolute fucking gall of the man. I balled my hands into fists. The anger felt good at least, breaking through the haze of numbness that had covered me like cobwebs after the last week. And at least if I was note-taking, doing something, even if it was for a reprehensible asshole, I'd prefer it to languishing away in this tower.

Voices sounded at the end of the corridor, drawing my attention. I'd thought the people in the dining hall were the only ones who resided up here. This space wasn't accessible to the public, only a select few people. Well, if I wouldn't be eating dinner, I might as well poke around. I was desperate for human interaction, but not desperate enough to deal with Cillian fucking Ashmore.

I slowed my pace the closer I got, two feminine voices growing clearer as I approached an open door with pale yellow light spilling out. While I didn't necessarily want to intrude on a private conversation, I also hadn't been given enough information from my less-than-forthcoming host about who was allowed up here.

An inhuman growl came from inside the room, and I stilled right beside the door.

"Come on. You've got better control than that, don't you?" The tone was sure and wicked in the same breath, a confidence there that I envied.

Another growl sounded.

"Calm down," she stated again. "Close your eyes. Deep breath in, then huff out."

A loud huff sounded, and my curiosity got the better of me. I peered around the doorframe. A stunning woman with dark flowing hair sat on the bed next to a massive silver wolf. Right there. In the middle of the room.

Panic registered in me, but I remained rooted in place.

"Good," the woman said, stroking her fingers through the wolf's fur. "You've got this. Fae, you've survived far more than a change of location. Breathe in again, then huff out."

The wolf complied, her big flanks shuddering as she followed the order. It wasn't hard to piece together that the wolf was a were, considering there'd been a second voice moments ago as I'd listened in. However, when I observed a little closer, I also caught sight of the raw red spots along her flank. The belabored, ragged breathing. The spotty patches around the ankles, as if she'd been chained. Her fur was matted and ragged, and she was thin—skeletally gaunt, like she'd suffered abuse. My stomach churned.

"Keep inhaling and exhaling, focus inward. I'll go get you some dinner, since you've got to be starved," the woman said, slowly rising.

Oh shit, she was heading out. I backed away from the door and pivoted on my heel, hoping I'd look like a passerby.

"You're less inconspicuous than you think."

I froze.

The woman from inside the room strode up beside me, a wan smile on her lips. "I haven't seen you here before. Are you one of Cillian's?"

"Does he often keep pets?" I asked, arching a brow.

She let out a bark of a laugh and tilted her head to the side. "Walk with me on the way to the kitchen."

I didn't have anywhere else to be, so I shoved my hands into my pockets and joined her. She wore long, flowing purple skirts and a black corset top, her dark hair so shiny in the light that it gave off a midnight glow. Unlike Amelia, who hadn't given off what I viewed as witch vibes, this woman screamed it.

"I'm Sofia," she offered. "And you?"

"Beau," I responded. "Cillian's new personal assistant." Who had yet to assist him with damn well anything.

Sofia arched a brow as we strode down the hallway together. Thankfully, reaching the kitchen wouldn't take me past the dining hall. After the way I'd stormed out of there, I wasn't keen on running into any of them again at the moment.

"You're a pretty thing, aren't you?" she teased.

A flush heated my cheeks. She wasn't the first who'd commented on my looks, or even the dozenth. The remarks had been a pattern my entire life, but then I'd usually run admirers off with my stubbornness or sharp tongue. Damian was the only one too self-absorbed to take the hints I'd been dropping.

"Don't worry," she said. "I'm not interested. I've got a gorgeous girl waiting for me when I head home tonight."

"You don't live here?"

Her laugh echoed through the hall. "God no. The Spires are far too gloomy. My place is much livelier."

"What's your place?" I asked, desperate for any scraps of information from the stranger who walked these halls like they were familiar.

"Haven Diner," she said. "On the opposite side of town."

Where I'd been a little over a week ago. Where this had all begun. I sucked in a shaky breath. "Good food there." Her eyes softened slightly, even though the intimidating air around her hadn't lessened. "Is that where you met Cillian?"

She shook her head, a hint of a smile clinging to her lips. "Oh no. He and I go way back, beyond these businesses we've established. Let's just say when I first arrived in Peregrine, the city wasn't as considerate to our kind."

"And the wolf back there?" I asked.

"You ask a whole lot of questions for a personal assistant." Her eyes danced, hinting that she teased.

I shrugged. "I was a librarian."

Her eyes crinkled at the edges with a broad grin. "That explains it."

We reached the kitchen, and she offered a nod.

"Thanks for the company. Hopefully I'll see you again, Beau." With that, Sofia disappeared into the kitchen, the dismissal clear.

I ran my fingers through my curls, annoyed that I'd spent the time getting ready for a dinner I hadn't even been able to enjoy. Maybe I'd come here later and raid the kitchen. It was what I'd been doing a lot lately, since it remained regularly stocked. A heavy sigh escaped me, and I headed back down the corridor in the direction of my room—my prison.

When I rounded the corner, I almost stopped midstride. Amelia waited for me by the door, a bowl in hand.

She took the first steps toward me. "I wasn't sure where you'd gone off to, but I figured you might return here eventually." We met midway down the hall, and she handed over the bowl of beef bourguignon I'd abandoned, still warm. "I owe you an apology."

"For what?" I asked. "You weren't the one who was rude."

She shook her head, and her lips twitched as if she fought a smile. "You're far mouthier than I expected."

"Didn't realize meek subservience was part of the job description."

"It's not," she said. "I think...you'll be a good fit. I owe you an apology for not starting your work earlier. We assumed you'd want time to transition."

The bowl warmed my hands, and combined with her apology, some of the anger flaring through me ebbed. "All this free time isn't helpful when I'm locked up here."

Amelia's brows dipped. "Right. This is...an unprecedented situation. Bear with us for a little bit, okay?"

"Not used to keeping prisoners?" I asked, unable to keep the sarcasm from my tone.

She shook her head. "I think it'll be good to have you around here, Beau Taylor. Good for him too. Get some rest. You'll start work in the morning." She offered a flash of a grin—a real one—and then turned on her heel, heading back down the corridor.

I stood in front of my door, holding the soup she'd offered me.

Tonight hadn't delivered any answers, just more questions, ones that bubbled under my skin, igniting my curiosity.

Well, I had plenty of time to try to dig up the truth.

Cillian Ashmore would regret ever holding me hostage.

CHAPTER 7

F or the first time all week, I woke up with the sun.

I wasn't sure what to expect working as Cillian's assistant, but I wanted to be ready for when Amelia summoned me. Energy flowed through me at the prospect of being able to focus on something again. My entire life, I'd been goal-oriented, unable to stay still unless I was reading, digesting information, helping archive dusty tomes. At least if I could find some purpose, this situation might not feel as confining, as restricting.

Even if I was still a prisoner.

I slipped out of bed, and a thump sounded as the book I'd been reading hit the floor. This one—*Forbidden Desires*—had appeared like the other one, and was a romance between demons of different class stations, whose system was a bit different from ours, based on ancestry and the type of horn they possessed. Not that I'd scrutinized demon horns often, but apparently the black polished type that arced up like Cillian's indicated a higher station.

I slipped into a pressed button-down and slacks and then into neat black business shoes that probably cost more than most of my wardrobe back home. After running some product through my hair, I was ready.

A knock rapped at my door.

I opened it and found Amelia waiting on the other side with a coffee in one hand and a laptop bag in the other.

"You'll be taking your notes electronically. Do you need to be debriefed on those skills before the first meeting?"

I shook my head. Between my library sciences degree and my time working at the library, it was a tool I'd used often. "I'm fine on that front."

"And for you." She offered over the coffee, which I accepted gratefully. My three favorite things in the world were coffee, cats, and books, and I'd been sorely missing all three. Despite being able to find meals in the kitchen, I hadn't figured out how to use a lot of the fancy-ass equipment, like the coffee maker, and I didn't want to risk breaking anything.

"Thank you," I said, clutching the warm paper cup close. I took a sip, and the sweet, creamy coffee coursed through my veins like sunlight. "Damn, where did you get this from?"

"Downstairs. The café in the casino," she said. "Which is where we'll be heading for this meeting."

Excitement prickled through my veins. "You trust me out on the floor like that?"

She lifted a brow. "Planning on running? You won't get far."

Her words were cryptic, but I had to remember she was a witch. Chances were, she had a spell in place I wasn't even aware of. Locator spells were a dime a dozen in that community, so she'd probably popped a witchy LoJack on me. The chance to go downstairs shot pure adrenaline through my veins. Even though I was stuck inside the Spires, this offered the chance for something different, and I'd cling to it.

The elevator lay at the end of the corridor, the bane of my existence up until now, because I'd stared at the way to my freedom while being blocked from it. Amelia snagged a key card from her pocket and held it in front of the fob. A green light blinked on, and the elevator doors opened. When we got into the elevator, she used her fingerprint on a pad, and then the buttons with the floors lit up. I locked every detail into my memory.

So even if I stole the card, I'd still need a fingerprint to escape. Damnit.

The elevator moved with a *whoosh*, and giddiness soared through me at getting to escape the confines of the upper areas of the Spires, even if I was still trapped in this casino. Amelia passed over the laptop bag, and I slung it over my shoulder.

"Needed coffee that badly?" she commented, a slight smirk on her lips. She might be my father's age, but she was far sharper than him—probably far more dangerous too.

"Absolutely. Would it be possible for someone to show me how to use the contraption in the kitchen?" I took another delicious sip, savoring it.

"Of course. Damn, we really didn't know what to do with you," she murmured. "Trust me, we haven't had a personal assistant in a long while."

"Why now?" I asked.

Amelia's gaze darkened. "Suppose Cillian's changed his mind."

"On what?"

The elevator doors opened, but instead of answering, Amelia left me with more questions. Of course. That seemed to be the modus operandi of everyone here. I should be annoyed, but the burst of color and general hubbub around the casino stole my attention. Even this early in the morning, people were standing by the slots, gambling their life savings away, humans and monsters alike. Had my father been gambling? Did he have debt? Or had he been charged for something he didn't do?

I'd tried to ask via text, but he'd just stated he was unfairly accused. What for, he hadn't clarified. With the number of cryptic answers I'd received over the last week, I was desperate for any clarity.

"Over here," Amelia said, leading me past the high-roller tables. There weren't too many patrons clustering around them at this time of day, but the dim lighting from frosted sconces, the rich red and yellow carpeting, and the polished mahogany tables and detail all created a lush picture. Far different from the overly black décor in Cillian's "lair."

Amelia bypassed the room for an ornate door in the back right corner. When she tugged it open, a huge official-looking room stretched out before us, just as rich as the high-roller area and with more of the same motifs. This room had bookshelves filled with old leatherbound books along the wall, though, and brass fixtures that glowed under the yellowed lighting. Runes I recognized as demonic from the books I'd read were painted along the wall in decoration, though I didn't have a hope of deciphering their meaning.

"Cillian will be sitting here," she said, gesturing to the head of the table, as per usual. I withheld my eye roll as she gestured to the seat next to him. "And you'll be there, mostly because it'll piss off Chadwick."

I arched a brow. "There's someone actually named Chadwick?"

She shrugged. "Who can fathom the whims of the wealthy?"

"Ah, my assistant's arrived before me?" The rich voice sent a shock of electricity through me, and I looked up to see none other than the asshole in charge.

Cillian was in full boss mode again today, a gleam to his obsidian horns, and his suit a tailored charcoal one that fit him like a glove. Everything he wore accentuated how large he was, and a shiver rolled down my spine again. His jaw was sharp and defined, his dark brows wicked, and his black hair was tamed and swept to the side. Even in the genteel clothes he wore, there was no denying the man's predatorial nature, and I could guarantee even this shareholder meeting would be interesting.

"I take my work seriously," I responded, looking him in the eyes and lifting my chin. I couldn't afford to show this asshole weakness.

A slow smile curled his lips, the sort that made my gut simmer. Those fangs poked out again, and I straightened, irritation welling inside me. The man might be gorgeous, but I wasn't swayed when it came to arrogant pricks. I'd dealt with them my whole life, and he was just another to toss onto the stack.

"Good," he said, his voice low and sensual. "I'm looking forward to putting you to work."

Fuck him. Even as my anger flared, the pulse in my groin was undeniable. Because as much as I hated it, I had my own secret fantasies, ones I'd never admit to. Ones I wasn't sure I even wanted fulfilled. I sucked in a sharp breath.

This was my captor.

The reminder delivered the ice water I needed, dousing any complications.

"I'll leave you to it," Amelia said. "Contact me when the meeting's over." She glanced between Cillian and me. Right. So that she could return me to my cage.

I didn't bother responding, just settled into the seat with my coffee and then extracted the laptop from the bag. Once I got it started, a bolt of normalcy shuddered through me, something I'd been craving for so long. The idea of just settling behind the keys, losing myself in typing and notes, sounded like total bliss right now.

Silence spread between us because the man was as sociable as a kumquat.

"Any preferences for the notes?" I asked as I opened the software on the laptop.

"Most of what my business partners have to say is drivel. They don't understand the inner workings of the Spires, and the way they run their casinos repulses me."

What a gem this guy was. It was a marvel that anyone showed up to these meetings in the first place. I shook my head, continuing to stare at the screen.

"Holding back?" he asked, his voice low with a dangerous edge. "How unlike you."

"How's there any room for your business partners when your ego's taking up all the space?" I commented dryly as I set a header for today's notes.

His chuckle reverberated through the room. "Careful, Beau, unless you want to find out if the rumors about me are true."

Even though a frisson of fear trickled through me, I stared him square in those golden eyes. "Well, if you dispose of me, you'll be out one hell of a personal assistant."

"That remains to be seen." He settled at the head of the table, dripping pure arrogance.

And I had to sit beside him for the next three hours.

I swallowed another gulp of coffee to protect my sanity.

***

"The upper areas are a waste of prime real estate," Frederick, one of the owners of Red's Casino, spoke up. While I agreed they were a waste, I didn't think the space needed to become yet another hotel or casino. We could do so much more, something productive for the denizens of Peregrine City.

"What I do with the upper areas of the building I own is none of your damn business," Cillian growled, as sociable and charming as ever. He'd been surly and disagreeable throughout the entire meeting with just about everyone at the table. Why did he even bother entertaining them?

"You know Thorin's expanding his territory here. It won't be long before the Spires loses its steady stream of clientele. He's going to make a grab at installing more of his people in the Pits too," Chadwick complained.

Cillian's brows drew together, his gaze stormy. "What do I give a damn about Thorin? Let him try to press in on this space."

"The rest of us are concerned," Frederick said. "You might have the reputation of being 'The Beast,' but that will only go so far."

Most of these men were human and older, though a vampire and a naga sat at the table as well. It was refreshing to see the variety, though it made sense that a demon like Cillian would include other monsters in the mix. While Cillian was as stubborn and unyielding as the rest of them, I could admit the whole meeting felt a bit pointless. Still, my notes were detailed yet succinct, and I utilized necessary bullet point lists and summaries for each section.

We'd paused for breakfast when it had been delivered, which had resolved my question about food, and I'd even been able to refresh my coffee. The buffet had contained a variety of pastries and fruit, including the usual danishes and croissants, but the inclusion of saltwater tarts—a New Atlantis delicacy—for the naga, and blood biscuits for the vampire, was surprisingly considerate.

"We need to wind this meeting down," Cillian said. "Our time's almost up, and I have other matters to address."

A few of the guys bristled, annoyed at the way Cillian dismissed them, but the others heaved a sigh, as if they were used to his rudeness and also eager for the meeting to end.

I made some quick readjustments to the notes I'd taken while the guys made a few more attempts at pushing their agendas, which Cillian promptly blocked. I tucked away the name Thorin, though, curious as to why he'd elicited such a strong reaction. In this mode, digesting information, I operated at my greatest function, and I felt the best I had since I'd first agreed to take my father's place.

"Since you've got better help now, can we get a copy of the notes your assistant's been taking?" Chadwick asked.

I withheld my lip curl, barely. These men treated me like I didn't exist, which told me everything I needed to know about their merit. "I can provide copies," I announced, stepping in without invitation.

Cillian arched a brow at me, and I arched one back at him. If he wanted a docile, submissive thing, he'd picked the wrong man.

He turned and stared down at the group still at the table. "You heard him. If you want notes, send an email. This meeting is concluded, so see yourselves out."

Wow, what a charmer. I saved the notes and shut off the programs before powering down the laptop. Rustling sounded all around me as everyone started to meander out, some leaving and others chatting with each other in quieter tones. Cillian remained seated next to me, as looming and ominous as ever. I slipped my laptop into my bag and rose, and he did as well.

"Come with me," he rumbled, his tone brooking no argument.

"A please wouldn't hurt," I responded, not bothering to sheathe my tongue.

The intensity of his stare almost caused my limbs to betray me, my legs quivering, but I held my own.

"I'm not begging you to do the job you were hired for," Cillian responded, pushing up and heading toward the door.

I chewed on my lower lip, tasting blood, but followed.

As much as he was insufferable and arrogant, I didn't want to sent straight back upstairs. If I could extend my time down here, I'd claim every damn second.

And eventually, I'd claim my freedom.

CHAPTER 8

P art of me was concerned Cillian would march to the elevators and usher me back up to my prison, but to my surprise, he headed in the opposite direction. The sheer arrogance of not even looking behind him to see if I followed rankled a little. I was tempted to try to make a break for it across the casino, just to see what he'd do, but I had the feeling that would increase my shackles.

I skimmed my gaze over the floor around us, noting how security was stationed in every corner, clear from their black uniforms. Right. "This place is teeming with cameras, isn't it?"

Cillian slowed and glanced back. "Contemplating your chances if you run? I wouldn't."

"Casino security. Right," I commented, slipping my hands into my pockets as we bypassed chandeliers dripping with crystals, gleaming brass fixtures, and lines of slot machines, half of them jangling.

Cillian snorted. "As if I'd have something so simple watching over you."

Which meant magic. I didn't doubt Amelia held the key. She was his right hand, and he seemed to trust her in most things.

"Over this way," he said, his tone brusque and demanding as usual. The temptation to drag my heels rose, and I did slow my pace to a meander as I soaked in my surroundings. Most patrons at the slots weren't paying attention to us, but every employee stared wide-eyed. Apparently they weren't used to appearances from Cillian, and a few all but leapt out of his way as he swept by.

He stepped into a corridor to the right, along which lay massive windows with bright, cheerful sunlight streaming in. I soaked it in, the feeling so close yet so far away. I longed to be out there in the world, in the city, not trapped in the Spires like some fairytale damsel. Still, even sitting in on a meeting and taking notes was a drastic improvement to the wasting away I'd done over the past week. I'd been spiraling when I needed to be sharp.

But shadowing Cillian would keep me sharp.

I stilled in front of a window as the gardens emerged into view. Fountains sparkled under the sunlight, and blooms in an array of pinks, purples, yellows, and reds stretched out, swirling in every direction. The tapestry of explosive color mesmerized me, careful craftsmanship in the layout. How such gorgeousness could exist in Peregrine City was beyond me, especially in this district, but the flowers and greenery seemed to have carved their own space here.

"Are you going to just gawk at it or join me?" Cillian asked, paused at a door that led outside.

My heart raced. He was taking me outside? I licked my lips, not willing to question the chance when I wanted the opportunity so badly. I quickened my pace to catch up, and he pushed the door open with a creak.

The air was fragrant, and the beams of the sun warmed my skin. I drank in a long, slow inhale, and the panic in me quieted for the first time since I'd arrived here. Fuck. Heat pricked at my eyes, but I refused to cry over stepping outside right now. Not in front of him.

"Your notes were thorough," he commented.

"I worked as a librarian until I was unceremoniously plucked from my life," I responded, walking a little faster to keep pace. "Note taking, cataloging, are basic skills in my repertoire."

"You're well read, then?"

I wasn't sure whether it was the fact I couldn't leave or the knowledge something odd was afoot with his choice of keeping me as his personal assistant, but my internal thoughts kept erupting from my mouth. "No, I'm a librarian who hates books."

A rasping noise sounded from him, suspiciously resembling a laugh. Though that couldn't be correct, as Cillian Ashmore was a heartless demon who couldn't see past his own ego.

The soothing sound of water flowing in the distance calmed me, and watching tulips sway in the gentle breeze added to the serenity. The occasional passersby wandered through these gardens, but they seemed to be wildly underutilized compared to the casino floor.

"Why is anyone in there when this exists?" I asked, not expecting an answer.

"People mistake city lights for the stars," Cillian said. His words were simple, blunt, but they settled deep in my bones with a resonance I didn't want to admit.

"Then why spend so much time lurking at the tip-top of your Spires?" I asked as we meandered past a burbling fountain, the water droplets sparkling like cut diamonds. Whether it was the cozy rays of the sun or the warm breezes loosening my tongue, something unwound in me despite the monster I walked beside.

"Do you always ask this many questions?" he asked.

"Why do you think I became a librarian?" Even saying the words summoned some slight sadness, though, as I already missed Peregrine City's. It had become a second home to me, and there was a comfort in the stacks I rarely found elsewhere.

He lapsed into silence as we wandered through the gardens, the red and yellow tulips bright and eye-catching. The light, sweet fragrances from the flowers drifted my way, and I drank them in deep, keeping pace with "The Beast," as the corporate world called Cillian Ashmore. Though keeping pace with him was putting me a bit out of breath as his massive legs carried him much faster.

Up ahead, a massive fountain with a pale limestone base and large basin splashed high in the air, and white benches were laid out around it in intervals. Clematis vines twined around them, the bright purple blooms a stark contrast.

"They'll meet us here," Cillian said cryptically, because the man couldn't seem to deliver a straight statement. Truthfully, I hadn't met a single person in his employ who did. Maybe they took a seminar on it. He headed for the nearest bench and found a seat.

I sidled up next to the bench, not bothering to sit. I'd just spent the last few hours right next to him, and I'd been overwhelmed enough by the power rolling off him, the sheer intimidation, the scent of brimstone and amber and musk.

Cillian spread his arms over the back of the bench, his massive shoulders on clear display. He arched a brow at me. "Afraid of monsters?"

"No, just can't handle whatever cologne you've got slathered on," I responded, unable to keep the bite out of my tone. His presence kept me on edge, something I was aware of yet hated in the same breath.

A low rumble emerged from his chest, but whether I'd pissed him off or amused him wasn't clear. I swallowed, my throat dry.

"Sit," he said.

"I'm not a dog." Why I couldn't seem to hold my tongue around him was beyond me, but he hadn't lashed out yet. Another mystery to add to the stack.

"If you were a dog, you'd be far more loyal and much less inquisitive," Cillian responded.

"Spoken like someone who's never met a dog before," I said, crossing my arms. "But I'm more of a cat person anyway."

"Figures."

Annoyance flared through me, and the urge to push back rose up hard. This was the man who held my future in his palm, and the smart move would be to remain quiet, to sit back and observe, but he sparked my temper like no one I'd ever met.

A few employees, clear from their navy-blue suitcoat and cream blouse uniforms, headed in our direction. I hadn't sat, and I wasn't planning on doing so with Cillian taking up far too much space on the bench. They hauled over a few bags and cup-laden carriers, which sparked my curiosity.

"Here's everything requested," one of the employees said, a slight tremble to her voice. "Do you need us to set it up?"

Cillian jerked his head no.

They dropped off the bags as well as the carriers, all three of them buzzing. One of the guys offered a salute, which seemed so ridiculous I had to bite back a laugh. Their fear of him was clear, and maybe I was insane for not having the same reaction to this massive demon beside me.

"Let us know if you need anything else," he said before darting off.

"Thank you," I offered.

The fact Cillian hadn't even said a word to them didn't escape me, and I bit back a few choice opinions regarding that. However, my stomach rumbled at the scents rising from the bags they'd brought over. Given his level of consideration, though, the meal was probably for him while I would be left to fend for myself.

He leaned forward and grabbed one of the bags, then passed it over to me. "For lunch."

I blinked in surprise, the gesture enough that I took a seat on the bench beside him and accepted the bag. The box inside was marked as being from one of the restaurants in the Spires, and I opened mine to find a ham and brie baguette sandwich. The salty scent made me lick my lips, and I didn't hesitate to take a bite. The flavors exploded on my tongue, and I withheld a groan.

Cillian's stare bored into me. His bag rested on his lap, but his golden gaze locked onto me with an intensity that made me shiver. I swiped at the side of my lips, sure something had to be clinging there.

"Going to eat or just brood?" I asked.

He opened his mouth, closed it, and then shook his head. "Here." He passed over one of the drinks from the holder. "If you don't want more coffee, I can get one of the staff to bring you a water or something else."

"I'll happily accept coffee." I placed the sandwich down to take the warm drink. After going a week without a good cup, I was desperate, even if I'd most likely be jittery later. "Your fancy kitchen contraptions for brewing some don't make a lick of sense to me."

"You could do a search for the model," he commented. "Most instruction manuals are online."

I shook my head. "I'm more liable to break it. Definitely not safe in my hands." I took a sip, the sweet, creamy liquid coursing down my throat. Combined with the sunshine and fresh air, this was the best

I'd felt since I first arrived here. The birds whistled and chirped in the background, and the steady thrum of the splashing water soothed my soul.

I stared out at the surrounding nature, and words bubbled to my lips. "How did you start all this?" While he clearly had some business acumen, guaranteed he hadn't launched with only a few pennies and a dream. The Ashmores were an old money family, not new to wealth by any means. "The Spires, I mean. What drew you to owning a casino?"

He let out a slow hiss of a sigh. "You never stop with the questions, do you?"

"Terminally curious." I busied myself with taking another bite, expecting silence to follow. Not like anyone had bothered giving me straight answers so far.

"I wanted to branch off from my father's business," Cillian said. "Make a name for myself." His tone hardened, his gaze far off, as if he were lost in memory. What had happened with his father's business?

"And you thought casino?" I asked. "If you really wanted to stick it to him, you should've become the ultimate disappointment and opened up an obscure bookstore or café."

"Is that a secret fantasy of yours?" he asked.

"Obviously," I responded, taking another sip of coffee. "Although I'd also be happy to work the rest of my days at the library." The reality that I no longer had my job slammed me in the gut, but I forced myself to stay in the present rather than give in to the crushing wave of anxiety that loomed. "At least if I can find another position once I'm free."

Cillian glanced away, the air between us tensing. "You'll still have the applicable work experience."

"Right, with an awkward ten-year gap as a personal assistant to the CEO of a major casino. Because that makes so much sense to employers."

"Makes more sense than a ten-year stint in the Pits," Cillian said, a hint of a growl in his tone. The hint of his fangs poking out should've terrified me, but irritation flowed through me again, clashing with any sense of warning. "And the burden belonged to your father."

I opened my mouth but then shut it again. Did I want to know what he'd done?

Cillian cocked his head to the side. "You stepped in for him, but are you aware of why he was about to face that sentence?"

No, no, no. I didn't want the answer. Because if Cillian said something I didn't like, I couldn't speak to my father face to face and ask for an explanation. And no amount of video calls, texts, or emails could replicate having that conversation in person.

"I'll wait on the answer until I can ask him myself," I responded, my tone firm. "He's been my only support for years, the only parent I've had. Of course I'd step in for him."

Cillian shook his head. "Just because he raised you doesn't mean he deserves loyalty."

"Speaking from experience?" I shot back, unable to help the sharpness that slipped in.

"Yes," he rumbled. His golden eyes locked onto me again, and I forgot how to breathe. "I would never have taken my father's place. I didn't owe him a damn thing."

My stomach twisted at the heat in his voice, at the deadly tone. A story dwelled there, one I was desperate to learn about, but I had the feeling he'd snap to silence or redirect if I asked.

"So starting a casino was your chosen form of rebellion?" I asked, guiding the redirection myself. "Couldn't just dye your hair and get some piercings like the rest of us? Ah, to be born wealthy."

Cillian shook his head, his jaw clenching. A storm brewed between us, and my shoulders tensed. I must've pushed him too far, but I couldn't take the words back.

All of a sudden the tension dissipated, and he lifted a brow. "And what piercings did you get?"

"Wouldn't you like to know?" Once those words escaped me, I wanted to bite them back. His eyes widened, and his gaze turned probing, penetrating. I'd gone through the whole rebellious phase, for as buttoned-up as I dressed now, but none of my piercings were easily viewed. In fact, they were in a place only a select few saw.

"Well, now you've struck my curiosity." His voice turned low and rough, like liquid sin, and I hated the way my skin prickled with awareness. His eyes roved over me, as if he were trying to assess what lay beneath my clothes. I shifted in my seat and sucked in a sharp breath, my body humming with awareness.

A buzz sounded from his pocket, and he plucked his phone out to glance at it. His expression darkened. "Business matters. We'll have to cut this lunch short. Let's head back upstairs."

I didn't respond, as there wasn't much to say. I could stay out here forever, but it was clear that wouldn't be allowed without supervision. As much as the melody of the birdsong and the breeze had lulled me into a false sense of security, the reminder slammed in a little harsher after the respite.

No matter how much I wanted to be free, I wasn't.

And I wouldn't be for a long, long while.

CHAPTER 9

The weeks passed far quicker once I'd started getting to utilize my skills, and soon months had gone by. Note-taking was easy, and I absorbed a lot of the information about the casinos in the city that I wouldn't normally be privy to. And Cillian remained as hot and cold as ever—brief moments of normal conversation one moment and then rude dismissiveness the next. My head spun from all his mood shifts, as fickle as spring weather.

"This meeting is concluded," he announced to the table of different humans and monsters, this time vendors he worked with for the Spires. As per usual, Cillian waited for me to get up first before rising himself, and I wasn't sure if it was to remind me he was my jailer or because he had another meeting involving me. We'd been eating lunch afterward some of the time, while other days he'd bustle out and leave me to my own devices. Which I wouldn't mind, except that Amelia would inevitably show up to fetch me and escort me back upstairs.

Far too quickly too. It was like the woman had a psychic pulse on things. Or at least, whatever her witchy magic did.

Everyone made quick work of leaving the room, unlike at some meetings where the business owners loitered. I watched the guy on the right side of the room, Nate Silvers from my notes. He was one of the last to leave, taking extra effort with his briefcase.

Once it was just Cillian and me remaining in the room, I shifted my laptop to face him. "Nate Silvers contradicted himself in a few different spots regarding the budget. I highlighted it in the notes."

"I've had a suspicion he's been trying to skim off the top for a while," Cillian said, stepping behind me to peer over my shoulder. "This should give me the direction of what to check out." His proximity sent a reflexive shiver up my spine. The way he loomed wasn't like the average human, not with the sheer size of him, and the brimstone and musk scent rolled off him, surrounding me. The amount of time I'd been here plus the amount of time we'd spent working together had started to addle my mind. I'd become used to his presence, even if I still loathed him.

"I'll send you a copy of the notes," I responded before closing down the document and shutting off my laptop. A normal person might say thank you, but I wouldn't hold my breath that Cillian would bother. He said the bare minimum and not much more, unless it was a rare occasion when he shared.

"Hey, boss," Charles said from the doorway, his smile as easy as ever. "Here to provide my escort services."

Right. Back to my prison.

Cillian grunted, which was his way of dismissing me, because the man hadn't learned basic decency. I slid the strap of my laptop bag onto my shoulder and didn't bother acknowledging him as I headed away to follow Charles.

The second we stepped outside the private meeting room, Charles led me straight out onto the casino floor instead of making the sharp right in the direction of the private elevators we normally took.

"Theo's waiting for us over at Sinspiration Deli," Charles explained. "Thought you might like some more time away from upstairs."

His kindness made my chest squeeze tight. As much as Cillian could be brusque and rude, Charles, Theo, and Amelia had made life in this new space tolerable. All of them tried in their own ways to make my time up there a little easier. Charles, with his random rambling and the coffee chats we'd started to have. Theo making sure I had food, as well as asking for book recommendations on the regular. Amelia had been a little tougher to crack, as she wasn't the sociable sort, but her regular check-ins had come to mean a lot. Maybe they all helped in order to ease their own consciences, but regardless, I appreciated the attempts.

"Thank you," I said, tugging on the strap of the laptop bag.

"Boss has a big luncheon out in Peregrine, so Theo's off the hook for cooking until later," Charles said. "He always snags the opportunity to grab meals elsewhere when he doesn't have to cook for himself."

"You're not going to cook him a meal?" I asked.

Charles barked out a laugh. "Unless we want the Spires to burn down around us, no. Me and the kitchen don't get along."

"Convenient that you're dating a chef," I said, keeping pace with him as we wandered past different rooms filled with gambling tables.

"Happy coincidence," he said. "The second I met Theo, goddamn. Have you ever hooked up with a werewolf? Hot doesn't begin to describe it. And that *knot*."

I snorted. I should be surprised by Charles's overshare, but I'd begun to see that was his nature. I appreciated it. "Can't say I have. My dating and hookup history is a bit sparse."

Charles blinked. "No way. With baby blues and golden curls like yours? Plus, your ass is like a work of art."

Heat flushed my cheeks at the compliment. "My coworkers always said I was too picky."

Charles shrugged. "Do you feel like you're too picky?" He swiped at some longer strands of his dark brown hair, which had begun to drift over his eyes.

I licked my lips, his question settling deep inside me. "No, I don't. I'm not interested in hookups with assholes, which means dating, and it's a cesspool out there."

My phone buzzed, and I glanced at the screen. Speaking of the cesspool—Damian.

"What was the wince for?" Charles asked.

"My neighbor, who won't take no for an answer," I responded. "Even though I've turned him down dozens of times, he still thinks he has a shot."

"Well, that's unattractive," Charles commented. "Is that how guys normally act with you?"

I opened the message.

Where have you been? There's an eviction notice outside your apartment. Did you move?

My stomach dropped. Of course. While I wasted away here, my normal life had fallen by the wayside. I'd contacted the library at least, to tender my resignation, but I hadn't contacted my landlord, because part of me wasn't sure whether I should try to keep my place or not. Apparently the decision had been made for me. However, that meant everything in my apartment would likely be tossed.

"What's wrong?" Charles asked, placing a hand on my shoulder and gesturing toward the overhang featuring Sinspirations Deli in neons. "We're here."

I sucked in a sharp breath. "Oh, you know, the normal quandaries that come with abruptly being locked away in a tower. My landlord posted an eviction notice, and I didn't have the chance to get my things before I came here."

Charles frowned just as Theo strode up to us.

"That's bullshit," Charles said.

Theo slid an arm around his shoulders. "What is?"

"Beau's about to lose his belongings, since his landlord's evicting him." Charles's brows drew together, and the indignation on his face made me like him even more. He was the best person I'd met here so far, and I latched eagerly onto any connection I could.

"Well then, we go get them," Theo said with a shrug. "I've got some free time later."

Charles stared at his boyfriend, an adoring look in his eyes. Jealousy flared through me. Fuck, what I wouldn't give for someone like that—a protector, someone who lifted me up and saw the real me...and accepted it. I'd been searching for so long that the prospect felt wearying and futile at this point. And with my next decade to be spent locked up in a tower, I wouldn't stand a chance at finding anything that resembled love.

Not even a good fuck at this point.

"Thanks," I said to Theo as we meandered over to the tables.

"Don't thank me for basic decency," he said. "It's uncomfortable. Anyway, I ordered a few sandwiches for the table, so you can all pick what you like." He plunked into one of the steel-framed chairs facing the four-seater pine table. The vibes here blended neon and loud casino noise with the chill ambiance of a lounge. The lighting was low, the back part of the deli featuring a stretch of red vinyl booths while the tables lay in the middle area.

"Cillian won't be upset if you grab my belongings?" I asked. I didn't want him getting angry at them over helping me out with this.

Charles snorted. "What will he do? Brood at me?"

Theo mussed his hair, a rueful grin on his face. "You're trouble."

"That's why you love me," Charles responded. My heart twisted tight. Their relationship was exactly what I longed for.

A server brought over a tray laden with sandwiches and placed them on the table. Theo had ordered a feast, which shouldn't be a surprise from the resident chef upstairs. He and Charles didn't hesitate to dive in, and I nabbed what looked like a roast beef sandwich on a crusty roll and dragged the plate in front of me.

"Do you need us to tell your neighbor to back off too?" Charles asked, talking as he chewed with his mouth open.

I shook my head. "It'll be a non-issue. Don't suppose he'll be bothering me for the next ten years."

The mood dampened at the statement, like I'd splashed black paint across the table.

"Damn, that really sucks," Charles said. "What you did for your dad, though—that was pretty selfless."

"He's all I have." I took a bite of my sandwich and savored the tang of the horseradish, the savory taste of the meat. "My mother passed away when I was a kid, and he worked hard to raise me on his own."

"Still a selfless act," Theo said, his demeanor a bit more serious. "You could've just walked away. You had a choice."

"For me, there was never a choice." The resolve settled in my bones all over again. I couldn't imagine letting my father hang.

"No wonder Cillian didn't want to send you to the Pits," Charles said. "I was surprised he took you as personal assistant, though. He hasn't had one since Olivia—"

Theo elbowed Charles in the side. "Which is his personal business."

Charles wrinkled his nose. "Right."

Who was Olivia? I filed the name away to memory, to dig into later. I'd started researching some of the businesses and names that had come up during meetings, ones that Cillian purposefully avoided or had a strong reaction to. Everyone danced around certain subjects for his sake, and I had a feeling those secrets were a pivotal key to understanding what was going on around here.

"Did you hear about Jessica, one of the dealers downstairs?" Charles asked, switching to gossip that wasn't about his boss. I nodded where needed but mentally checked out as my mind percolated with the information I'd received. I needed to do a little more investigation.

Given all the free time I had after Cillian finished needing my help each day, I'd been putting more and more effort into trying to untangle the web of secrets around the Spires. As well as avenues of escape.

The idea of running out of here and never turning back burned like a beacon in my mind.

Sure, I might be separated from my father for a spell, but if I were in a different country far from Westia, somewhere like the Lyrelands, he could find me. We could be reunited somewhere safe, somewhere far away from Peregrine City.

I polished off the rest of my sandwich, Charles occasionally poking at me with questions, but for the most part, the conversation at the table was light and superficial.

"We'll escort you upstairs and then head out to get your belongings," Theo said. "Can you send me the address?"

I typed it into his phone, and we rose from the table. No one came to collect a bill, though maybe Theo had already paid. If he even paid at all here, given his high station in Cillian's employ.

The tension grew as we headed toward the elevator, the way it always did when they were taking me back to my prison. Everyone apart from Cillian seemed to be aware I was a captive, and to their credit they were uncomfortable with the situation, yet none of them did a thing to set me free.

The ding of the elevator passing floors echoed as we zoomed to the top of the Spires, and I sucked in a sharp breath. Every time we rose up here, the weight grew heavier on my shoulders. When we reached the top and the doors opened, I stepped off.

"We'll see you later," Charles said. "Join us for dinner tonight?"

"Sure," I responded, tucking my hands into my pockets as I headed down the hallway in the direction of my room.

Except this time I had purpose.

When I stepped into the room I'd become far too comfortable with, I headed straight over to the simple desk in the corner, which had a clock with neon numbers resting on it. I set up my laptop and settled into the seat. A different book sat on the nightstand this time, and I wasn't sure whether Amelia was the one leaving them or not. However, *Lupine Fairy Tales* had been a fascinating read thus far, so different from the stories I'd grown up with.

I turned on my laptop. I'd already searched for Thorin in association with casinos, and the primary one I'd found in Peregrine City was Thorin Glass, who owned Glacier Enterprises as well as Spectacle, the rival casino of the Spires. Cillian disliked him, but based on the articles and information available about Thorin and Spectacle, it was hard to discover why, unless he simply didn't like the competition.

Cillian had also become irritated when the name Henrik had been mentioned, and from what I'd discovered, it would seem he was another Glacier Enterprises employee. Except, when I'd researched him, I couldn't find much beyond discovering that he was one of the top technomancers employed by the company.

However, that wasn't the name I was most curious about. On a hunch, I typed Olivia into a search as well as Thorin Glass.

Her name alone would be an impossibility to search for, but I'd keyed in on the topics Cillian tended to avoid.

Results turned up immediately. One of Glacier Enterprises' lawyers was Olivia Waverly.

Hmm. I glanced at the shut door, as if any moment someone would burst in and try to stop me. Not like too many strolled through these halls, though, and I needed to understand what was going on here.

I typed Olivia Waverly and Cillian Ashmore.

Old headlines splashed across the screen.

Of them as a couple, spotted in locations across Peregrine City.

Of a messy breakup.

Of Olivia parting ways with the Spires, going to work for Glacier Enterprises.

I clicked out of the tabs and leaned back in my seat. Was his surliness, his avoidance, all over a broken heart? It seemed like an impossibility for the callous demon I'd met. However, the breakthrough sparked my mind to life. Adrenaline pumped through my veins, as if this discovery gave me some sort of foothold in my current situation. Any clarity beyond the murky non-answers and immediate avoidance.

An email notification appeared on my laptop. From my father.

I hate the idea of you stuck there, Beau. I spoke to a friend, who told me the West Wing holds the answers. I'm not sure what that means, or if the information will help you, but if it gives you any way to break free, please try.

Love,

Dad

My heart thumped in double time.

He might not know what the West Wing was, but I definitely did. And I had a map to it. If the West Wing held the answers, did that mean it held an avenue of escape?

Cillian was gone at the moment, on a business meeting, and Theo and Charles were out helping to get my belongings. I wasn't sure where Amelia was, but this might be the only chance I'd have to learn what they were all hiding.

Time to go to the West Wing.

CHAPTER 10

I didn't bolt out of the room straight away.

No, I took my time.

I changed into black sweats and a black shirt that would allow me to slink about in the shadows better, and I tucked the copy of the layout Amelia had printed for me into my pocket. While I wasn't sure exactly what witchy measures Amelia had placed on me, I was certain they were only to keep me on the premises, not ward me out of the West Wing.

My heart thudded harder. Was I actually doing this? What if Cillian found out?

However, no one was here at the moment, so this was the one chance I'd get. Dad was trying to help me from the outside, in whatever way he could, and snooping around the West Wing might be the key to unlocking my escape.

If Dad had help, he probably planned on leaving the area as well. Because once I was gone, the deal would fall through and Cillian would come for him again.

Complacency had already started to seep through my veins after spending only a few months here, which now sent my alarm bells ringing. The sooner I started to sympathize with the people holding me captive, the more I'd give them allowances and the less I'd fight back and try to find a way out. And yes, I'd agreed to stay here in my father's stead, but I didn't care what debts he'd incurred at the Spires. Nothing justified sending him to the Pits.

I shut off the laptop and slipped my phone into my pocket. I had what money remained in my wallet, which wasn't much, not for a grand relocation, but if the West Wing held the secret to my way out, I wouldn't waste the chance.

I paused at the doorway and stared back into my room. The laptop was closed on the desk, and my bedsheets were rumpled from this morning. The latest mystery book lay on my nightstand, and the wardrobe full of clothes sat open. While this was where I'd been living for the past few months, none of it felt like mine. No mugs of coffee and tea were scattered throughout, no stacks of teetering books or heaps of papers I sorted through like at my old apartment.

Leaving all this behind would be like waking up from an odd dream, not like reality.

That was *if* I ended up finding anything of use. This could be a big risk with no reward. But I'd never know if I didn't try.

I stepped out of the room, my senses on high alert. Quiet echoed through the hallway, an odious and devouring thing, but today the emptiness was in my favor. Despite it being midday, a midnight quality existed in this section of the Spires, so different than the rest of the place, as if I were wading through an eternal night.

My footsteps were too loud for my liking, and I slowed my pace to a deliberate one, making sure each step grew softer and softer until they were unnoticeable. The dim lighting lured me down the corridor, toward the shadows crawling at the end where it was intersected. The left would lead me past the normal areas I'd already explored before curving around to the area that had been marked as "do not enter" territory.

This could be a terrible idea. If Cillian discovered me here, guaranteed he'd send me to the Pits. The tentative freedoms I had would be stripped away to nothing, and I'd be struggling like the rest who were shunted down there.

Yet, if I didn't try, I'd lose my mind wondering.

The unknown of what the West Wing hid had burned inside me from the moment Amelia decreed it forbidden.

I turned to the left, glancing behind me to make sure no one approached from the opposite side of the corridor. Empty. A light spilled out from one of the rooms up ahead, so I crept forward carefully. I hadn't run into Sofia again, or the werewolf who had been in the room that one night, but occasionally when I wandered by, lights were on in the rooms and the doors were shut. I'd like to think the woman who ran Haven wouldn't be involved in human or monster trafficking, but I couldn't come up with an explanation for why these rooms were sometimes occupied.

All the mysteries settled uneasily beneath my skin.

Voices sounded from the corridor I'd just come from—including the familiar one of Amelia's.

Panic rushed through me, and I sped up to the nearest open door and slipped inside. It was dark in here and smelled like lemon cleaner and chalk, but I pressed myself behind the door against the cool wall.

My heart thumped so hard I could swear the sound was audible from the halls, but I forced my breathing to regulate so I didn't give myself away.

Footsteps grew louder, and so did Amelia's voice. If she had some kind of tracking on me, she might discover me now and this whole endeavor would be over.

I held as still as possible, trying to make myself invisible. Too fast, the situation brought me back to grade school where I'd done the same, hiding away in a classroom in the hopes Ken and Jake—two of the guys who'd decided to make my life hell—wouldn't find me. My stomach roiled. For as far as I'd come, I was still cowering, still hiding away.

The footsteps started to fade, so she must've headed in the opposite direction with whoever she'd brought up here. My heart thumped at a wild pace, my legs begging me to move even as I remained still. If I stepped into the corridor now, I'd risk detection.

But now I knew where Amelia was, which worked in my favor.

When silence descended again through the area, until all I could hear were my own shaky breaths, I peeked out past the doorframe.

The halls were empty once more.

I resumed my trek down the corridor, past a couple of closed doors that were clearly occupied if the light and slight shuffling coming from behind them was anything to go by. Whoever was in there didn't want to be identified any more than I didn't, though, since this area was handled with the utmost secrecy.

I followed the curve of the corridor, which led me to more rooms along another stretch stained by shadows where I stopped and pulled the layout from my pocket.

Up ahead, a short set of steps led to an elevated area, more closed doors and corridors branching from there. It was elegantly roped off with a clear "Do Not Enter" sign.

I slowed down, my heart thumping so hard it reverberated through the room.

Cillian was such a drama queen, his personal area barred, as if a sign would deter anyone. And besides, the only ones who resided up here were his staff, me, and whoever the rotating people in the spare rooms were. Though he could house a large portion of Peregrine City with the sheer volume of empty rooms in the Spires.

I sucked in a sharp breath and slipped under the velvet rope.

Into the West Wing.

What I searched for was beyond me. I didn't want to dive into his personal life or endeavors. I simply wanted to uncover anything that would signal a way out. A way to escape.

Unlike the rest of the corridors, where some of the doors remained open, everything here was shut.

I walked up to the nearest one and turned the knob. Locked. Right. That should be expected. Dust coated areas around here, as if Charles wasn't allowed to come clean, which again felt a bit ridiculous. What was Cillian hiding here that he had to keep from those closest to him?

A slight scuff was clear on the floor from the lack of cleaning, and I followed the trail, which led deeper down the corridor. One trail stopped in front of a door to my right, and the other went to the end of the hall, where a massive black door loomed. It looked forbidding and all-consuming, as if it held every secret trapped inside this place.

When I tried the door to the right, it opened. The room before me was an ornate bedroom, featuring more of the twisted black branch décor Cillian seemed to love. Mirrors on the ceiling and along the walls reflected scraps of light from the windows. The contrast of his white pillows and black silken sheets stood out, intimate in a way that made me shiver, and the bed was far larger than a king size, but demons had their own businesses that catered to them. This room wasn't what I searched for, but I was mesmerized nonetheless.

On his nightstand stood an odd sculpture of a rose, metal and flattened, and his shelves held books and oddities, glass cases that gleamed and snagged my curiosity, some with demonic runes imprinted on them, but I couldn't be deterred.

I pulled myself away from the room and shut the door behind me. My goal had to be behind the hulking door at the end of the corridor. The tension grew the closer I neared, as if the secrets and power inside it grew so immense they could barely be contained.

I stopped in front of it, a chill settling inside my bones. I was at the point of no return.

I tugged, but of course it was locked.

Disappointment fluttered through me. Had this all been for nothing? I traced the carvings across the front of the doorway, ornate and detailed.

One was deeper than the others, right beneath the doorknob.

I crouched and squinted at it, trying to discern its shape in the dim lighting. I traced my fingers along it again, trying to commit the shape to memory—a bulbous top, a long line beneath it.

Like a rose.

My heart thudded hard, and I sucked in a sharp breath. Should I try it? My whole body felt jittery, as if I'd downed too much coffee on an empty stomach. I stood and pulled away from the door, my footsteps careful and quiet as I headed back toward his room. When I stepped inside, a sense of the forbidden washed over me. This was intrusive and invasive and wrong. Yet so was holding me captive in the upper Spires.

I picked up the flattened metal rose on his nightstand, its weight hefty. Yet the shape of it reminded me of what I'd just traced with my fingertips. It was worth a try. I strode back down the corridor, my senses on hyperalert. Each creak or whisper of a breeze from outside made me stiffen as I slowly approached the massive door.

Cillian wasn't here. He was at a business meeting.

Yet I couldn't shake the sense I was being watched. The thickness in the air, as if I stepped through fog. I swallowed, but my mouth became dry as I reached the door. This time, I placed the metal rose where those deeper divots were. It sank into the space, fitting there perfectly.

A click resounded throughout the corridor.

My heart in my throat, I turned the knob.

The door creaked open.

An enormous room spread before me. It was filled with computer servers, wires, and screens—a large one hung on the right side of the room. The bookshelves were filled with a tightly packed mixture of files and hardbacks, all neatly coordinated. This must be the heart of his operation. My pulse sped as I stepped inside. The air in here was crisp, as if this area was better maintained than the rest, and the hum of electronics was ever-present.

On the other side of the room lay a darkened doorway, which piqued my interest. I took out the printed layout—which didn't extend past here. I wasn't sure where it headed, but it wasn't listed in the information I'd been given.

The main screen held a set of numbers on it: *52 days, 12 hours, 45 minutes, 32 seconds.*

What the hell did that mean? I stared at it, watching the seconds count down until the minutes changed to forty-four. Something seemed vital about it, and I wandered over to scrutinize it closer. The screen was navy blue, the numbers in bright white font that glared against the gloom through the rest of the room, just barely lit by the electronic screens that were still running.

"The Rose Protocol" was written at the base, but what the countdown was leading to mystified me.

I wandered over to the files—they were company files for the Spires, which wasn't of any interest to me. When I neared the largest computer tower by the black desk overtaking the left corner of the room, it was clear from the blinking blue light that it was on and connected to the major screen hanging on the far wall.

My skin prickled as I walked through the room, step by careful step. Dust clung to the corners, yet the desk was clear of it, clean in a way that implied frequent use. A few black orbs looked like paperweights, but when I glanced closer, electricity flickered in their depths. Magic? In a place like this, I could believe it. The hum of the electronics filtered underneath my skin.

How was this supposed to help me escape? Why would Cillian keep this room under such fierce protection? It only seemed to multiply the secrets rather than offer any clarifications. The tick of the numbers made my bones hum, as if something significant lay on the screen, a truth in plain sight.

"What the HELL are you doing in here?"

Cillian's voice boomed through the room, with a deep and feral fury I'd never heard before.

I whipped in the direction of the door. He stood there, shoulders heaving, his golden eyes half crazed and his fangs on full display, sharp and deadly.

Oh, fuck.

Fear rushed through me in a dizzying sweep. I'd been discovered.

There was no explaining this. He'd kill me.

The crazed look in his eyes, the ragged breaths, the growl pouring from his lips confirmed that. If I stayed, I was dead.

My gaze snagged on the blackened doorway. He blocked the other one, so the only shot was this one—in the dark.

Cillian took the first booming footstep forward.

I ran.

CHAPTER 11

A nother growl burst out of him, but I didn't dare turn around.

I plunged through the doorway into liquid darkness, expecting a door, a room, to have to bar myself in and buy seconds before my imminent demise.

Instead, I stepped onto the landing of a staircase.

It coiled down into pure shadow.

Except it traveled *down*.

My heart swooped. I didn't hesitate, bolting down the steps. The shadows swirled around me, like living entities. The sound multiplied as I flew as fast as possible, the winding staircase turning in dizzying circles as if I descended a private tower. I couldn't stop, though. Not now. Cillian's growl sounded from above, echoing all the way here, and loud stomping gave a warning signal of his descent.

If he caught up to me, I was dead.

I'd been intruding in the one area I'd been told to avoid. It was dangerous, yet I'd done it anyway.

My heart lodged in my throat as I flew down the unending staircase, sweat bursting out on my temple. My breaths sawed out of me, and my legs burned, but I moved on borrowed energy. Once the adrenaline died, I'd falter, but until then, I raced down the staircase at faster speeds than I believed possible. The clatter sent reverberations up my shins, but I didn't stop. Couldn't stop.

How many floors did this descend? His casino was twenty floors up, the upper tiers all part of his expansive castle. I couldn't manage twenty flights of steps. He'd catch up to me well before then.

I reached out for the wall and ran my fingertips along it, as if it might hold some secrets I could miss—if a doorframe, an emergency exit, cropped into view, I didn't want to pass by it. Not with the rapid way I raced down the steps. My feet ached from the pounding pressure, my chest burning from the heaving breaths that escaped me with every passing second, every step onward.

But I couldn't stop now.

Not if I wanted to live.

While he was clearly intimidating, clearly dangerous, I'd somehow along the way begun to view Cillian differently—maybe the conversations, working alongside him day by day. Another roar resounded throughout the stairwell, booming loud enough to make the stone walls tremble. Any illusions of safety were dispelled.

As I wound around the stairwell again, a landing came into sight, even though the stairs continued down past it. If I remained on the steps, I'd lose steam far before he did, but this way, maybe I could find a place to hide.

I skidded to a halt, slamming into the wall as I tumbled forward to the door. I fumbled with the knob, my palms slick, but it didn't turn. Those booming footsteps grew louder and louder. I tugged on the handle again, and this time it opened.

Yes!

I burst through, and the brightness of the light made me blink. Patterned, rich red carpet. The clink of machines. Casino. I was on one of the casino floors. Fuck, I needed to hide. Any second, not only would Cillian be after me, but he could easily sic his security on me. I'd be crushed by them in a hot second.

My vision adjusted enough to note the balcony to my right, and to my left, farther down, the glare of a light and the sheen of the golden doors of an elevator.

My legs moved unbidden.

Gasps sounded around me as I rushed toward the elevators at top speed. The people blurred as I passed, since I was running too fast to absorb details. Guaranteed, at any moment I'd be garnering attention from security, but whether I evaded them depended on how quickly I could get inside the elevator. Once there, I wasn't sure where I'd go, but my window of escape narrowed before my eyes.

I skidded to a halt right in front of the elevator doors and slapped the button.

Shouts, chatter, and the *clink, clink, clink* of slot machines echoed behind me, but I didn't dare turn around. Once I saw my odds, I'd freeze. My forehead dripped sweat, my throat bone-dry, and my shoulders heaved. My whole body begged me to keep running, to surge forward, but I waited for the elevator.

I'd fucked up. I'd fucked up so badly.

But all I could do now was run.

Those metal doors opened up, and I dove inside.

A few people were already in there, one guy exiting, but I smashed the "close door" button as fast as possible, then the ground-floor one. I pressed myself against the wall, casting a quick glance at the other people in the elevator—two women about my age wearing sparkly sheath dresses and an older guy in a suit, who all stared at me. I returned my gaze to what floor we were on—the seventh.

Maybe ground floor wasn't the place to exit. Cillian might be expecting that. Especially if he had alerted the guards.

The second floor had exits out to the street.

I chewed on my lower lip, hard enough that I tasted copper. Sweat was pasted on my forehead, my arms, everywhere, and the stares of the other people in the elevator bored into me, but if this was the worst they'd seen in this stretch of Peregrine City, they clearly hadn't been around here long enough. My breathing hadn't evened, still shaky as the elevator dropped floor after floor.

It stopped on the fourth floor, and I sucked in a breath. Fuck it.

When the doors started to creak open, I pressed "door close" and jammed the second-floor button this time. If security awaited me on the other side, I couldn't risk letting them in. No one in the elevator argued my decision, but they glued themselves to the other side, watching me with wide eyes. Right, away from the maniac.

Third floor. *Ding*.

Second floor.

It was go time.

The elevator doors slid open, and I slipped out and swept to the side of the main atrium as fast as possible. I didn't want to break into a run on this floor, didn't want to attract any attention. On the far side of the room here, security moved in a sweep across the floor. They were thorough and quick-footed. I needed to escape, and fast.

To my right lay a corridor that ran adjacent to the main floor in the center. I needed to find a side exit. They'd be expecting me to head to the front of the casino.

I darted down the corridor, walking at a quick clip but not quick enough to draw immediate attention. Granted, with my wild hair, heaving shoulders, and the sweat pasted across my skin, I was a neon-red warning sign.

The security guards would spot me in seconds.

People strolled by at a leisurely pace, couples and groups of friends murmuring to each other as they enjoyed their time at the Spires. I glanced behind me. No security in sight. Yet. My calves squeezed tight, begging me to bolt. My heart hammered so hard I could hear it in my ears, the sound deafening. God, I was so close.

So close to leaving the Spires.

The corridor opened to the left, and I made the turn. A few yards away lay a glass door. My pulse pounded. Could that be an exit? A way out of here?

A shout sounded from the hallway I'd traversed, and my blood turned to ice.

Someone must've spotted me.

I tossed away any attempts at blending in and bolted for the door. The second I neared, I skidded to a halt, slamming into the cool glass. Beyond the door lay a busy street—lay my freedom. *Thump, thump, thump.* My heart threatened to burst out of my chest.

I glanced back. Security hadn't emerged yet, but those pounding footsteps grew louder, mingling with my heartbeat.

I yanked the door open and vaulted outside.

The sunlight slammed into me at once, and I squinted. The Spires often distorted my sense of day and night, being trapped inside, and the upstairs featured so much shadow and darkness it was easy to drown in it. Yet out here, Casino Alley was as loud and vibrant as ever, without the allure the night delivered.

Shit, I needed to move.

The exit dumped me out into a stairwell that led to an alley, major streets filled with bustling cars on either side. I clattered down the steps, but when I reached the bottom, paralysis struck again. Which way did I go? I should've spent more time studying the layout outside the Spires and the area beyond. My calves spasmed. I pivoted to the right, hoping the direction would lead me to the light rail—how I'd first arrived weeks ago. My footsteps echoed, and shade obscured me slightly, though it wouldn't hide me from anyone peering through the windows lining the place.

My heart slammed so hard I was shocked it didn't just pop out of my chest. I jogged forward, my shins aching. When I reached the traffic, I'd try to cross the street, create some barrier between me and the Spires. The shadow of the building was immense, and a shudder rushed through me, as though no matter how far I ran, I'd never escape.

I gasped in a breath as I neared the edge of the alley.

So close.

A group of men stepped into view, blocking my way.

I skidded to a halt. They were dressed in different suits—not the standard security black.

"Well, well," the guy in the middle stated, crossing his arms. He was taller, with broad shoulders, a steep brow, and a square jaw. He had a thick beard and sour scowl that fit the rest of his cruel features. The sight of him jogged my memory, but I couldn't quite place from where. "Who's the lost lamb?"

"Ashmore's new personal assistant." The slender guy to the right of him looked familiar too—from one of the meetings, even though his name evaded me.

"He's taken on personal help again?" The man in the middle grinned, an ugly, vicious thing. His eyes held a malevolent darkness. While Cillian could be terrifying, it was in more of a force-of-nature sort of way, a wildness to him that couldn't be replicated. Yet the look in this man's eyes held a premeditated and visceral cruelty that shook me to my core. "If you've escaped your master, I can introduce you to a new one."

No, no, no.

I whipped around and surged forward.

A hand clamped down around my wrist.

Another guy rushed around to step in front of me—bulky, broad, and blocking my exit. "Where do you think you're going?"

"Make sure not to damage my new goods," the bearded guy proclaimed. "That's my job."

Ice shot through my veins.

No. No. No.

I had to get free. Except I was surrounded.

If I didn't escape here, I was in for a worse fate than being imprisoned in a tower.

The bearded man grabbed me by the shoulder, his fingers curling in like hooks. There were five of them, and two snagged onto me with rough grips, the others obstructing any clear path to freedom. The stench of their body odor and oppressive cologne surrounded me. My heart lodged in my throat.

I had to leave.

Had to break free.

"Quick, let's get out of here," the bearded man ordered. "Before we're spotted."

My whole body locked up, and even my breath remained stuck. Yet the moment they pushed me forward, it was like they hit a button. I thrashed in their grip, letting out a holler that echoed through the alley.

"Shut up." The guy to my right smacked me in the face, the sting barely registering in the face of sheer panic.

Fuck. Fuck. Fuck.

I thrashed again, trying to kick out at the nearest shin.

They started to drag me forward, toward the edge of the alley. If they got me into a vehicle, my chances diminished drastically. Who'd be searching for me anyway? Dread coiled through me, even as I lashed out and struggled every inch of the way.

No one would find me.

No one would come looking when I vanished.

I tried to shout again, and one of the assholes smacked me in the side of the face—hard. It stung. My cheek throbbed. Their rough grips formed steel bands around me, and the more I resisted, the tighter they held on.

Fuck.

Then a roar sounded through the alley, with enough power to deafen.

CHAPTER 12

"**G**et the fuck off him." The bellow quaked through the alley, enough that even the stones trembled.

The grip on me loosened, and the man standing in front of me stepped to the side.

A lone figure approached, but it was the only one needed to dispel a crowd.

Cillian Ashmore.

Mere minutes before, I'd been terrified to see him, but to my surprise, relief rushed through my veins. The hands restraining my wrists and shoulders retracted, and my knees trembled. I didn't bother holding myself up, just sank to the ground. My knees thudded against the hard surface.

Cillian strode forward, each step deliberate and echoing through the space.

The sunlight glinted off his black horns and highlighted the deep reddish hue of his skin. His hair was a mess, his suit and button-down mussed instead of pristine. His golden eyes were wild with rage, but in this moment, his gaze wasn't directed at me. Cillian's hands balled into fists as he approached, and the sheer danger he emanated was like witnessing a live bomb.

"We caught someone who evaded your security," the bearded man said. "Thought you'd be grateful."

He bared those long and wicked fangs, and a literal growl rolled through the space. "Thorin. What are you doing here?"

"Just wandering by," Thorin responded. "No need to be so hostile when we're simply trying to help."

Oh fuck. That was where I recognized him from. After all the running, the capture, and whatever was to come, I didn't have the bandwidth to process the magnitude of this man's relevance.

"And Chadwick, what are you doing with him?" Cillian asked, his voice crashing down like thunder.

Chadwick—from the meetings.

"We were walking through town and happened to see your personal assistant on the run," he said, a tremble in his voice he couldn't quite mask. "We figured we were doing you a favor."

"And Henrik," Cillian growled. One of the men who'd grabbed me—middle-aged—straightened up, his lips thin.

Cillian stared them down, and by his lack of response, he clearly didn't believe them for a second. I opened my mouth but it was dry, the words withered up. What I could even say was beyond me, as I was guaranteed to face punishment after my escape. Now that he'd caught me, what would he do? Send me to the Pits?

At this point, even that sounded better than going with Thorin. The cruelty in the man's voice wouldn't leave me any time soon, and I'd seen enough of bullies and beasts to recognize the difference. Cillian was wild, mercurial, but not malicious—a beast. Thorin—he was cruel, like the bullies who used to gang up on me in school. My limbs trembled.

"Thorin, Henrik, have you forgotten you're not welcome on my premises?" Cillian said, his voice simmering. "Chadwick, our associations are now dissolved as well."

"But—" Chadwick started then stopped.

The look in Cillian's eyes was deadly. He loomed over all five of these men, casting a long-reaching shadow. "Get away from him, and get off my property," he intoned, the threat in his voice not hidden.

For a moment, silence reigned, the tension growing in the air like a bomb about to drop. I didn't move from my spot, unsure which way the pendulum would swing.

"Come on," Thorin said. "Let's leave Cillian to being alone and miserable."

A few mutters sounded, but Thorin led the way as the group departed, the shuffles and scrapes of their feet on the pavement resounding through the alley. Relief saturated me at their departure.

As much as Cillian had kept me locked away in the Spires, at the end of the day, I'd chosen to take my father's place. He just enforced the bargain I'd made. Guilt tangled with the anger and fear that roiled inside me.

And I'd broken into his chambers, rifled through his secrets.

He stared at the retreating men, arms crossed, not budging an inch or saying a word, as if waiting until he was sure they'd vanished. His focus wasn't on me, thank fuck. I sucked in a long slow breath and pushed myself to stand. My body felt like it'd been tossed in a washing machine and spat out. My legs barely kept me upright, my shins throbbing.

Cillian's gaze swept my way, pinning me in place. "And you."

I gulped hard. Was I sorry? I still wasn't sure. I'd been so desperate for freedom that it'd pushed me to action, and I'd seized the opportunity. However, I could admit one truth. "Thank you."

Because if he hadn't intervened, the situation would've been a lot worse.

He stared at me for a moment, those full lips pursed. The sunlight brought out aspects of him the shadows couldn't—the richness of those golden eyes, the subtle weariness there as well. His presence alone was a forbidding, intense thing, but after the way he'd come to my defense, I experienced something new.

Safety.

He'd come in and saved me when he didn't have to. I'd run away, and he could've cast me off to the wolves. Instead, he'd rushed to my defense.

Granted, he still might eviscerate me, but in that moment, I stole the seconds of calm while I had them.

"Let's go," he said, tilting his head toward the steps. "Time to head back."

A mere hour ago, all I'd been able to think about was escape, but when he said those words, further relief rushed through me. Because I'd been unprepared for the level of danger I was in from the rest of the world now I was associated with Cillain Ashmore. Maybe the precautions to keep me in the Spires hadn't just been about my captivity.

Maybe it had been to keep me safe.

The newfound understanding rippled through me, rocking me to my core.

I trailed up the steps after him, forcing my pace to quicken even though my body protested. He didn't look back, just expected me to follow, but I didn't want to remain in this alley in case Thorin and the others returned—I didn't trust that they'd be obedient. The moment

I stepped inside, the air that had stifled me before my escape caressed like a reassurance. Shame flushed through me. Would I have to face Charles and Theo? Amelia? And they'd know I tried to make a run for it.

Or maybe he was leading me inside to negotiate sending me to the Pits.

We walked the halls I'd run through mere moments before, as if nothing had happened. My breathing calmed, even though the crash of adrenaline brought aches and pains, and my legs trembled like they were about to fall off. How I'd run as fast and far as I had was mind-blowing, considering I'd never been at the pinnacle of athleticism.

Cillian, of course, looked rumpled, but he breathed evenly and walked steadily, like he hadn't just chased me through the entire casino. Bastard.

Sweat cooled on my skin like paste, and I was dying to scrub it off. However, I was about to face whatever fate lay in store for me. Not only had I disobeyed his direct order to stay out of the West Wing, but I'd tried to escape.

We reached the elevator, and he swiped his card and pressed his print on the pad before he pushed the button for the upper floors. The elevator *whooshed* up. I leaned against the wall, hoping it'd keep me upright. Fuck. So much had happened since this morning that my mind spun. It felt like a lifetime ago.

The silence stretched between us, reminding me of the first time I'd gotten into this elevator—except back then Amelia had been there as well. I had no idea then how much my life would change. Cillian leaned on the opposite side of the elevator, his arms crossed and his gaze veering toward me every few minutes.

"What happened?" he asked at last, breaking through the quiet.

I swallowed hard. "I thought...well, I didn't think after you discovered me there I'd still be standing. So I ran. When I made it outside, they found me."

"Thorin doesn't just appear," Cillian said, a hint of accusation lurking in his voice.

"I know I'm not making a case as being trustworthy right now, but that's the truth. I'd never seen the man before in my life."

"Hmm." The rumble sent a vibration through the air, and I shivered. For as terrifying as Cillian had been, he hadn't scared me in the same way Thorin had.

I tipped my head back and looked at the top of the elevator. No matter what case I pled, I wouldn't appear anything but guilty. Not after I'd broken into the West Wing and tried to escape the Spires.

The elevator let out a *ding*, and the doors opened.

The hallways were familiar, ones I'd roamed plenty of times at this point. We weren't far from the kitchen and dining hall. I followed Cillian, not saying a word. What could I even offer? When we reached the open door to the dining hall, he stopped and strode in. No one else was in there to witness my shame, thankfully.

Cillian chose one of the nearest tables and sat. I followed suit, the hushed quiet settling over me. The second my ass hit the seat, I almost sobbed in relief. After what I'd put my body through today, I'd be feeling the soreness for a while. My muscles still slightly trembled.

"Why?" he asked. His golden gaze bored into me, as though he'd know if I tried to lie.

I swallowed hard. The truth dwelled deep within me, but I wasn't sure I wanted to unleash it. However, this was the chance to explain myself, for better or for worse. "I'm not free."

He settled in his seat, scanning me over. "And going to the West Wing?"

"I hoped I'd find answers there," I said, shocked my voice remained steady. My throat was bone dry, and when I swallowed, my tongue stuck to the roof of my mouth. I would kill for water. "I've been in the dark from the moment I stepped foot in here."

"And what illumination did you find?" he asked.

My shoulders tensed. His calmness unsettled me. I'd been prepared for him to roar at me, to call security to drag me to the Pits. Instead, we were having a direct conversation. And I was as sure of his aim now as I had been when I'd first arrived here.

"Truthfully, very little. I saw the massive computer screen you have tucked away in there, and some old books, but I barely explored. Thorin...that's your rival, right? He owns the other casino?"

Cillian's expression darkened. "Thorin Glass is one of the most despicable people in the entirety of Westia."

"I caught as much," I said, a shiver rolling through me. "Thank you again."

"He views you as mine," Cillian said, his voice low and husky. "Therefore, he will stop at nothing to obtain you."

The way he'd said "mine" curled around me and squeezed tight. While Cillian meant it to mean a possession, the rasp in his tone held a fierceness that...I didn't hate. After experiencing his protection out there, how he'd swept to my defense and scared away Thorin and his cronies, I couldn't help but see him a bit differently.

All the wildness about him was terrifying, but directed in my defense? My pulse raced in a way it hadn't for quite a long time.

The quiet settled between us again, but one question burned stronger than anything else.

"So, what now?"

Cillian arched an eyebrow. "Now you get some rest, because you'll be up early tomorrow. We've got a long day of meetings."

Wait, what?

"But what about repercussions?" I asked, regretting the moment the words left me. Why had I mentioned anything?

A slight smirk lifted his lips. "Seems to me you're wanting punishment."

Heat rushed to my cheeks, and I shifted in the seat and glanced away. "Just needed to clarify."

"Mm," Cillian responded, rising from his seat. "Are you planning on running away again?"

After what I'd encountered out there, knowing Thorin and others might have a vendetta against me, I'd come to a decision on that as well. Like it or not, my life had changed completely the day I stepped into the Spires, when I'd agreed to take my father's place.

"No," I said. "I'm not."

Cillian skimmed his claws along the surface of the table before meeting my eyes, a light scratching noise echoing there. "Good."

With that, he turned and walked out of the room.

I sagged in the seat, the weight of everything that had happened today crashing over me. My feet became cement blocks, my mind slowing to a crawl in the wake of everything I'd been bombarded with. My whole body ached, and the first thing I needed to do when I got up was grab some water, but for a moment, I just stayed here at the table.

My perception had been tossed on its head today. When I'd come here, I'd been sure Cillian Ashmore was pure evil—that the CEO of the Spires was every whispered rumor I'd read. However, the experience of witnessing him today in contrast to Thorin allowed me to peer behind the veil. Cillian held multitudes behind the curt responses, the glowers, and the snarls.

Somehow, in some way, he'd managed to spark my curiosity.

And that was a deadly thing.

CHAPTER 13

"Come on, Jailbreak." Amelia's voice rang through the room. I'd just emerged from the bathroom in nothing but a towel, and she stood in the open doorway, waiting for me.

"Cillian's summoned you for breakfast," she said. "I wouldn't keep him waiting. Not after yesterday." Amusement danced in her eyes. I swallowed a gulp of relief. I'd thought for sure Amelia would hate me after I'd not only violated her order to avoid the West Wing, but had also tried to escape. And clearly, she already knew about it.

"Right, let me get dressed," I said. When she didn't move, I lifted an eyebrow. "Unless I'm supposed to go like this?"

"Your choice," Amelia said, pushing off from leaning against the doorway. "I'll see you later."

"You're not going to be there?" I asked.

She shook her head. "No, I've got to give the security team an extra debriefing, since somehow, a lone man managed to escape them yesterday."

Embarrassment heated my cheeks. Right, that had been my fault. "I'll see you later, then."

She slipped away as fast as she'd arrived, and I shut the door behind her before I rummaged through the wardrobe. I pulled on a pair of charcoal slacks and a white button-down that fit my frame nicely, then I ran a brush through my curls, spraying them to tame them a bit. Even though my muscles ached from yesterday, no other signs remained that I'd bolted.

Yet a fundamental shift had occurred in me.

I was aware the situation was unethical—that my father and I shouldn't be beholden to Cillian—yet I still wasn't sure what my father had done. And if it was a matter of jail time or this, well, this might be the kinder solution.

I left the bathroom and slipped on some black loafers. Since I wasn't sure if we'd head to a meeting right after breakfast, it was better to be prepared. At least, that was what I told myself.

My heart thumped a little harder as I stepped out of my room and made my way down the hall, and my feet dragged as though I waded through mud. Just last night we'd been here, after a hellish day. Today, it felt like a fever dream, even if my body carried the strain and fatigue from yesterday. Everything ached.

My footsteps echoed through the corridor, yet I didn't have the same reservations as the last time I'd been summoned for a meal. After seeing Cillian at his most terrifying, I'd come to realize I didn't fear him in the same way I had.

Because he could've aimed all his power and viciousness at me, but instead he'd come to my aid.

When I stepped through the door to the dining hall, I half expected Theo and Charles to be there as well. However, only Cillian sat at the table, waiting for me.

My pulse sped up.

He'd cleaned up from last night, and was now in the polished and professional attire I'd come to expect from him. His jaw was freshly shaved, his horns gleamed like obsidian, and his black suit fit snugly, highlighting the man's bulk. He leaned back in his seat, facing away from me, and his casual sprawl ensnared me, the way his thick thighs spread and he dominated the space he was in. I licked my lips, my mouth suddenly dry.

Even though I approached, he didn't budge or look back, yet I had the feeling he knew I was here the moment I stepped up to the door. Something about Cillian suggested a predator's level of attention, and nothing I'd seen dissuaded me from that.

"I've been summoned?" I asked, needing to break through the quiet. I settled in the seat beside him on instinct, after doing so as his assistant so many times. I regretted the proximity at once. This close, I couldn't ignore the power radiating from him, the intensity in his sharp, golden eyes. The scent of him, all brimstone and musk, threatened to overpower me, but I sucked in a shaky breath and focused on the food before us.

An array of breakfast fare had been left—eggs, bacon, and toast with a purplish spread that had a savory sort of taste. Apparently a demon delicacy, which I'd tried a few times. There was also a carafe of coffee and cups. I poured myself some at once, needing the hit of caffeine if I were to survive this breakfast.

"Sore today?" Cillian asked with a light lift of his brow.

Heat rushed through me in a fierce torrent. He referred to the great escape I'd made yesterday, I was aware of that, but the sensuality in his tone was hard to avoid. "Remind me to start working out on a regular basis. My body was not prepared for that level of exertion."

"You're aware we have a gym up here, correct?"

"I suppose you spend hours a day there," I commented, not thinking.

Cillian's grin widened, a few fangs poking out. "Noticing my muscles?" The wicked glint in his eyes was unmistakable.

I choked mid-swallow of coffee. Placing the mug down, I did my best to recover even as I spluttered on the hot liquid.

Cillian's coolness had been manageable, easier.

Cillian's full attention? I was underprepared. My whole body charged like I'd been plugged into an outlet.

"Look, I was a librarian," I muttered. "The gym wasn't high on my list of concerns."

"Ah, so you can't be well read *and* work out?" he asked before taking a sip of his coffee.

I chewed on my lip. This was the chattiest he'd been since I'd met him, and I wasn't sure whether he'd had a personality replacement in the span of time between my discovery of the West Wing and now. As though last night a lightning bolt had struck him and *bam*, he was suddenly sociable. "It's possible, but I prefer to spend my spare time curled up with a book, not running laps like a madman."

"Did you look at the library here?" he asked.

I stared at him. "What?"

"It's farther down this wing, around the corner," he said.

"You've known I was a librarian from the very beginning, and you're mentioning this now?"

Cillian shrugged. "I figured you'd found it already. You've spent plenty of time exploring, and I'm aware of your innate curiosity."

My cheeks heated again. The fact no one had scolded or reprimanded me for yesterday affected me more than I realized. I kept bracing myself for a comment, for censure, for them to be livid with me for breaking the rules, for trying to escape.

Instead, Cillian and even Amelia were...kinder? I couldn't for the life of me understand why.

"If I'd known you had a library, you would've had to pry me away from there daily," I responded, a blip of excitement coursing through my veins. While his collection couldn't possibly compare to Peregrine City's library, the chance to be around a large selection of books again, to smell the slightly sweet almond and leather pervasive in those spaces, was one I wouldn't pass up.

"Tomorrow," he said. "I can take you to the library tomorrow."

"You're assuming I won't have the time to find it today," I challenged. "You've told me where it is, so I'm not likely to let that stone go unturned."

Cillian's grin widened. "And you're assuming I'm not going to keep you busy the entire day. Yesterday was quite disruptive for my business, and you've got a lot of fires to douse—and apologies to security staff to draft." Even as he said the words, they were light, like a tease not a censure, and I couldn't help but wonder if this aspect of him had been hiding there all along.

"Fair," I responded, hiding behind another sip of coffee.

Cillian took a bite of toast, the delicate move almost comical with the way he clutched it in his claws. Now that my sheer hatred of him had been stripped away, I couldn't help but acknowledge how my attention strayed to him far too often. How his appearance was arresting, and not just due to how formidable he was. His golden gaze landed on me, and he winked.

I incinerated.

Playfulness wasn't ever something I would've expected from Cillian Ashmore, to the point I wasn't sure if I'd hallucinated it. My whole body vibrated with tension from his presence, from the liquid-smooth gesture from a man who should loathe me. And instead, he seemed to have not only forgiven me for my grand escape, but we'd also made some sort of breakthrough.

"You going to eat your breakfast?" Cillian asked, arching a brow. His gaze was knowing, as if he understood the devastating effect of a simple wink. "We will need to get going soon. The first meeting for the day will come fast."

"Please tell me Chadwick won't be there," I muttered as I crunched down on a piece of bacon. Thinking about how the man who I'd been in plenty of meetings with had flipped on a dime sent a shudder through me.

"He's not allowed to step foot in the Spires again," Cillian rumbled. "He should've thought twice before double-crossing me. His life's about to become hell."

"Don't tell me you have some underground operation to dispose of your enemies," I joked, but the joke dried on my tongue because of the potential truth there. With his level of money and resources, that was likely a truth.

Cillian didn't respond, but his lips twitched in amusement. Right. If Amelia, Charles, and Theo were innocent staff, I'd eat my hat. Each of them were deadly in their own way—even Charles, who masqueraded as innocent and friendly. I hadn't missed the control in his movements, the honed grace there.

"So, I'm guessing Thorin did more than just piss in your oatmeal," I commented. "Or steal a business from under you—whatever wealthy guys like you do to form grudges."

"The lows he's capable of have yet to be discovered," Cillian said, his expression darkening. The mention of Thorin summoned storm clouds. "Trust me when I say he's not someone you ever want to get involved with."

I pursed my lips and leaned back in my seat. "Oh, I'm supposed to trust you now?"

"Clearly," he responded, cracking a grin. His fangs poked out, his golden eyes wicked, and the breath rushed from my lungs.

The wildest thing, though, was that I did trust him. I'd grown up being beaten up, having to defend myself from assholes left and right. And the whole time, I'd wanted someone to step in, to stop them.

Yesterday, Cillian had done just that.

"Maybe," I responded, meeting his gaze.

His eyes widened in surprise, but then his lips curled into a smirk. "Dangerous thing to do."

I sipped at my coffee, not looking away from him. "I'm not as scared of danger as you think."

"I'm well aware, Beau," he said, the low rumble of his voice coursing right through me. The way he said my name, drew out the word, was pure danger. "Why do you think I made you my personal assistant? You'd be wasted in the Pits."

"Then why was my father getting sent to the Pits?" I asked. My stomach soured at the reminder of why I was here, of the bone of contention between us in the first place. How quickly his actions had caused me to forget.

Cillian's easy demeanor grew colder, and he finished his toast in a few bites before responding. "Because he was a coward. I can admit I will never understand your allegiance to him, even if I can admire your bravery in taking his place."

My shoulders tensed. My father had tried to get me to leave the Spires. He'd told me not to take his place. This had been my choice. Which was an ever-present reminder whenever I got angry at my current situation. Because in a fucked-up way, I'd chosen it. "You don't know him like I do."

"I could say the same," Cillian responded, his arrogance sliding right under my skin.

I bristled. I must've been under some spell to have found him attractive before.

I finished off some eggs and toast in quiet, following it up by crunching on some bacon, a little more spitefully. Cillian polished off his coffee and dabbed at his lips before rising. Of course he didn't make a move to clean up after himself, he had staff for that. I swallowed the few last gulps of my coffee before getting up from my seat as well, assuming the cue meant our day was about to start.

"Let's get this first meeting over with," he said. "They'll be needing comprehensive notes, since they can't seem to retain anything we've said in the prior meetings."

I bit back the snarky comment rising to my lips. Today would be long and wearying, and my body was still rundown from yesterday. But I'd earned that on my own, and I'd get through the hours without complaint. Cillian didn't wait for me—no, he acted just as he had before, turning on his heel and striding out of the room. I had to hustle to follow after him, and our footsteps echoed through the hallway as we headed for the elevator.

I hated that I missed the sudden ease that had emerged between us last night into this morning. Given the amount of time I spent around this man, if our situation could be marginally less hostile—damn. I couldn't imagine what that might be like day in and day out. Except, I'd caught a glimpse of where his charm, his teasing might lead me, and it struck me to my core.

Because Cillian was the exact sort of intense, powerful beast I feared...and craved.

CHAPTER 14

The day prior had been grueling, and I hadn't missed the myriad of times when Cillian would glance my way and smirk. Even though he still had his cold moments, he'd definitely melted. He'd lean in to whisper a private comment to me during a meeting, or his gaze would linger on me longer than normal. And I wasn't immune.

"Conflicted" summed up my view of him.

Yet from the second I got out of bed today, excitement had thrummed through my veins. Because Cillian had promised to show me the library. And even if his library was small or poorly curated, the chance to sort through titles again was an itch I couldn't deny.

A knock sounded at the door, and I lurched up from where I lay on my bed in the between phase of "dressed but not motivated."

Charles and Theo stood in the doorway, both of them holding boxes.

"Hey, Jailbreak," Charles said, an impish grin on his lips.

"Is that my new name now?" I said with a groan.

Theo shrugged, though his features gleamed with amusement. "Seems fairly earned."

I chewed on my lower lip and pushed up from the bed. "That's fair. And I'm sorry."

"What are you apologizing for?" Charles asked as he swept into my room and dropped the box by the side of my bed. "It wasn't like you rooted through my personal belongings. And Lia said Cillian pulled out the snarling, chest-thumping bullshit, so he had to see it coming."

"Speaking of personal belongings." Theo popped the other box on top of the one Charles had set down. "This was what we were able to retrieve from your apartment. Damn, man, you keep things sparse."

I'd only been in the apartment for the past few years, as I'd lived the first year after I moved here with my father while I was finishing up school. And in that time, I hadn't been able to accumulate much in the way of possessions. Hadn't even been able to adopt a cat like I'd always wanted.

"Mmm, apart from a few items," Charles said, glancing at the bottom box. "They'll be our secret, though."

Oh god, what could they have found in my place? Kitchenware, books, a handful of electronics? A small clothes collection, same with shoes?

Unless they'd gone into my bedstand drawers.

Heat rushed through me, my cheeks burning, and Charles's wicked gaze confirmed my suspicions.

Right. My toy collection. The dildos I kept weren't...average by any means. Nor were they all human cocks. And my toy collection wasn't sparse. My mouth grew bone dry.

Theo mimed zipping his mouth shut, though his eyes twinkled too.

"I'll melt into the floor now, thanks," I muttered, scrubbing my face.

"Hey, you're not the only one who likes his guys girthy." Charles waggled his brows and glanced at Theo, who rolled his eyes and clapped a hand on his shoulder.

"Come on," he said. "You promised you'd be my sous chef today. We've got extra meals to make."

"Ugh, fine," Charles said. "You're mean to me in the kitchen, though. I only like that in the bedroom."

I bit my lip to keep back my laugh. Something about him was infectious and fun. He was unrestrained in a way I wished I could be.

"If you get bored, you can always join in," Theo said as he began to guide Charles out.

"I just may," I called after. While I hoped Cillian would show me the library, there was no guarantee, and with no meetings on the docket today, I would rather occupy my time with a project than nothing at all. They both vanished from sight, and I slipped into the bathroom to at least wash my face and brush my teeth before I started to roam. I was dressed down today in a soft gray Henley and fitted cargos. I ran my fingers through my curls, which behaved today even without product.

A creak sounded from my door. Had Charles or Theo swung back in?

When I stepped out, a new visitor awaited me.

Cillian leaned against my doorframe, his horns brushing the top, and his massive shoulders taking up most of the space. His arms were crossed and the sleeves of his button-down were rolled up to the elbow, displaying his veiny forearms. I all but swallowed my tongue. My heart thumped harder. In the time I'd been here, about a month at this point, Cillian had never once swung by my room.

And having his presence in my bedroom...fuck.

"Did you make a wrong turn?" I asked, unable to help myself.

He arched a single brow. "In my own casino?"

I shrugged. "It's a bit dramatically large. Do you need a room for every day of the year?"

"Speaking of dramatic," he commented, amusement in his low, husky tone. "Did you want a tour of the library or not?"

"Yes," I responded, taking a few steps forward automatically. His eyes crinkled in amusement, again, showing me dimensions I never would've expected from the callous demon I'd first met.

"Come on," he said, pushing up from his lean.

The fact he'd taken time out from his busy schedule to give me a personal tour of the library hadn't escaped me. Nor had the fact he was giving me longer lingering glances, or that he'd made an exception for me in the first place. My chest heated, the warmth suffusing my whole body, and I did my best to ignore it. The more time I spent around him, the more I grew aware of his presence, his scent, his graceful movements.

All of it was far too dangerous, and yet I followed him out the door anyway.

Even in the early morning, the dimly lit corridors cast their midnight quality to the upper Spires, as if Cillian couldn't bear to face the sun. Although, maybe that was a demon preference I was unaware of. My time here, working as Cillian's personal assistant, had made me realize how little I knew about monsters. I'd lived among them, worked among them at the library, but our interactions were sparse. Which was a shortcoming of mine, if anything.

We passed the kitchen, the dining hall, all the familiar areas we proceeded by. While I'd explored, I'd kept to open areas, not wanting to burst in on anyone's private space, especially after stumbling into Sofia and the werewolf girl that one night. Which I still had a theory about. Cillian's footsteps boomed through the corridor, his tread heavy.

"Here we are," he said, coming to a halt in front of a set of double doors. They weren't anything too ornate—probably why I'd walked past them by so many times. "You ready?"

"You know, whenever men hype something up too much, it usually ends up being disappointing," I responded.

Cillian's fangs poked out with his grin. "Trust me, I never leave anyone disappointed." The heat in his voice had to be my imagination, but his golden eyes scorched into me. He took the first steps into the library, and I strode in after him.

And then came to a dead halt.

I wasn't sure why I'd thought the man who owned the Spires would have a paltry, commonplace library, maybe a few bookshelves lining a room.

This was...well, exquisite barely summed it up. The room was about as huge as the dining hall, and the middle of it held polished wooden desks with chairs, as well as a few sofas by the windows that offered a cozy appeal. However, the entire walls of this huge room were stacked with books. Shelves stretched to the ceilings, ladders stationed near one end of each wall, considering you'd need them to be able to scale the breadth of these stacks. Smaller glass-covered cases were interspersed throughout the room, with backlit open tomes inside them that made me wonder what sort of treasures he possessed.

The breath snagged in my throat as I soaked it all in. Dust motes sparkled in the air under streams of light, and combined with the citrine chandeliers, the rich mahogany wood and wine-red accents lent the room the studious, hushed feel I adored about libraries. The place held the rich almond and leather scent I'd been craving, and joy bubbled up inside me as I took my first steps in.

"How is it organized?" I asked as I wandered in, trying to scan the stacks.

Cillian snorted. "Why am I not surprised that's your first question. The fiction section by genre, and the non-fiction section by topic. Though the stacks get a bit convoluted. I don't have the time to constantly reshelve or change the order around."

"You realize you have a personal assistant, right?" I said, bypassing him to head over to the nearest shelf. This seemed to be classics, leatherbound editions, ones that would be the envy of any library. "Why was I wasting time wandering the halls when I could've been organizing in here?"

"Why indeed," he murmured, stepping up beside me. The books spanned in every direction, the sheer sight of them sending a frisson of excitement through me, and yet the enormity of this gigantic library was somehow dwarfed by the presence of the man at my side.

"How often do you come here?" I asked. The idea that this knowledge sat locked away in waste simultaneously repulsed and intrigued me. He was a mystery I still hadn't been able to unravel.

"It gets used, librarian," he murmured, the rich tone sending a shiver through me. "If not by me, then others."

Who those "others" were remained yet another unknown about this man and this space, but I had a few ideas that circled around, some outlandish and others fanciful. I skimmed the titles on the shelves, and to my excitement, the classics weren't the same old human ones found in Peregrine City's library. No, this was a richer selection, many written in languages other than Common. I tugged at one with a deep red cover that featured white whorls like tangled roots. The language wasn't one I recognized.

"Demonic," he said. "You're not going to find much monster representation in the libraries out in the cities or the countryside. But the stories of my people deserve to have a home. They deserve to be shared."

I swallowed hard, humbled in the wake of his words. When I thought about what we stocked, he was right. They were mostly human stories, human concerns. We didn't have tome after tome from werewolf or harpy authors, or non-fiction books about issues pertinent to vampires or minotaurs. Truthfully, we barely had anything at all.

"Then I'm honored to be in the presence of a rare library such as this." Hunger roared inside me to devour all these unfamiliar stories, all this information I'd never been exposed to. They were similar to the books that had been landing on my nightstand every once in a while.

When I glanced at him, hunger reflected back in his gaze. Except he only looked at me.

"You're remarkable, Beau Taylor." His words held a reverence to them I'd never experienced before, as if I were as sacred and breathtaking as this place. He took a step closer, and I sucked in a sharp breath.

I was unable to pull my gaze away, but I found I didn't want to. Here, in this moment, a subtle tension was exposed, one that had lingered under the surface all along. The air thickened, as if with the secrets this room carried. As if with the laden potential that existed. As if with the sheer life that pulsed beneath the surface, begging to be set free.

I licked my lips, the unspoken words hovering in the air between us.

Mere inches remained between Cillian and me, and my whole body vibrated with the need to close the distance.

He was my jailer. My captor. My guardian.

And yet....

Cillian loomed over me and placed a hand on one of the shelves, bracing himself, and a dark thrill rose inside me as I stared up at him. One of us would walk away. One of us had to. His golden eyes roared with lust, his lips lush, full, and alluring. The magic that existed in this library wasn't something that could be replicated—a quixotic brew of desire and curiosity. Of fear and lust. Of secrets and truth.

And god, I longed to be set free—if not from him, then through him.

He leaned down, and his lips met mine.

This wasn't a mere kiss. It was a transformation. Cillian kissed with a firmness I craved, with a fervor I'd always longed for, and I surrendered to him at once.

One moment had always stuck out in my memory. We'd moved a lot growing up, just me and my father, and for as long as I could remember, I'd always lost myself in books, in imagination—in other people, other stories, ones that weren't as lonely and sad as mine. And I'd never forget the earliest book I fell in love with. When my consciousness was no longer on this plane, my entire self immersed in the magic stirred up by the print on the page. The trembling anticipation, the shockwave of feeling so strong it couldn't exist in real life.

Yet as those intense sensations, those intense emotions crashed through me, I discovered that they existed here in this kiss.

Cillian let out a low growl and grabbed my hip. With his quick motion, my back thudded against the bookshelf, and he crowded me against it. I loved how he loomed over me, how this predator reduced me to mere prey. His massive hand remained on my hip, radiating heat there, and he kissed me hard and fast again, leaving me dizzy in the wake. His scent consumed me as I drank it in with each gasped breath.

Cillian drove his tongue into my mouth, deepening the kiss. Yet his didn't just lap against mine. No, his longer tongue trailed along mine with a slithering caress. My whole body melted from the way he teased, all while he continued kissing me over and over. His fangs scraped against my lower lip, and a gasp escaped me. My cock throbbed at the sensation, a sudden longing to feel those teeth *everywhere*.

A live-wire energy zipped through me, awakening parts of me, parts of my body that had been dormant my entire life. He kissed with as much demand as he lived in his normal life, yet he gave even more in return. Like this, sides of Cillian I never expected to see emerged, and I gladly handed myself over.

He pinned me there against the stacks with his hand on my hip, the firm wood digging into my back. His body pressed against mine, and his rigid length against my stomach lit me on fire. God, I was so hard my cock ached, the throb there growing more intense by the second. Cillian ravaged my mouth over and over again, with fangs, with his long tongue, with his lush lips. His kisses were consuming, drugging, and I wanted to lose myself in them.

The brush of his mouth against my sensitized skin, the puff of breath against me when we both pulled back for air—everything elevated me higher. I melted for him, my body putty in his hands as he took me apart kiss after kiss.

This was what I'd feared from the moment I met him.

Because Cillian didn't kiss casually, he possessed, and from this moment on, I didn't know how I'd be able to resist the draw. The low rumbles coming from him turned me on even more, and at some point I'd gripped his shirt, not even realizing I'd moved my hands to brace myself. Because as much as I'd fought this, I wanted him with every ounce of my being.

He nipped my lower lip again, the sting sending adrenaline through my bloodstream. My whole body sang under his dedicated assault on my senses. I wanted to roll around in his scent and lose myself in his heat.

Cillian drew back far enough that I could stare into his golden eyes, at the wildness there that had lured me in from the start.

He crooked a brow. "I'm not sorry."

I licked my lips, a slight tang of copper there from how kiss-swollen they'd become. "Neither am I."

He looked me over for a moment, a slow grin rolling to his lips. "Good." Pressed against him like this, I could feel the rumble of his words, the vibrations traveling through me. I was so turned on I could barely breathe right now. My cock tested the confines of my pants, brushed up against his massive thigh. How easy would it be to rut against those muscles until I came?

"You look needy, pet," he murmured.

The endearment sent an immediate bolt of lust through me. His deep, rich voice, that word—everything about it veered close to the fantasies I kept locked away.

"Desperate," I gasped out.

His lips twitched, and he reached down to cup my length. His firm grasp made me incinerate. Fuck. A few tugs and I'd unload in my pants. A whimper escaped my lips, and his grin widened enough that those fangs were on clear display. He was so damn gorgeous he stole my breath away.

"Too bad I've got a meeting to get to," he said, a tease lingering in his voice. "Guess you'll just have to be patient for me."

"Maybe I'll handle it on my own," I challenged.

He reached up and rested his massive hand around my throat, which tipped my chin up. The devilish glint in his gaze sent a shudder through me. "Trust me, pet. You'll want to wait."

I licked my lips, the slight pressure against my throat making my adrenaline spike in the best damn way. He relaxed his grip, but not before he pressed a light kiss to my lips again. Then he stepped back, and the lack of his body against mine was like plunging into cold water. Cillian slipped his hands into his pockets as he turned on his heel.

"I'll see you soon, Beau."

With that, he stepped out of the library, leaving me there amongst the stacks, my world flipped upside down.

CHAPTER 15

C illian was gone.

After all the big talk of being patient for him, he'd had to leave today for an emergency meeting. Amelia had been very hush-hush about who it was with, and I took her avoidance as a cue that whatever he'd gotten involved with was trouble. Danger lingered around the man like an aura. Too bad for me I was addicted.

I lost myself in the stacks for the day, since he'd given me free reign to organize as I saw fit, and the variety of books overwhelmed me. I'd expected to find some comparable to those in Peregrine City's library, but no. This held unique books for almost every monster species I could think of, though my knowledge was clearly limited as I discovered new types all day. And yet, despite the thrill of searching the stacks and starting to flip through some of the books, the place also reminded me even more of his presence.

The way he'd kissed me yesterday had been nothing short of trans-formative, as if I'd been sleepwalking through life only to jolt awake.

When I'd been back in my room, the temptation to jerk off and find release myself had risen in a strong way, but I'd tamped it down. Because the curiosity of what he might deliver if I waited held an even stronger appeal.

Except now he was gone, and Amelia had been vague about the timing of his return. I placed another book on the shelf, in its new location, one that made a bit more sense. The stacks clearly hadn't been organized in an age, and even when people had put the books back, they hadn't all placed them in the spots they belonged. The golden rays of the setting sun tapered in through the windows, casting their gilded light across the surfaces.

Yearning tugged deep inside me. And the truth of who I yearned for still elicited complicated emotions, because my situation with Cillian was anything but ordinary. Yet those stolen moments here with him remained in such bright and evocative color inside my mind.

Was he okay? He rarely left his tower, apart from furtive meetings down in the casino, but he seemed almost as trapped as I was some days.

And my escape had taught me that the man had dangerous enemies out there.

A knock sounded at the door, drawing my attention.

My heart raced, but when I spun around, Amelia stood in the entrance. She was dressed down in a muscle shirt, black pants, and combat boots, looking far more herself than when she donned a staff uniform. For a woman who was probably in her fifties, she was fit enough to take me down in a fight.

"If you're bored later, we've got our monthly game night. We're playing Sparks. Even though Cillian hasn't come back yet, if he makes it in tonight, he'll join us." Her eyes softened, and I couldn't help but wonder how much she'd pieced together.

I chewed on my lower lip. I hadn't played Sparks in a long while, and I'd never been good at it in the past, but the idea of a diversion sounded perfect right now. "You'll have to refresh me on the rules."

"We ordered pizza too," she said. "Since Theo's with Cillian right now."

I hadn't realized my shoulders were tensed until they relaxed. If Cillian wasn't alone, that made me feel marginally better, even though I suspected what they'd headed into wasn't as simple as a business meeting. And whoever it was with wouldn't be docile. No detours to go and pet puppies or frolic through a garden.

"I'm down for pizza. Is it just you, Charles, and me then?"

Amelia grinned, one that made her look younger than her years. "Oh, no. Game night is when everyone else comes to visit."

I lifted my hand in a mock gasp. "You're telling me Cillian has friends?"

She smirked. "Shocking, I know. This is tradition spanning decades if you'd believe that."

I sucked in a sharp breath, envy stabbing me in the chest. Truth be told, now that I was beginning to see other sides of the demon, I could believe it. I'd witnessed how differently he acted with Charles, Theo, and Amelia compared to his business partners, and I wished I had the sort of friendships that lasted over a decade, or even ones that could last years. Deep down, I'd known it, but coming here had made me realize how superficial and fleeting most of my relationships were.

After the first week or so, messages had dried up from coworkers and acquaintances, confirming that was all I'd ever had. Nothing deeper. Nothing true.

The only one who still contacted me was my father.

"Come on," Amelia said. "The books will survive a night alone."

I shook my head, as if I could clear my mind somehow, and pulled away from the stacks. Maybe it was from being trapped up here, maybe not, but the truth was, Charles, Amelia, Theo, and even Cillian were the closest interactions I'd had in a long while outside my immediate family. "You already sold me with pizza. Though how many people should I anticipate?"

Amelia shrugged as she walked in step with me down the corridor. "It varies every month. Depends on obligations, who needs an outlet or an escape. Sofia won't be attending—though she mentioned she met you—but Ursuline has arrived. Jaffar might be in town tonight as well."

"You throw these names out as if they should have some meaning to me," I joked as we slowed closer to the dining hall.

"They will," she said, placing a hand on my shoulder. "I have a feeling you'll fit right in."

My heart squeezed tight at her acceptance. While Charles was affable and easy to like, and gave as much in turn, Amelia didn't seem as easily won. Her approval meant more than I could vocalize, especially with how much of a right hand she was for Cillian. "Thank you."

"Don't thank me," she said. "I plan on wiping the floor with everyone in Sparks tonight. Adding another head at the table just makes for a more enjoyable victory."

We stopped in front of the dining hall, which had been transformed for the evening. The lights were dimmer, with a reddish glow that cast a hazy club vibe to the whole room. A few of the tables had been pushed together, which made a larger one to sit around even though there weren't a great number of people here. Charles sat at the big table along with three newcomers. The lack of Cillian's presence in the room was noticeable, as if I hadn't realized how much space he took up until he was absent.

My heart thumped a little harder.

"Did you order the pizza yet?" Amelia asked Charles.

"Yeah," he said, lounging back in his seat. "I chose different toppings on each one, so no one needs to fight."

"We'll always find a reason to debate," a handsome man said. He had a pallor to his skin despite its brown tone. When he grinned, fangs poked out, clarifying the situation at once. Vampire. The man wore casual clothes like formal wear—a slouchy beige shirt and white chinos—and his black hair was artfully tousled.

"Who's the newcomer?" An almost regal voice sounded, and I glanced over to the opposite side of the table where a cecaelia sprawled out by the table, their tentacles taking up the space where seats would be on either side of them. Their pale blue skin looked a little purplish in the dimly lit ambiance of the room, and their short silver hair, sharp jawline, and fierce, dark eyes were lethal.

"I'm the personal assistant," I introduced myself.

"Never expected to meet you here," the third person at the table announced. I hadn't recognized her on sight, but the voice was familiar. I blinked for a second, until I registered it was the server from Haven—Gretel. Her dark brown hair was pulled back into a ponytail, and she seemed a little more lethal in this environment, even though Haven hadn't dulled her sharp edges.

"Same could be said of you," I responded, taking a seat in one of the open spots next to Charles.

"You must be the innocent waif wandering the halls my wife ran into," Gretel murmured.

My eyes widened. I shouldn't be surprised Gretel was married to Sofia, given her ties to Haven. Yet the web here was more intricate than I could've conceived.

"Will Cillian be joining us later?" Ursuline asked.

Amelia plunked into the seat on the other side of Charles. "Unlikely, though that's the goal. He got tangled up responding to Glacier *business*."

Jaffar scoffed. "They're despicable. Their pretense of tolerating our kind is flimsy at best."

"Olivia will learn that the hard way someday," Ursuline responded.

My attention perked up at the name of Cillian's ex. What was Glacier? I'd already filed away the name to research later—it rang a bell. Whatever business Cillian and Theo were dealing with tonight was clearly dangerous, but I remained in the dark. Even if all I had were scraps to work with, I'd uncover what was going on.

"Fuck that bitch," Charles said with a smile on his face.

"Enough yammering," Amelia said, casting a quick glance in my direction. Was there something she didn't want me to know? "Let's get a few games of Sparks in."

"You ready to get your ass beat, old woman?" Gretel teased.

"Please, you like them older," Amelia shot back, a flirt to her tone that shocked me. I'd seen Theo and Charles relaxed before, but Amelia was the most businesslike out of the three. It seemed that this was the place she let her hair down.

"Then you'll love me," Jaffar commented dryly. "Long life's one of the many perks."

"I'd love some pizza if it would hurry up and arrive already." Charles leaned back in his chair and patted his stomach.

"Missing Theo?" I asked.

His lips twisted in a wry grin. "He always makes sure I'm well fed."

Gretel rolled her eyes. "No one wants to hear about your sexcapades, Charles."

"I'd rather hear about yours, Gretel," Ursuline teased, their voice low and alluring. "Guaranteed Sofia's a wildcat in the bedroom."

"Wouldn't you like to know." Gretel's smirk said everything.

"Chances are, we'd be incompatible," Ursuline responded, their full lips twitching. Based on their firm tone and the suggestion there, I had a feeling the cecaelia had a dominant streak. Like a certain demon I knew. I sucked in a sharp breath at the memory of how he'd kissed me until I melted. What would he do when he got his hands on me? Fuck, the idea made my whole body immolate.

The fantasies that had haunted me last night were lurid and demanding, and I'd barely been able to sleep, my cock hard and dripping, and my balls desperate for release. My being vibrated with the need to be around him, yet he was gone.

Risking his neck for gods knew what reason.

My stomach flipped. I wasn't sure if I'd be able to eat much tonight.

"How good at Sparks are you?" Charles asked, leaning in.

A grin lifted my lips. Thank fuck for distraction. "I'm terrible. In fact, I need a complete refresher."

"Oh, perfect," Gretel said, her eyes meeting mine. For some reason, seeing her here calmed a part of my soul. Maybe because she was someone I'd met outside of here, a reminder of my former life before I'd entered the Spires. Or maybe because the air of sharpness around her reminded me of myself in a way. Prickly, like a thorn. It was a foundation block of my personality.

"Okay, okay," Charles said as he brought a stack of cards and the multi-hued glass pebbles over. "I'll update you on how to play, and then you can kick everyone's asses. Except for mine, of course."

"I'm in."

***

To my surprise, Sparks wasn't as difficult as I'd built it up to be in my head. Maybe because the last time I'd played had been as a child, but the strategy made sense now, and I lost myself in the patterns and playing against the talented people at the table. Amelia hadn't been bragging for nothing—she excelled at this game. However, so did Gretel and Ursuline. Jaffar and Charles seemed to be having a bad night, or they just weren't good players. I couldn't quite gauge yet.

The pizza, beer, and camaraderie made the time pass faster than I'd realized. I hadn't looked at my phone or the door in a while, even though an ever-present tug remained in the back of my mind.

After being devoid of companionship for so long, far earlier than when I'd come here, this sort of gathering should've been tougher. And yet, I felt comfortable here in a way I didn't amid the bars and coffee shops of Peregrine City. It helped that the company was better than I could've chosen myself. Ursuline was sharp and witty, often exchanging barbs with Amelia, and Jaffar had a dry sense of humor that I appreciated as well, a good counterbalance to Charles. An understanding flowed between Gretel and me, but whether it was due to a shared prickliness or not, I wasn't sure.

"Damn, we should probably clear up the game," Amelia said, stretching her arms over her head. "Tomorrow morning's going to come early."

My stomach churned as I glanced at the door again. Still no Cillian.

"Not all of us are ancient, Lia," Charles teased.

Amelia took another sip from her beer, not dignifying him with a response.

"I should be getting back to Sofia," Gretel said, rising from her seat. "She's a harsh mistress."

"Just the way you like it," Ursuline teased, their voice low and seductive.

Gretel smirked. "Don't be jealous."

"I'm jealous," Charles complained. "My boyfriend's still out there, dangling his pretty werewolf ass in front of trouble."

My heart thumped hard at Charles stating the words aloud. Because I'd felt Cillian's absence acutely all day.

"Oh, so my ass is pretty?" Theo's voice sounded from the doorway.

Everyone's heads whipped in that direction. Theo leaned against the frame, arms crossed. His hair was ruffled, questionable streaks across his skin, and the tears in his jeans weren't a style choice. My chest squeezed tight.

"Where's Cillian?" Amelia asked the question I wanted to ask.

"He's in a mood," Theo said. "At least, too much of one to socialize. He's going to head back to his chambers."

"Big bad demon heading off to brood?" Jaffar commented. "Color me shocked."

"I think I'm going to call it a night." The words escaped me before I could rein them in, and I rose from my seat. Sure, the excuse was flimsy and transparent, but I needed to see him. I needed to remind myself that what happened last night hadn't just been a fever dream. My footsteps echoed as I swept across the dining hall, not bothering with goodbyes. Theo smirked as he pushed away from the doorframe where he leaned.

"Go get him," Theo murmured before he strode past me.

My heart lodged in my throat, but I stepped out into the corridor. Cillian's heavy footsteps were audible from here, as he headed down the opposite way. His silhouette was clear, and I strode in his direction, unflinching.

The shadows from the hallway seeped into me, a velvet dark I was growing accustomed to. The *thump, thump, thump* in my chest was so loud I was shocked he couldn't hear it, but I quickened my pace.

Even still, he moved faster than me from the sheer length of his strides alone.

"Didn't think you were the type to hide," I called out. My words echoed through the corridor, amplified even louder.

Cillian stopped.

Then he turned around.

Feral didn't quite describe him. When he took the first steps toward me, I froze. The wildness to him had drawn me in and unnerved me from the start. Yet tonight, that was elevated. His shirt was torn, his slacks too, and the blackened streaks across his skin looked like gashes. His shoulders heaved, and his golden gaze was so intense I swallowed, an audible gulp.

He strode in my direction, step by careful step, but I didn't dare move.

I'd called him over here, so I would face the demon whose attention I'd snared.

"You'd be safer to run tonight, pet," he growled, his voice low, deadly. "I'm on edge." Still, he continued, closer and closer, until we were mere feet apart. This near, his presence overwhelmed me, and yet the tug inside me finally calmed.

Cillian was back, and he was in one piece.

I licked my lips, my heart thumping out of control at this point. "Maybe I don't want safe. I don't want to wait any longer."

His lips curled into a smirk that revealed his sexy-as-sin fangs, and my cock throbbed at the sight. Fuck. His presence was an accelerant to the fire begging to combust inside me. "Careful what you wish for. If I take you tonight, pet, I won't be nice."

My blood scorched.

"What about me made you think I wanted nice?" I responded.

His low growl simmered through the space between us, and a second later, he closed those few feet. One second I was standing staring at him, and the next he'd scooped me up in his arms.

"Then come on," he said. "We've got a long night ahead of us."

CHAPTER 16

U nlike the first time I'd headed in the direction of the West
Wing, when I'd been filled with nerves, this time a different
anticipation flowed through me. The easy way Cillian carried me made
my head swirl, the sheer size difference between us something that had
turned me on from the start. His scent of sweat, of musk, of brimstone
surrounded me, and goddamn, every inhale sent a tingle through my
body.

"You're persistent, aren't you?" he murmured. "Most run when I
get like this."

"I'm here, aren't I?" I responded. Whether it was bravery or stupid-
ity was questionable some days, but I had a stubborn streak I'd never
been cured of.

"Have you ever been with a demon before, pet?" he asked.

"I haven't." I delivered the truth, hoping it wouldn't make him
change his mind.

"And what makes you think you can take me?" he asked, arching a brow.

Maybe because most of my toys at home were monster-sized if not shaped. I'd been a size queen for a long time now, but no one had ever measured up. Except the confession felt a little too personal. "Trust me."

"Mm, we'll see," he said as he carried me up the short steps and onto the platform that had been forbidden to me mere days ago. He headed in the direction of his bedroom, and my heart thumped harder. "And you're okay with restraints?"

I blinked, surprised at the turn—but not deterred. "Is there a reason?"

Cillian licked his lips, the tip of his tongue lingering over the point of his fang. "Exerting control is about the only thing that'll keep me from going feral at this point. If there are elements I can't anticipate, like someone else touching me, I'll be unpredictable."

I swallowed hard. As much as part of me lusted for the unpredictable, to see him feral, I also valued my life. "I'm fine with restraints."

If anything, the idea of being bound and fucked by him amplified my need even higher. My cock was hard and leaking at this point, and I shifted the slightest bit in his arms. He nudged the door open with his elbow, his pupils dilated, his breaths coming out a little heavier, as if he were mere inches away from snapping.

Cillian swept into the room and deposited me onto the bed, the silken sheets feeling like sin against my skin. "Undress."

"With that sort of seductive talk, how can I help myself," I commented as I undid the first button of my shirt.

Cillian whipped my way, wildness in his eyes, his movements. "If you won't strip yourself, I'll handle it." He closed the distance between us, and his claws glinted in the dim lighting. With a lightning-quick movement, he lashed down the front of my shirt with a single talon. Buttons popped off, and the fabric fell to either side of me. His claws attacked my waistband next, and he had it shredded in mere moments. The breath caught in my throat.

Cillian tugged the frayed fabric from me, my boxer briefs as well, and I kicked off my loafers and socks, my mouth dry. My cock was harder than ever at the display of effortless strength, and the ache that built inside me quickly grew into an inferno. I sat on his silken sheets, stripped down while he was still dressed, and a shiver ran through me. I reached down to palm my cock, pre-cum welling at the tip.

Cillian walked over to the center of his room and reached up to the ceiling. What had seemed like a black patch in the paneling undid into thick black straps that attached to a hard point. I swallowed hard. Oh god. Was he going to hoist me up in those? The sight of them thrilled me, feeding into those fantasies I'd never believed could become a reality.

"Come here," Cillian said, the firmness in his voice brooking no debate. "If you need me to stop, tell me. Otherwise I'm going to taste you and tease you and fuck you until you're screaming my name."

My eyes just about rolled back in my head. Fuck. Every word from him shot right into my bloodstream, quickening my pulse. Even though I had no idea what was in store for me, I strode forward, my feet bare on the cool tiles beneath me. When I stopped in front of him, he slowly scanned me, his golden eyes burning with banked heat. He licked his lips, his long pointed tongue slipping out. Ngh.

He undid one of the straps, binding it around my torso and clasping it in the front. He then wrapped one of the thick black straps around my thigh, a circular restraint there, and another around my other thigh. Finally, Cillian bound the smaller ones around my wrists, until they were securely in place. All of them connected to a bundle looped around the main hoop.

"Are you ready?" he asked.

My heart thumped, but I didn't have any idea what he planned next—and that excited me even more. The restraints were snug around my torso, my wrists, and my thighs, but they weren't cutting off circulation.

Cillian wrapped his hand around the bundle of straps that looped through the hard point, and he tugged.

One moment I was on the floor, and the next I wasn't. My knees bent, my arms lifted, and my ass dangled out in the air, placing me in a more vulnerable position than I'd ever been in before. A sinful thrill rushed through me, the craving I'd always longed for simmering under the surface. The restraints around my thighs and waist kept me pinioned in place, almost like I was seated—except I was exposed.

"Perfect," Cillian murmured. "You're being so good for me."

He ran his claws along my thighs, and my skin prickled in response. The tips weren't sharp enough to break skin, but the sensation sent warning flares of danger that collided with lust.

"Oh god," I gasped out.

"There are no gods here, pet." Cillian stepped between my spread legs and nipped at my earlobe, at the side of my neck. The scrape of his fangs against my skin sent another full-body shiver through me. Like this, I couldn't reach down and touch my cock, which was hard and aching. I couldn't do anything but receive whatever Cillian bestowed upon me.

This was everything I'd dreamed of.

He continued to drag his claws along the inside of my thighs, up my chest, scraping around my sensitive areolas. His warm breath hit the side of my face, my neck, as he nipped and tasted my skin, and the pleasure that rippled through me had me wanting to wriggle. But every shift tugged at the restraints, and even though I could move, I settled in place. His sensual mouth was an addiction I didn't know I had until I experienced it.

"You taste delicious," he commented as he dipped his head down. His long tongue extended out and curled around my nipple. It squeezed and then tugged, and the sensation sent a pulse of need through me. I whimpered as he continued to tease my nipples with his tongue, his claws tracing lazy circles across my skin. I tilted my head back, wanting to surrender to the shivers rolling through me. Against this onslaught— the scratch of his claws, the tease of his tongue and fangs—I was reduced to just feeling, just experiencing.

It was bliss.

With the amount my mind churned, with how much had jangled around in there over the past month, the ability to surrender to him gave me everything I'd needed. I craved more, though. I wanted him unleashed, thrusting inside me with his thick demon cock. I wanted to feel his tensile strength wrapped around me, that formidable presence enveloping me. God, I'd been curious for so long, and at last those desires would be sated.

Cillian let out a low rumble in his chest as he pulled back. He tugged off his shirt, the fabric letting out a rip, then he yanked off his belt and shunted his tattered slacks to the floor.

He stood before me completely bare, and I salivated.

His body was pure muscle, a work of art. He was all broad shoulders, a massive frame. The dim lighting in here cast shadows that accentuated each dip and curve, and the vee that led to his cock drew my attention. And gods—his length jutted out in all its full glory, better than I could've fantasized. His balls hung heavily beneath a thick, long cock that was ridged and bright red and girthier in the middle. His legs were gigantic, as were his arms, and the idea of them wrapped around me or bracing me up amplified the heat pouring through me.

Fuck, I wanted to taste him so badly. I wanted to lick his skin and swallow down that giant length. Except tonight I wasn't doing any initiating at all. No, I was his to tease and touch and use. Lust roared through me at the thought.

He dragged his claw along my ass cheek until he stopped close to the sensitive furl of my hole. "You said you can take a demon's cock, but can you take my knot? Or do I need to come all over this pretty body?"

Ngh. God. Both of those options sounded divine.

However, there was one I'd longed to experience for a long time now. "I can take your knot," I gasped out as he nipped at the side of my throat.

"Ambitious, aren't we," he murmured, the heat of his breath against my skin making me shiver. Each squirm tugged at the bonds around my thighs, around my wrists, around my torso, reminding me I was suspended here for his pleasure. The pressure of them tripped my brain in the best way.

"Always," I responded, my voice breathy. My balls throbbed, my cock ached, and my whole body hummed with life, as if an electrical current coursed through me.

"I'll make sure you can," he said, lowering to his knees. In his current position, his face was level with my bared hole, and the vulnerability sent another rising thrill through me. My body flushed, as if I were embarrassed or ashamed, when in fact I was the furthest thing from. Instead, the longing expanded inside me, threatening to consume me. Because I wanted to be hunted, pinned like prey, and taken hard.

And Cillian was the first lover I'd been with who might be able to deliver.

"What's this here?" he murmured, his claw lightly skimming along my taint until he gave the jewelry there a light tug.

"Oh," I gasped out, the sensation strong. "I told you I had piercings."

"Full of mysteries, aren't you."

The flickering lamps cast a sheen over his obsidian horns, ones I itched to touch, and when he looked up at me, his golden gaze had me ensnared. The sheer hunger there was consuming, and that same hunger was taking over me as well. His massive hands wrapped around my thighs, as if they weren't already spread open, and he gripped tight, the tips of his claws digging into my skin with the slightest sting.

Then he leaned in and licked my hole.

"Oh, fuck." Pleasure rushed through me at the sensation, at the smooth, hot, wet glide. His tongue writhed against my hole, having far more control than a human's. He lapped circles around the furled skin until the breaths shuddered out of me, until my thighs started to quake. Fuck, fuck, fuck. Cillian knelt in front of me, unmaking me piece by piece, and I savored every bit of his attention.

His saliva coated my hole, and it relaxed further, more than normal at least.

"Is there something in your saliva?" I gasped out.

Cillian pulled back, and I regretted asking, simply because I didn't want him to stop. His lips were shiny from spit as he grinned. "It'll relax you. Now be a good pet and let me continue."

Fuuuuck, that was hot. I whimpered in response and tilted my head back in surrender. He leaned in again, but this time the tip of his tongue slipped into my entrance. My thighs tightened from the sudden sensation, and my cock ached even more. Cillian slowly pushed his tongue deeper and deeper inside me, farther than I'd ever experienced from any of my human lovers. The thick, wet slide of it, the control as he thrust in and out, had me panting. My whole body lit on fire from the sensations as he ate me out like he was starved, like he couldn't get enough.

Cillian circled his tongue inside me, making it move in an electric way that hit all my buttons—prostate included. I gasped out another ragged moan, not caring how loud I was here. He had me hoisted up and splayed open at his mercy, and I lived for every second of this. The way he thrust his tongue inside me felt so damn good I could barely breathe.

Except it wasn't enough.

"More," I moaned.

Cillian retracted his tongue, taking the time to lick around my entrance in those intoxicating swirls. He let go of my legs, and I felt a slight sting along my thighs from where his claws had dug in. Then he pushed up and strode over to his nightstand. The click of a bottle was instantly recognizable, and my adrenaline spiked at the sound. At the anticipation of finally getting his thick length inside me.

Cillian stepped in front of me, running the lube up and down his mouthwatering length. The ridges there, the girth that promised to stretch me wide, and the sheer size of it would send me vaulting into the stratosphere. His lips quirked in a sexy-as-sin smile. "Is this what you were begging for?"

I licked my lips, still breathless, but I managed to nod.

"Mm, no, I want to hear you ask for it," he said, standing right between my legs, the tip of his length inches from my hole. It was so close, and I tried to rock a little in my bonds to see if I could nudge against it. That just made Cillian grin wider, those sharp fangs protruding.

"Please," I groaned out. "I need your cock. I need you to fuck me."

"Damn, you beg so prettily. Who would've thought?" Cillian's husky words stroked right through me, and he pressed his tip against my hole. The second he began to push in, the stretch intensified. I had large toys, but fuuuuck, he was larger. I swallowed hard. He eased in the first inch and then grinned. "Regretting saying you could take me?"

"No," I shot back. "I can take more."

Cillian's eyes glinted, a smirk curling those lush lips, then he pushed in farther, and I hit the wall of the thick middle of his cock. The breath rushed from me, the sting of pain and pleasure melding. I gritted my teeth, breathing through my nose.

"Fuck, you're so tight," he purred. "Such a gorgeous little pet with such a greedy hole."

Those words made my head spin, at the sheer amount of want and need roiling through me. My cock had somewhat deflated from the sting, but this underlying desire to take all of him had seized hold of me. Determination worked itself into my bones, and sweat prickled across my brow. He shifted forward and back, loosening the area, each pass moving him a little deeper. His muscles were corded, everything tense with how he held back right now—as if by a thread.

Cillian pushed in again, and the muscle relaxed. His cock sank all the way inside me, and I howled. Pleasure raced through me at being stretched like this, at being filled this intensely. I was at my edge, my limit, but the endorphins flooded through me, vaulting me higher than I'd ever gone before.

"Fuck, you feel like sin," Cillian grunted out. "The way you're gripping me."

I whimpered, unable to form a sentence with how he scrambled my brain. And then he started to move.

Another scream ripped from me as his thick middle, the ridges, traveled along my channel, sending a cascade of sparks through me. He managed to glide against my prostate with every slow and deliberate pass, and sparks flared inside me over and over. From his tight hold on my thighs, the corded muscles of his neck, and the harsh breaths coming from him, I could tell he was still restraining himself. Letting me adjust to his size.

"Take me," I gasped out. "Take me hard."

Those words sparked an inferno in him, his eyes lighting up, his nostrils flaring.

"You don't know what you're asking for, pet," he murmured.

"You needed to unleash tonight," I forced out between pants. "So take me."

The last thread holding him back snapped.

It was as if Cillian transformed before me, truly "The Beast" he got called. His eyes all but glowed, and his fangs lowered further. His claws dug into my thighs, but I relished the pain. It kept me grounded in the moment. A feral growl rumbled up his throat until it split the air.

And then Cillian thrust in hard.

The rush of sensation made my whole body buck, and a cry escaped me. He started to hammer into me with faster momentum, the bonds insubstantial with the way he speared me on his cock. I felt weightless, just a rag doll, as he fucked into me like he needed me to survive. Each thrust in as his thick middle glided over my prostate had me screaming out. Tears leaked from my eyes, and my balls ached, my cock so hard I could scream. But with my hands bound, I couldn't find relief.

Growls poured out of Cillian, the smack of skin on skin echoing in the room. My cries came unbidden as he tagged my prostate again and again and again. My whole body had become one raw nerve that he kept pressing, the mixture of pleasure and pain keeping me breathless.

He leaned in and sank his teeth into my shoulder. Heat and bliss rushed through me, and I screamed so loud my throat went raw. All the while, he hadn't stopped fucking into me, the steady thrust of his cock threatening to make me unravel. I surrendered to him completely, my mind vacating the room. Right now, all that existed was his cock inside me, his massive body surrounding me. It was just the sting of his thickness, those ridges, his claws digging into my thighs, his teeth into my shoulders.

It was him and me and this inevitable collision.

His growls vibrated through me as he fucked like he was possessed, like an animal rutting into me. My eyes rolled back in my head, the onslaught of sensations growing beyond what I could process.

Fuck. Fuck. Fuck.

My skin smacked against his with every collision, as he railed into me hard and fast, the intensity building inside me. My balls ached so badly I could feel the pressure through my whole body, my prostate so oversensitive that tears streamed down my cheeks. Yet I wanted it all. I wanted this claiming more than my next breath.

Like this, the complexities between us faded away. We were just sweat and motion and moans.

"Mine," Cillian growled out. "You're mine."

His words struck me square in the chest, this wild possession reaffirming them. He consumed me body and soul in this moment, and I let go. My arms were suspended, my thighs, the band around my torso helping keep me upright, but even if the bonds weren't there, Cillian's strong arms would've lifted me up.

He thrust inside me a little faster, the cords of his neck taut. His jaw was clenched, and the sheen of sweat covering his limbs gave him away. I floated on sensation, awash in the bliss that rolled over me again and again. My cock wept at this point, my balls painful, but I was at his mercy.

Cillian buried himself in me, and a loud growl echoed through the room, reverberating in the air. His cock pulsed inside me, and a moment later, wet heat flooded me as he came. The stretch followed, taking my breath away, as his knot expanded at his base. He sagged forward, strands of his sweaty hair dangling down, his shoulders heaving.

"Don't worry, pet," he rasped. He wrapped his hand around my cock, and I keened in response, my whole body a live wire at this point.

Cillian stroked my sensitive cock, and after a few pumps, my balls threatened to unload. His palm was large, callused, and so warm, and it felt like heaven wrapped around my length.

The cries poured out of me unbidden as he continued to jerk me off, his knot inside me, keeping me in place.

The tension spread, growing, growing, growing until finally...my balls drew up, and I came.

The orgasm hit me so hard that my vision blacked, and the sheer force of the pleasure barreling through me held my breath captive as my cock spurted load after load of cum. My muscles tensed, my body locked up, and I released everything I'd been holding back. Cillian didn't stop working me through my orgasm, the heat and pressure of his palm coaxing more from me. The rush of bliss that coursed through me was so intense it felt like too much, my body threatening to shut down.

I let out a whine, reduced to mere noises as his knot throbbed inside me. Everything grew oversensitive at this point, but he was lodged in me, and I loved it better than any fantasy.

Cillian let out a long, deep breath that sounded like it was pulled from his core. "Fuck, you're...more than I could've imagined, Beau."

His praise rained down on me, and I basked in it, even though my eyes closed, the heaviness settling over me. Sheer exhaustion rocked through me as the adrenaline that had been keeping me on the edge crashed.

"Let me take care of you now," he murmured, a calm in his voice, in the air, in the wake of the frenzy.

Slowly, the snap of the bonds around my arms released, and they sagged by my side. I didn't bother trying to keep myself up. Cillian's arms wrapped around me, holding my weight with ease as he undid the straps around my torso, my thighs. I was locked onto his knot, attached to him in the most intimate way, and I wanted to linger in this space for as long as possible.

The weight of everything slammed in even harder, and my eyes felt like lead. A heaviness lulled me toward oblivion, and as Cillian's arms tightened around my body, my forehead rested against his chest.

Safe. I felt safe.

Blackness stole me away.

CHAPTER 17

When I blinked my eyes open, I lay tangled in silken sheets, and there was a massive warmth plastered to my front. My hole was sore as hell and...full? I tried to move, but I was stuck, and the jostling planted my face against a wall of muscle.

A laugh rumbled in the air, the vibrations traveling through me. Cillian.

Heat rushed through me. I lay in his bed, and he was still buried inside me after he'd fucked me until I couldn't feel my limbs anymore.

"My knot takes a bit to relax," he said, running his claws through my hair. The tips along my scalp made me shiver, soothing me at once. "I cleaned you up already, but you're not going anywhere yet."

I swallowed hard. This was one of my fantasies come true, and I loved it more than I wanted to admit. My throat was wrecked from all the screaming I'd done, and I had the feeling my hole would be the same after his knot relaxed. Cillian's arms surrounded me, and he breathed with a steadiness that relaxed any of my residual anxiety at once. With the way his cock was lodged inside me, his knot keeping us together, he was right—I wasn't going anywhere.

"Thank you," he murmured, brushing a kiss onto my head. The tender motion sent a shiver through me, unexpected to say the least.

"For what?" I asked. He hadn't been a selfish lover. No, he'd taken me apart piece by piece, even when he was straining at the seams, and he'd made sure I was okay throughout. How such wildness could co-exist with such care added yet another contradiction to this confusing man.

"Normally I hide away," he murmured. "Find an outlet, but never...with someone."

The sheer loneliness in his statement made my chest ache. For as much as he had closer and more loyal friends than I'd ever experienced, he clearly struggled to let them in.

He reached down, running his palm over where he was still buried inside me, my skin tender and stretched to its limit. "Fuck. You've been one surprise after another."

"Glad to keep you on your toes," I said dryly, luxuriating in the feel of his chest against my cheek, of his hand caressing the area where we were joined. He'd fucked me so well it would be on replay in my mind from here until eternity. "Any time you need to let out some aggression, you know where I am."

"Oh, you've got another thing coming if you think I'm letting you slip through my fingers." He nipped at the top of my ear, his fang scraping there after. "The way you took my knot—you're a rarity, pet."

That term again. "Pet" should've made me angry, especially with how I was stuck here, and yet something about it soothed me at my core, made me want to curl up on his lap and purr. Everything about our arrangement was confusing, conflicting, but I sank into the comfort of here and now. I was in his bed, in his arms, his knot inflated inside me, and I reveled in the moment.

"What if I run?" I teased, not sure if I was playing with fire. However, it brushed against the desires I'd held secret for far too long.

He tilted my chin up so our eyes met, and his sensual lips curled into a smirk. "Then I'll chase you."

Heat poured through me in a ferocious torrent, and the breath hitched in my throat.

Cillian's eyes danced. "Someone likes the sound of that."

I licked my dry lips.

"You're far too pretty," he said before leaning down to press his mouth to mine. I savored the taste of him, the contact sending a ripple of lust and comfort through me as he continued to kiss me, a languidness to his movements, as if we had all the time in the world. His knot was starting to deflate inside me, and I hated it. I wanted to stay knotted to him all night, stay entwined in his arms.

He kissed me breathless, his long tongue teasing mine, gliding in the same sensual way he'd eaten me out. I sank into the sensation, much calmer in the wake of the frenzied way we'd crashed together. His knot finally deflated, and he withdrew from my hole with care. I felt it gaping without him there, and I whimpered against his lips.

Cillian pulled back, his white teeth stark against his red skin with the way he grinned. "Miss me already?"

He ran his fingers across the tender skin of my hole, careful with his claws, and a rush of his cum trickled out, some of it trailing down my thigh. A shudder rushed through me, of want, of desire. He smeared it around my hole, his movements surprisingly delicate with the wrecked skin.

"Fuck, I want to cover you in my cum," he murmured, nipping at my lower lip. "Fill you up with it, spread it all over your skin."

"Yes," I rushed out, heat flooding my cheeks. I didn't care how shameless I sounded—that was what I wanted.

"Another time," he said. "Right now, let's get you in the tub."

I barely had time to blink before he rose off the bed and hoisted me in his arms. He carried me with an ease that reminded me how strong he was, and that sent a torrent of need through me all over again, even though I was depleted and wrecked from the way he'd claimed me. The trickle of his cum from my hole sent another flutter through me.

He strode into an attached bathroom, and I drank in the sight of it—black tiles and a massive clawfoot tub. The polished silver fixtures gleamed in the light, and the room smelled crisp, like lemon and ozone. Cillian set me down beside the tub and turned the taps on. Steam rose from the water that began to fill the tub.

"Get in," he said, placing a hand on my shoulder.

"You're really not one for niceties, are you?" I arched a brow.

"I'll use them when I see a point." He smirked and lifted me off my feet again before lowering my body into the water. The heat surrounded me at once, the scalding water soothing my sore muscles, and a deep sigh escaped me. The tub was the biggest I'd ever seen, more like a hot tub than a bathtub, and big enough to fit us both, which felt like an impossibility.

"Are you getting in?" I asked. I didn't want to seem needy, but I also wasn't ready to have him out of sight yet. Besides, he was the one who'd shown up bloodied and beaten. Surely he needed this as much as I did.

"I will," he said, slipping a towel around his waist. "I'll be right back. Get comfortable."

I settled my back against the porcelain and tipped my head up to stare at the glossy black tiles of the ceiling. The pale white grout glared from between each one, a pretty offset that ensnared my attention.

Cillian's footsteps were heavy enough I could hear him thumping around in the other room. The door creaked, and he must've headed out into another area of the West Wing. I closed my eyes and tried to focus on the thunder of the water pouring from the faucet, and on the hot water caressing my tired and aching body. My hole would be beyond sore tomorrow, and my throat as well.

Still, in this moment, with my whole body relaxed, my world was calm and my mind remained quiet.

And I'd treasure every second of it.

Cillian's footsteps returned, and he stepped in through the doorway. He'd brought a tray of fruit as well as a few bottles of water, and my heart skipped a beat. I never would've expected this level of attentiveness from the man who'd gained a reputation for his harshness, who'd been cold and callous when I'd first arrived. Who'd also ravaged me until I was incoherent. The hot water stung around the scratches on my thighs, and the bite on my shoulder ached, but I savored those marks as reminders.

"Are you just going to hover around the tub or get in?" I asked, pushing up from where I lay back.

Cillian shook his head and placed the plate and water by the side of the tub. "That mouth."

"And you haven't even felt it yet," I challenged, my gaze traveling to his thick cock that hung limp between his thighs. Gods, how had I managed to fit all of that inside me? And already I could imagine taking it again and again.

Cillian gripped my chin and tilted it up. He pressed his lips to mine again in a claiming kiss, and I melted in his grasp.

When he let go, he climbed into the other side of the tub and turned off the stream from the faucet. Water sloshed, some over the sides, and his legs tangled with mine. The touch comforted me at once.

"Come here," he said. "Onto my lap."

As much as I was tempted to retort back, I wanted that too badly. I pushed up from my spot, which took far too much effort with how taxed my muscles were, and settled between Cillian's thighs. How I'd gone from overwhelmed by his presence to somehow comforted by it mystified me, but the shift had been drastic and transformative. Cillian wrapped an arm around my chest, drawing me back to rest against his, and my eyes fluttered shut.

The heat from the water didn't settle me as much as the heavy weight of his body, the firmness of his muscles. He made me feel protected, which was something I'd craved for longer than I could remember.

"Why me?" I asked the question that had been burning in my brain. "You mentioned not having an outlet with anyone, but you're stunning, powerful. You could have whoever you want."

Cillian reached to the side of the tub and grabbed one of the bottles of water and passed it to me. I took it and drank, grateful for the coolness against my parched and wrecked throat.

"What about me says inviting?" The rumble of his voice vibrated against my back. "I'm not a fan of letting people in."

"And yet here we are," I responded, closing my eyes again, as if that might allow him to open up further. Each hint I got of Cillian, each little scrap of the person behind his persona, had me craving more.

"I used to date," he offered. "Once upon a time."

"What happened?" I asked, trying not to hint at how badly I longed to know. Had it been Olivia? Had she soured him to relationships?

"An ex of mine," he murmured. "I...well, she grew frustrated with the lack of reciprocated feelings. I warned her. Told her I wasn't capable of what she wanted."

"What did she want?" My heart lay in my throat, but I kept my eyes shut.

"Love." Cillian let out a bitter little laugh. "Some have it in abundance, but I never have."

"Why stop dating, though?" I asked, ignoring his self-judgment. He seemed to think he was incapable of feelings, of emotions, but I'd collected so many glimpses of him throughout my months here.

"Olivia, she...well, I'd let her in more than most. She'd even worked for me. But then when I broke up with her, she made her betrayal loud and public. Left me with a reminder to never piss off a witch." His arm shifted around me, and I blinked my eyes open. He rubbed against the black tattoo of a rose on the inside of his forearm.

Olivia. That was the woman who'd caused him to retreat in on himself. My heart twisted tight. "She works for Thorin?"

Cillian stiffened behind me. "How do you know?"

"I heard her name around and looked her up. The information's not difficult to find for a librarian." I shifted in his lap so our eyes met. His golden ones were wary, as if he expected I'd stab him in the back. "This is a terminal case of curiosity. That's it. If you remember, Thorin was about to capture me in the alley because he'd learned I was your personal assistant. My skillset is research, not duplicity."

His muscles relaxed, and he sucked in a sharp breath. "I wasn't aware of how much you independently researched."

"How else will I get any answers? The lot of you lock up tight about most things, and the amount of half responses and avoidance I've received has left me with an abundance of questions."

His chest rumbled with his laugh. "You asked why you? That's one reason. You've been not only tenacious but clever from the moment I met you. Yet you're not as narrow-minded as many of the other humans I've come in contact with. Too many times, I've developed relationships, business or other, only to discover they're harboring an anti-monster sentiment beneath it all."

"I may be a little naïve at times, but there's too much to learn out there in the world to be narrow-minded," I said, meeting his gaze. "Though I know the exact types you're referring to." My coworkers who'd been so eager to push me into the arms of an asshole like Damian were the same ones who'd ignored the occasional monster patron who'd come in, giving them clipped responses and the bare minimum of effort. Those attitudes were still rampant, so I didn't blame Cillian for his caution.

"So, does all this progress mean you're going to start answering my questions?" I asked, a smile rising to my lips.

Cillian snorted. "If anything, I'll evade them even more. Make you work for it."

"Bastard," I shot back, even though my grin didn't falter.

One small question prickled in my mind. One that had emerged ever since I'd seen his library. "Are you the one who's been leaving me books?"

"Why deprive a librarian of the thing he needs most?" he responded.

My heart thumped hard. Those small gestures—they'd burrowed deep into my heart during my early days here. And it'd been him all along.

He leaned in and pressed his lips to mine, the calmness there the total opposite of the frenzied way he'd returned to the Spires. I wanted to ask him what he'd been up to in the first place, how he'd gotten those wounds, but I was well aware he'd evade. I sank into the solidness of his body, the heat of the water around me, the utter relaxation that settled inside me after he'd given me the best orgasm of my life.

"We should probably get out of the tub at some point," Cillian said, pointing to the fruit and water he'd brought.

I stiffened. "Right, I'll head back to my room."

"What makes you think I'll let you go, pet?" Cillian wrapped an arm around my torso and drew me against him. My whole body relaxed again. While I was no stranger to hooking up, after what I'd experienced with Cillian I wasn't sure how I'd handle being back in my room in the aftermath. Not after tonight.

He scraped his fangs over my shoulder, and the contact made me shiver. Fuck, I shouldn't still be turned on after the way he'd taken me, but my body raced with a newfound electricity around him.

Admitting how much I wanted to stay here made me feel a little bit too vulnerable tonight. "What if I try to run?"

"Haven't you figured that out yet?" Cillian responded, rich amusement in his voice. "I'll catch you."

CHAPTER 18

S leeping with my boss and captor was making me view this arrangement in an entirely different light.

It could've been the regular sex or that he fucked me so hard I couldn't walk straight after—those endorphins were nothing to be scoffed at—but my outlook on being here had shifted since we'd first fucked a few weeks ago. And more often than not, I'd been spending my nights in Cillian's room. We hadn't discussed the parameters of our arrangement or what this might mean, but I wouldn't turn down the contact I'd craved for a long, long while.

I brewed some coffee in the kitchen, which this late in the morning was empty. Cillian didn't have any meetings today that I needed to attend, and he'd locked himself in an office, so I'd wandered off to get myself food. My ass was sore, although the more I took his massive cock, the more I adjusted to the girth, the heft, the...knot. Ungh. I leaned against the counter and closed my eyes for a moment, savoring the memory.

"You've actually come up for air?" Charles's voice sounded from the doorway, and I blinked. "Thought you'd gotten lost in the West Wing."

A laugh escaped me, followed by a frisson of vulnerability. Would Charles, Amelia, and Theo look at me differently? I'd run into them over the last few weeks, but only for brief interchanges, and mostly regarding business. However, their knowing glances made it clear they'd pieced together what was going on between me and Cillian.

It didn't help that I was covered in marks now. The visible bite marks on my shoulders leading up to my neck were a dead giveaway, as the only other person up here with fangs was Theo, and he was spoken for. I resisted the urge to press my fingers against the bruises like I'd been doing from the moment I received them.

"I needed coffee," I said, gesturing to the percolating machine beside me. I pulled out another mug for him, since Charles seemed to have an addiction as big as mine. "Want a cup?"

"Yes, please," he said, finding a spot to lean beside me at the counter. "I'm sure you need the extra energy." His grin was instantaneous, a twinkle in his eyes that I enjoyed.

I shook my head, a mirroring grin rising to my lips as I poured myself a cup of coffee. "Don't know what you're talking about."

"Do you see me complaining? I've known Cillian a long time, and he's never been this sociable or pleasant. Keep up the good work. For morale."

"For morale," I said, lifting my mug in salute.

"What are you conspiring about in here?" Cillian's rich voice came from the doorway, and my body and mind perked up in unison. A cord tethered us together, one I didn't want to sever, and I couldn't help my reaction any more than I could help my next breath.

"Oh. *Coffee and Conspiracies*," Charles said, pouring himself a cup. "That's the perfect title for a podcast."

Cillian snorted as he swept into the room, his presence dominating my attention the way it always seemed to.

What would we do here? I licked my lips, the urge to kiss him, to fall against him threatening to consume me. However, we hadn't discussed how to act around his staff and friends.

Cillian answered for me, stepping into my space and leaning down to claim my lips in a kiss. Surprise exploded within me, as well as a burst of lust from how he consumed me without a care who watched. My heart thudded hard. Actions like this left a deeper mark on me than he might ever realize, after spending years of my youth being bullied and ignored.

Charles let out a whistle. "Damn, you're going to make me have to hunt down Theo if you keep being all hot up in my space."

Cillian's rumble of a laugh vibrated against my lips, and he slowly pulled away. "Go find your boyfriend. I'm stealing this one away for the day."

A thrill rose inside me at the idea of what he might have in store. "Oh? Do I get a say in where we're going?"

"Outside the Spires." He arched a brow, as if daring me to challenge him.

The reality of his statement crashed down on me like a bolt of lightning. Leaving the Spires? I never could've imagined he'd allow that.

"I can trust you to not run off, right?" he asked, a teasing in his voice that implied he already did.

"Believe me," I said. "I've seen what would happen if I did." The memory of Thorin's attempt at kidnapping me was fresh in my mind, even though it had happened weeks ago, as was the way Cillian had swept in to the rescue. The thought of going out into the world with him by my side made me feel as though I wielded a protection I hadn't had before.

"Have fun," Charles said, waggling his brows. "Don't do anything I wouldn't do."

I rolled my eyes, even though part of me loved that we weren't hiding anything from Charles. That Cillian allowed his closest to learn about us. "Do I get to know where we're going?"

Cillian shook his head. "You wouldn't know the place even if I told you."

I took a final sip of my coffee and put the mug down in the sink, my whole body vibrating at the prospect of leaving the Spires. The freedom to be out in the world was something I missed, even if the feeling had become tangled up in this newfound...thing with Cillian, and the fear of what awaited me as well.

Cillian had already taken the first steps to the door, and he waited for me there. I followed, and once I reached him, he slid a hand behind my lower back, guiding me forward. The subtle pressure of his warm palm there lit me up, my whole body humming at his proximity. He'd fucked me harder and better than I'd ever experienced before, and even his touch was a reminder of the orgasms he'd wrung from me.

We strode down the hallway and quickly made it onto the elevator, which I'd traveled on many a time with him at this point. Except Cillian pressed the P level, which wasn't one we'd gone to before. The elevator *whooshed* down, and I leaned in against him, reveling in the hard muscle beside me, the heat of his body, the possessiveness of his touch.

"What sparked this idea?" I asked, even though I wasn't sad about it in the slightest.

"I've been spending too much time in the Spires too," he commented. "It's about time we break free for a little bit."

In a way, Cillian sometimes seemed as much a prisoner here as I was, trapped inside this place. The statements he dropped on occasion made my heart squeeze tight, a reminder he was far more than he appeared.

The elevator doors opened to a parking garage, and we stepped out. The chill from the darkened area swept through me, a crispness there hinting of outside. It should be warmer today, which meant I'd get a glimpse of the sunshine and Peregrine City at its balmiest, as well as wherever Cillian planned on dragging me to.

He directed me over to a gunmetal-gray car, sturdy with sleek lines, and he pulled the keys out and pressed the button, the lights flashing.

"Get in," he said as he slipped over to the driver's side.

I complied, settling into the passenger seat, then passed him a look. "Clearly, please isn't in your vocabulary."

"Not when it's a common sense ask," he replied as he started the car and pulled out of the spot. As he wheeled around the parking garage, heading toward the exit on the lower level, my heart thumped a little harder.

Out beyond the Spires.

I believed I wouldn't see it for the next ten years, yet here he was, taking me out like the excursion was no big deal, when this gesture meant the world to me. He pressed a button on his keys, and the parking garage door opened, bringing in bright sunlight. The car zipped out onto the street, and the sense of freedom cascaded over me, effervescent. Today, Cillian was taking me out. We weren't boss and personal assistant, captor and captive. We were simply Cillian and Beau, and the ability to enjoy this with him sank into my veins, as heady as the sunshine.

"Are we going somewhere indoors?" I asked.

"I'm a bastard, but I'm not that mean," he teased, driving down the streets with ease. The sight of his thick forearms, his casual clutch on the wheel as he navigated was sexy as sin, and I couldn't quite look away. The cabin of the car was larger than a human model, clearly designed to fit bigger monsters, which fascinated me.

Right, so outdoors but somewhere I didn't know in Peregrine City. Which, truth be told, could be a fair amount of places. I'd lived here for the past few years, but I was more interested in adventuring between the pages of a book rather than exploring new areas by my lonesome. Maybe making more friends would've helped, but I'd never been apt at that either.

"Do I get a hint at least?" I asked as he zipped out of the casino district and nearer some of the richer areas I didn't often travel to.

"You'll enjoy it." Cillian winked my way and continued to speed along through the city, the vibrant life everywhere flashing around me. Passersby on every sidewalk, people shouting at each other, cars honking, the traffic breaking and swelling. The windows of the high-rises on either side of me glittered like diamonds. Part of me desperately missed being out there among all this, but another part had begun enjoying my time in the Spires as well. The people there I'd come to trust, the haunting corridors and gigantic library, the sense of safety I felt...and him.

I sank into the thrum of the engine beneath us, the car zooming through the city at top speed, and the intoxicating sunshine wrapped up with his presence. My whole body sparked with a liveliness I'd been craving for a long while now, since before I'd even been sent up to the Spires.

"Up ahead," Cillian said, starting to slow down. A massive metal gate barred the way, looming buildings on either side. I wasn't sure what he expected to show me outside, but it looked like we headed to another high-rise. He paused at a metal stand outside the gate and rolled the window down. "Mal, it's me."

A second later, the doors creaked open, and Cillian drove forward. A smug smile clung to his lips that I wanted to lick off, to run the tip of my tongue along his fangs, to drink in his intoxicating taste over and over again.

When I glanced forward again, my breath snagged. We drove down a narrow road, but at the end of it lay another wrought-iron entrance. Beyond that, though, all I could see was green. A tunnel lay past the entryway, surrounded by dangling wisteria with its pale purple blooms, and the trees that towered in the distance were majestic, ones that must've taken ages to grow. I rolled down my window, and the crisp, verdant scent traveled my way at once.

"What is this?" I asked as Cillian drove through the entrance and tunnel, the wisteria dangling overhead.

"The Slumbering Garden," he said, taking the tunnel at a leisurely pace. "It's a private garden my friend Mal owns, so there's a reason why you wouldn't have heard of it before."

"Ah, is this something only high society knows about?" I asked. The sweet breezes through the window enchanted me, and we hadn't even parked.

"Monsterkind," Cillian said. "Mal's a dragon shifter. Even though we're thinly accepted in big cities like this, that's not how the reception is farther out. And refuge is needed even here."

Heat flushed through me. How little I knew about the people I'd walked alongside for years. "I can see that. I grew up outside the city, and the views toward monsters weren't as tolerant...and that's putting it mildly."

"Surprising you turned out as open-minded as you are, then," he said, pulling out of the tunnel. A small stretch of asphalt made for a parking lot, and beyond it lay the entrance with a pale green and gold sign that read "Slumbering Gardens," along with more greenery than I could focus on.

"I was always the odd kid in my hometown," I murmured, my chest tightening at the memories. Books had been my steadfast companions through it all. "Changes your perspective."

Cillian pulled to a park and then placed a hand on my leg. "I hate to break it to you...but you're still odd."

I blinked. "Was that...a joke, Cillian Ashmore?"

He let out a bark of a laugh, as brilliant and sharp as sunlight, and cracked his door open. "You won't get another from me."

I stepped out of the car, and my knees wobbled for a minute, as the reality I was outside the Spires sank in again. The sun shone brightly today, the sky an aching blue, just puffy white clouds marching across the horizon.

"Come on, there's a lot to see." Cillian had started to walk toward the entrance, where the sweet breezes and the sound of trickling water beckoned. Flowers were in bloom, splashes of yellows and pinks, violets and blues, batches of them visible even from here.

We started down the pathway, where rosebushes of every variety and shade bracketed either side. The perfume was intoxicating, and I drank in the scent.

"This must be your favorite thing," I commented as I knelt to smell one of the butter-yellow blooms.

Cillian arched a brow.

"Your rose tattoo? Unless that has some other significance."

His eyes darkened. "They're pretty, sure. But I don't like them for their beauty—I respect them for their thorns."

The statement felt loaded with so much more, and I filed that away with every other detail I'd accumulated on Cillian—plenty at this point. In a way, his answer made me appreciate him on a deeper level, though. So many found it far too easy to fall for pretty things, which was why Damian had been in such hot demand. Except that had never drawn me in.

No, I craved a substance beneath the surface that he would never have satisfied.

Not nearly like the endless mystery of the man before me.

"My favorite gem in this place is this way," Cillian said, reaching back to offer his hand. I accepted automatically, but when our palms brushed together, my pulse raced. The effortless touch he gave, how tactile he was, surprised me every time. I'd never anticipated it from the ice-cold man I'd first met.

We meandered down the rose path, and I savored our time out here, in the sun, exploring somewhere new. Like this, my troubles were miles away, and I enjoyed every second of it.

"Did you always want to be a librarian?" Cillian asked as we walked along.

"Yes," I responded. "I used to hide away in the library at school. The librarian there took me under her wing. And books have always been a refuge of sorts." I cast him an arch look. "Did you always want to be the owner and proprietor of the Spires?"

"Not in the slightest," he responded, staring out at the expanse before us, the path lined by looming trees and interspersed with lilies of so many different shades and varieties. I soaked them all in with my eyes while waiting for his response. "I wanted to be an architect."

I tilted my head to the side. A silent thrill rose inside me at being privy to this detail. "Why didn't you pursue it?"

"My father had a strict path for me to follow. And he wasn't the sort of man you said no to." The grimness in his tone told the rest of the story, and I swallowed hard. "But he's gone. No longer a problem."

"Then why not now?" I asked.

Cillian shrugged. "I found ways to make owning the Spires mine."

My eyes widened as the realization set in. "You're the one who does most of the designing for it, aren't you."

He let out a low whistle. "Your sharpness is a constant delight."

"It would certainly explain the gothic brooding with a side of edgelord in the décor upstairs," I teased. Cillian's sharp bark of a laugh was as infectious as this gorgeous day. We strode down the lily-lined path, the thick, velvety petals catching my attention left and right.

"Up ahead," Cillian said, pointing to what lay farther down.

I squinted, a bright sparkle almost blinding me as the sunlight glinted off the surface of water. We got closer, and the sight before me took my breath away. The pond was huge and still, reflecting the brilliant blue sky above like a mirror. On the far side of the pond lay a white structure with a large overhang, hulled out like an amphitheater. I couldn't help but wonder whether anyone ever performed there, but they'd have to be exclusive, private situations, since I'd never even heard of this place in all my time in Peregrine City. Water lilies spanned the pond, dots of vibrant green and pale pink against the glossy surface of the water.

Cillian's hand was in mine, the clutch possessive, and I basked in his touch, in the beauty of the day, in the freedom I experienced in this moment. The past month had taught me not to take time like this for granted. I'd spent years in this city, cycling through the same routine, and when I thought back on it, had I really been free?

Beyond my father, I hadn't had any connections worth preserving. Those had withered away to dust.

"Worth it, right?" Cillian asked, tilting his chin in the direction of the pond.

The breath snagged in my throat. The sun highlighted the browns in his black hair, and the glossiness, the curve of his regal horns, and the lines of his chin, his neck were so clear I wished I had any drawing ability, just so I could capture them. His skin glowed a rich red, and that solid frame held a sturdiness I craved. But his eyes, when he stared at me with tenderness—fuck, the look curled inside me and settled there.

"Yeah, worth it."

I wasn't talking about the gardens.

CHAPTER 19

W e spent most of the day at the gardens, since Cillian had packed food in his car, and the fact we were undisturbed there by other people appealed to me even more. I appreciated my solitude more than most, and despite occasionally getting lonely, that didn't mean I welcomed crowds. It was the most perfect date I'd ever been on—if it was even a date.

We hadn't clarified anything about our situation, our relationship, and while I wondered what we were, there wasn't an urgency to define anything either.

Not when he made me feel claimed and possessed and *his*.

"Want to grab a coffee before we head home?" Cillian asked.

"Be still, my heart," I teased, placing a hand over it. I never in a thousand years could've imagined I'd be spending casual time like this with the demon I'd first met in the Spires. He'd seemed as forbidding as the peaks themselves.

We slipped into the car, and he started the engine before peeling out of the place. My heart thudded hard, the need for him rising again. I'd spent all day with him, but now that we headed home, my mind slipped toward the darker proclivities that dwelled there.

A few blocks away from the Slumbering Gardens, Cillian slowed to a halt in front of a coffee shop, Midnight Café. With the black banner out front and the neon white lighting for the sign, it felt like a perfect choice for him. The streets around here bustled, so different from the quiet oasis we'd escaped.

"How long has Mal been in Peregrine City?" I asked, as if I knew the person who owned the garden.

"His whole life. And he's lived a long one," Cillian said. "There's a reason he owns that much acreage in the city. It'd be impossible if it hadn't been in his family already."

"Damn, I can only imagine."

We stepped out of the car, and the moment we did, Cillian's alertness kicked in. His shoulders tightened the slightest bit, and the feral air around him increased. My body responded in turn, and I paid attention to my surroundings a bit more. Around every corner, someone terrible could lurk, a reality I was more aware of now I had a mark over my head as Cillian's personal assistant.

When we walked into the coffee shop, a smooth jazz swept through along with the quiet chatter of the customers inside. The décor was equally dark, black walls offset by painted star and moon motifs, and the globe lights around the shop gleamed like moonlight.

"What can I get you?" he asked me as we stood in line. His palm pressed against my lower back again, and I fought the urge to swoon. It made my stomach flip-flop in the best way.

"A latte would be great," I said. This was all so normal in a way that fucked with my head, and I found it far too easy to pretend we weren't stuck in the Spires, that this was just our normal life and we were out in the city together. The yearning that rushed through me grew fiercer than anything I'd ever experienced before.

He strode up to the register and placed our orders—a latte for me and a black coffee for him.

The barista set to work on the espresso machine, and we moved to the handoff pane.

The tension emanating off Cillian hadn't abated.

"You really don't go out in public much, do you?" I asked, keeping my voice low.

His expression darkened. "I used to. But that changed."

After her, I assumed. His ex-girlfriend who jumped ship to Thorin's business. Whatever was going on regarding that situation seemed to be a lot more dangerous and complex than I was aware of. I couldn't lie that I'd become more curious than ever.

The door creaked open, and my glance traveled that way.

I froze at the sight of a familiar face. What the hell was Damian doing on this side of town? He was perfectly coiffed, as usual, wearing a crisp button-down and a smarmy attitude.

His gaze landed on me, and his eyes widened in surprise—to be expected, since I'd all but disappeared. Part of me hoped he'd ignore me, pretend I wasn't here, but then his hands balled into fists. He marched in our direction, his footsteps determined, and I couldn't withhold my groan.

The slice of my past was jarring here with my present, as if I were two merged into one. The old me, the one who'd known Damian, who'd lived in the same complex as him, felt further away than ever, and I found I didn't hate that.

"Beau," Damian said as he closed the space between us. His voice echoed too loud in the coffee shop for my liking. "Is that you?"

"In the flesh," I commented dryly. My feet itched for escape.

He reached out and placed a hand on my arm. "Where have you been? I've been worried sick about you."

I tensed at once from his touch, not wanting him in my space, same as ever.

"Get your hand off him," Cillian rumbled, and his palm pressed harder against my lower back. He loomed over both of us, his presence multiplying, if that were even possible. A silent thrill rose up my spine at Cillian's command, at the way he stepped in and defended me, when in the past I'd tried to avoid persistent assholes like Damian. I'd simply deflected and endured when all I wanted was them to be gone.

"Who're you?" Damian asked, his upper lip curling in a sneer. As he scanned Cillian up and down, I recognized the flash of his gaze for what it was—not jealousy but disgust. If anything confirmed I'd made the right call about avoiding Damian, that did. Many humans in the city hid their monster hating under polite veneers, unlike in the countryside where people brandished those attitudes like weapons.

"Remove your hand, or I'll remove it for you," Cillian responded with his usual tactfulness. In this instance, I could admit to being amused. Damian's persistence had always unnerved me slightly in the past, since he knew where I lived, but with Cillian's hand at my back, with him at my side, I felt no fear. This was addictive.

I gave a slight tug, and Damian thankfully let go before he unleashed carnage. He'd never seen "The Beast" feral, but my god, it was a sight to behold.

"Latte and a black coffee," the barista called at the handoff pane, and I stepped past Damian to snag my latte.

"The landlord ended up renting out your place," Damian said, pointedly trying to ignore Cillian, as if that were possible. "Are you going to come back? I can always try to put in a good word."

"No, I'm not returning," I said, and for the first time since I thought about the prospect, I wasn't sad. That apartment never felt like a home, more just a place to rest my head. Stale blank walls, strangers behind every door, a view of the city that didn't feel familiar in a cozy way, just dull. I passed the black coffee over to Cillian, who accepted it with one hand while refusing to remove his other from my back. "I'm not at the library anymore either. You'll find your way."

"Is this guy coercing you?" Damian asked, jerking a thumb in Cillian's direction. God, he couldn't be stupider. He lowered his tone. "Guys like him—they're dangerous. You don't want to get caught spending too much time with them."

The threat lay heavy in his tone, in the flash of his eyes, and my anger toward him multiplied.

Before I could respond, Cillian spoke up. "I'm fucking him so well he doesn't want to return to his old life."

I licked my lips, not bothering to hide my grin. He wasn't wrong. Cillian's golden eyes flashed as they met mine, a hint of a smirk on his lips, and fuck. I was enamored. The way he brazenly barreled in like he owned every space transfixed me. When I'd first arrived at the Spires, I'd loathed his attitude the most. But used in my defense? Yeah, my feelings had changed.

Damian's face contorted as he stared at me differently. Like I wasn't the person he'd chased after for years. That look—I knew that look from growing up in a small town. I knew the ugliness that lurked beneath, the hatred that bubbled there.

"With a *monster*?" Damian's emphasis on monster lingered in the air, the censure evident. His volume was loud enough that I could feel the press of eyes on us from all directions, but I kept my back straight, facing him head-on.

Damian let out a disgusted huff. "Fine, Beau. Don't come crying to me when he's ruined you."

Tension roiled between us, especially from said monster who stood at my back, barely restraining himself. This wouldn't end well for any of us.

"You know, because I'm a commodity," I said dryly, trying to slice through the pressure.

Damian scowled and turned on his heel. To my relief, he marched out of the coffee shop, his stomps resounding through the place. I doubt he'd really heard what I said, but in all honesty, he never heard me anyway. Relief rushed in as the casual chatter throughout the coffee shop resumed, as patrons stopped looking in our direction.

Cillian took a sip of his coffee. "So, who was that?"

I snorted, and we stepped away from the handoff pane. "My old neighbor who refused to take a hint."

"I can see as much," Cillian said, pushing the front door open for me. I hated the loss of his hand at my back, as the steady warmth had grounded me better than anything else. The waning golden sunbeams cascaded down on us, and I soaked them in. I wasn't sure when we'd take another trip outside the Spires, so I wanted to savor every minute of this one.

We stepped toward the car, when movement in front of us caught my attention.

A woman strode our way, the clip of her heels on the sidewalk echoing. Cillian froze.

The thing was, I recognized her, but not from meeting her in person. Her ebony hair was pulled back into a perfunctory bun, and her red pantsuit clung to her body in all the right ways, a dip in the front showcasing her creamy cleavage.

"Olivia," Cillian growled, his voice half feral. "What are you doing here?" He stepped in front of me. Apparently it was a day for interferences. Annoyance rushed through me at the sight of her, and I hated that she was even prettier in person than the pictures depicted.

"Word on the street was that you were taking a jaunt through town today," she said, an icy coolness to her voice that coated a layer of frost over everything. "Enjoying the sunlight while you still can?"

"I'm on a date," Cillian said. "Which is none of your business, or Thorin's. Your jealousy is unbecoming."

Well, Cillian didn't need any of my help in being rude, as he'd perfected the art himself. Still, his mentioning it as a date sent a flush of warmth through me.

"Ah, so you're trying?" she asked, the words coming out in a taunt. "Good luck. The smarter move would just be to accept Thorin's deal."

"Never," Cillian snarled. "And tell your master to stay the hell away from Beau."

"This is him?" she asked, scrutinizing me.

"I'm right here," I pointed out. "It's bad manners to talk about someone in front of their face."

Cillian's arm wrapped around my shoulder, as if he thought I'd be taken from him. The possessiveness thrilled me but scared me at the same time, because Cillian's defense felt less like jealousy and more like protection. As if danger could be lurking around the corner.

"And pressuring me won't make me cave either," Cillian spat out. "So you can tell him to call off his puppets."

Olivia let out a small noise of amusement. "I have no idea what you're referring to."

"Of course you don't." Cillian was brimming at this point, the rage pouring off him. "Leave me alone, Liv. Haven't you already done enough damage?"

Her chin jutted out, and the first flicker of anything piercing her composure descended. "There's always room for more."

With that, she swept past us, her heels clacking on the pavement before she disappeared into the coffee shop. Cillian's arm wrapped protectively around me as he ushered us toward the car.

"Let's go home," he said. "I don't trust that she was here by happenstance."

A shiver ran down my spine at the thought she'd kept eyes on us, that Thorin might somehow be surveilling us. We strode toward the car, and even when I settled into the passenger seat, the sense of foreboding still lingered.

"So, did we have enough flashes from our past today?" I asked, trying to lighten the mood.

"I'd be happy to never see that flash from the past again," Cillian growled as he turned on the engine and peeled out of the parking spot. The tension radiated through the cab of the car, the disruptions from the outside world reminding me we were anything but simple. The afternoon sun was turning golden in hue, careening closer to night, and the car zipped down the street as we headed back in the direction of the Spires.

We drove for a few minutes in loaded silence before Cillian glanced in his rearview mirror.

"Fuck."

"What's wrong?" Before the words finished leaving my lips, I whipped around. A black sports car trailed behind us, closing the space with increasing quickness. The way they drove felt erratic, determined, and my intuition was shouting at me.

"Should I bother trying to spoon feed you a lie?" he asked as he pressed harder on the gas, and we shot forward.

"Considering your reaction and the expensive car behind us, no," I responded, my heart thrumming hard.

"Let's just say this isn't the first time I've been followed while outside the Spires." Cillian's tone was light, but his words landed with deadly impact. My pulse sped as I turned around to stare at the black sedan keeping close to us. What could they want? Was this one of Thorin's cronies? Someone Olivia had tipped off? The questions multiplied at the same rapid pace as my pulse.

"What's their aim?" I asked. "Intimidation?"

"I wish it were that simple," Cillian murmured, letting out a sharp breath. "Sit down in your seat. I'm going to attempt to shake him."

We slowed at the light, and even though he'd made the demand and I sat forward again, I kept an eye in my side-view mirror. The black sedan was almost on top of us with how close it had stopped, and it revved its engines. Fuck. That wasn't a good sign.

The danger that surrounded Cillian was beyond anything I'd experienced in my simple life before I'd arrived at the Spires. Car chases weren't even in the realm of possibility.

I gripped the door handle, mostly for something to distract myself with, and sucked in a sharp breath.

The light turned green.

Cillian zipped forward, his engine roaring. The car vaulted forward at top speed, blasting past the limit as we traveled down one of the narrow streets of Peregrine City.

Cillian hunched forward, his body poised for action, his grip tight on the steering wheel. With no signaling, he made the first right down an alleyway between two large, looming buildings. His car barely fit, but he zipped along the bumpy road. The jolting shuddered my bones, and my palms broke into a sweat.

The black sedan followed with a smoothness that unnerved me. These weren't novices at tailing—no, they were practiced.

They might not just be following us either. What if they wanted to get rid of us completely? A chill rippled down my spine.

"Want some getaway music?" I asked, needing to break the silence somehow. Needing to distract myself from the fact that an unknown driver was chasing us through Peregrine City.

"Sure," he murmured, and I was rewarded by the slightest twitch of his lips. I flipped through his streaming service, picking a French rap artist I liked to listen to. My fingers trembled slightly. The smooth strains poured through the speakers, even though they didn't quite deflate the tension circulating through the car.

We burst out of the alley and onto another larger street, and Cillian made a right. He zipped down a wide, bustling main street, weaving from one lane to the other as he passed a few cars. A couple honked at him from the fast lanes, but he quickly glided past them. I'd consider the driving reckless on a normal day, but given our situation—necessary.

I glanced in the mirror. The black sedan zoomed behind us at the same breakneck pace. Fuck. We hadn't ditched it. Somehow, the car continued to follow close behind us.

I chewed on my lower lip, my heart thumping a bit harder. The bright neon signs and some of the tall domed buildings signaled we were closer to the Casino District. Nearer to the Spires. Yet Thorin's place, Spectacle, was here too. Would any other cars join in the chase? How many had Thorin sent to follow us? The French rap glided through the speakers, smooth and effortless, a contrast to the way my internal alarms jangled.

No, I wouldn't take a deep breath until we were back in the Spires.

"Don't worry," Cillian said, making another sharp turn, the car tires squealing with the effort. We darted down another narrow street, the shadows sloping here, the squeeze seeming impossible. Would we scrape the buildings? "This isn't my first car chase."

"I don't know whether I should be reassured by that or not," I murmured, leaning back in the seat in a pitiful attempt to pretend my body wasn't tense. The riotous thump of my heart grew louder by the second, and I gripped the door handle a bit tighter, my palm slick.

The black sedan was almost on top of us again.

Cillian hopped onto the I-90, one of the busier roads close to the Spires, and then slammed on the gas again. We rocketed farther ahead, surrounded by cars on both sides, all moving at a rapid pace. However, when I glanced to my right, the black sedan was no longer driving behind us.

No, it was inching up to our side.

Cillian clenched his jaw, clearly biting back a curse as he sped up the slightest bit more, as if looking for an opening. How he remained so calm, so collected, was a mystery to me, but he possessed a deadly focus.

To the left, a small gap opened up—Cillian seized it.

Once he slipped into that one, he pushed on the gas, moving even faster to then launch into a spot in the middle lane again, ahead of where he'd been.

The black sedan was stuck a car behind us in the middle lane. My knuckles grew white on the door handle. Maybe we could make it.

Cillian veered to the right, sliding into place, and then slammed on the accelerator to zip off the highway, down into the side streets again.

How close were we to the Spires? We couldn't be far at this point. My heart hammered so hard it all but leapt out of my chest, and the squeeze of these smaller streets only amplified my nerves.

"They're not going to smash us off the road, are they?" I asked, wanting the reassurance, even though my gut proclaimed danger, danger, danger.

Cillian's silence was all the answer I needed. My palms sweated as I kept my grip on the door handle. He plunged down a few more random side streets until he blasted into a familiar alley.

I glanced out the window and up. The Spires were right next to us, looming above us in all their stony majesty.

Thank fuck.

As I looked into the side mirror again, the black sedan clipped around the corner.

Cillian sped up and clicked a button. Up ahead, a garage door began to slide open.

So close.

I bit my lower lip so hard it bled, not glancing into the mirror again to see where the black sedan was. Instead, I kept my gaze to the front and focused on the open garage ahead of us, one I now recognized as being attached to the Spires.

Almost there.

Cillian simmered in his quiet, but he remained calm and in control as he closed the remaining feet toward it.

He turned the wheel and made the sharp turn, a screech sounding as we entered the garage. Cillian jammed on the button. At once, the door began to roll down behind us as we flew forward into the dimly lit parking garage.

I took my first deep, full breath since the black sedan had begun following us.

The garage door clicked shut.

"They won't follow us here?" I asked, as Cillian slowed to a glide around the circle of the garage until he found a clear spot closer to an upper floor.

"Wouldn't dare," he said. "Amelia's got tricks up her sleeve."

Considering she was a witch, I could make a guess about protection spells, at least for the Spires. I sagged against the seat and let out a long, noisy exhale. "Thank fuck."

"Thorin likes to ruin things," he murmured as he shut the engine off.

"I'm catching the drift. No wonder you rarely leave the Spires. Has it been like that for a while?"

Cillian's silence was loaded, and for a moment I thought he would ignore my question. "It's only lately that it's gotten this bad. But Thorin Glass has long been a bane on my family."

"Maybe I should be glad I'm from a staunchly working-class family," I responded. "Feels a lot less dramatic."

He let out a snort. "Should we head back in?"

I nodded, even though my blood still thrummed. The adrenaline hadn't faded yet, and a craving I'd long tried to suppress rose again. I needed to unleash all this pent-up energy, and there was one way I wanted to, desperately.

Cillian lifted a brow. "What's going through your mind, pet?"

I licked my lips. Should I confess the fantasy I'd long held? If anyone could deliver on it, Cillian Ashmore would be the very demon.

"I've got an idea."

CHAPTER 20

We agreed to meet back in the hallway in an hour. It gave me enough time to shower and prep my hole, making sure I was nice and slick. My heart thumped hard but for a different reason than a car chase this time.

As much as Cillian had the potential to be terrifying, I wanted to let the monster out of the cage. I wore a pair of sweats and a loose tee that clung to my shoulders, my hair in ringlets from having freshly showered. I stepped out of my room, my pulse increasing, as if I'd be snatched from the corridor at any moment.

However, he'd told me to meet him in the hall near the library, and my mind reeled with the possibilities. All I knew was that this evening would be one to remember. My limbs vibrated with the need to burst into action, to run, to move, but I kept my pace steady as I walked down the corridor, the blue lighting giving it a subterranean glow.

Today had been a roller coaster—pinnacle of perfection and a fast drop down, but I was ready to rise again. I sucked in a sharp breath, my mouth dry.

I made the turn at the end of the hall, heading in the direction of the library. Amelia was working down below tonight, and Theo and Charles were out on a date themselves, so only Cillian and I were on this floor—and that privacy was what I counted on.

When I started down the corridor, the feel of a gaze on me had me hesitating. Walking a little slower, I glanced over my shoulder, but I didn't see Cillian at the opposite end. Nor was he in the kitchen when I passed it. Yet the feeling of being watched intensified with every step forward, and my heart thumped a little harder.

Where was he?

I stopped midstride and did a full circle in the middle of the hallway, but I didn't spot Cillian. The inky shadows grew so murky in sections that it made it hard to tell what was nothing and what corners and darkened doorways might hide someone. Yet Cillian wasn't small enough to obscure. Anywhere he hid would be obvious due to his size alone.

The prickle traveled across my arms, my legs. As if someone watched me, waiting.

The movement was so fast I almost missed it. From the corridor behind me, a huge blur emerged from one of the open rooms.

"Run," he bellowed, his voice echoing through the hallway.

My whole body jolted in surprise.

I couldn't help but obey.

My adrenaline kicked into high gear, and I vaulted forward down the corridor. We hadn't planned much more beyond the basics and rules, and my mind reeled as the panic crashed in. All too easily, I remembered running down stair after stair as he chased me, my body screaming in alarm.

Yet this time, the fear transmuted into something different. Something far hotter.

His footsteps boomed behind me, and just like before, he was the predator and I was the prey.

My heart thrummed from the chase, and my whole body lit up with electricity.

I passed closed door after closed door, my mind reeling. One destination shone in my mind like a beacon, though, and my feet carried me onward.

Cillian's growl reverberated through the hall, igniting my veins with liquid adrenaline.

Oh gods.

The double doors I'd been searching for neared, and I burst forward, almost flying down the hallway. I grappled for the handles and yanked. The boom of footsteps grew louder and louder as Cillian gained on me.

I plunged into the library—my refuge.

Before I could reach out to drag the doors shut, Cillian stepped into view. He loomed over me, stained in shadows.

"Poor choice, pet. There's nowhere to hide in here."

I raced away from the doors, a thrill rising inside me. He stalked forward, those golden eyes aglow, ever the predator. My cock plumped up at the sight of him, an automatic response at this point. When I reached the far wall lined with the bookshelves, I paused. There wasn't anywhere to run.

Cillian let out another low growl that reverberated around the room, his gaze locked on me. I whimpered as I backed against the bookshelf.

A slow smile rolled onto his lips, a surety there that sent a pulse of lust through me. I clutched the bookshelves behind me, plastering myself against those solid stacks.

He took his time closing the distance between us, each footstep with purpose.

His shoulders heaved, his pupils blown as he zeroed in on me. He moved with a singular thought in his mind.

Claim.

I whimpered again, shifting a few feet to the right. Cillian tracked my movements, his gaze never leaving me. The distance between us grew smaller and smaller.

"You can't outrun me," he said, his voice low and husky as he continued stalking forward.

My whole body rioted with the need to dash.

"I can try."

I burst to the left, aiming for the door.

One moment he stood feet away from me, and the next, a force tugged me backward by the shirt collar. The rip of the fabric echoed in the room, the pieces fluttering to the floor, and I tried to surge forward again. A hand clamped around my wrist.

I whipped around to face him, and all of a sudden Cillian was right in front of me, towering there. His whole body simmered with everything he'd been holding back, a wildness I craved, and I yanked, trying to escape his hold.

"Be a good pet for me and bend over." He tugged at my arm, and I dug my heels in. "Oh, you want to do this the hard way?"

I gulped, my throat dry. He grabbed me by the waist and dragged me forward, his muscles bulging. I thrashed in his grip, clawing and trying to get his arms off me. However, his strength was unwavering, like I was bound by iron bands, and he stopped right in front of the bookshelf.

Cillian plastered his body to mine, pressing me against the shelving as he brought my hands up. "You're going to be a good pet and take my cock."

"Fuck off," I spat, my heart thrumming.

"I'd rather fuck you," he said, pinning both my hands above me with one hand. I writhed back and forth, but my ass kept brushing against him. He didn't waver. Instead, he reached down with his free hand, grabbed my waistband, and yanked. The sweats tore off me, the force making my thighs sting.

My whole body flushed with the mixture of panic and lust that I craved. He had me stripped to nothing and pinned against the shelves. I writhed back and forth again, and Cillian grabbed my ass hard enough to bruise. A moan escaped me before I could bite it back.

"Looks like my slutty little pet likes it rough." His voice was gravel and sin.

"No," I gasped out. "Get away."

He nudged his thick length between my cheeks, separated by a thin layer of fabric, and another moan exploded from my lips. I tried to keep myself from grinding back against him, the memory of how good he felt thrusting into me flaring fast and hot. Ngh.

"No," I cried out again, twisting and yanking back and forth.

The shink of the zipper sounded behind me, and a moment later, the thick tip of his cock nudged between my cheeks.

Frenzy hit me fast and fierce, and I tried to whip to the side and sink my teeth into his arm. They sank into his skin, but he was undeterred. I writhed and lashed against him, but his grip was solid, his form behind me immense.

Cillian thrust his thick, ridged cock into me hard enough to knock the breath from my lungs. The mixture of pleasure and pain held me captive, and I unlatched from my bite, trying to breathe through the intrusion.

He pushed all the way inside me, his thickness threatening to split me open, and I howled.

"You can take me," he said, his voice husky and rough.

His grip around my wrists tightened, and he pulled back slightly and thrust in again. The ridges brushed against my insides. The shelves quaked with the force of the movement. My whole body flooded with sparks as he grazed past my prostate.

"Oh gods," I gasped out.

His grip on my hip was hard, his claws digging into my skin enough to pierce, and the pinpricks of pain kept me on edge.

"If you can't be a good pet for me, I'll make you," he said with a growl. He dipped down and sank his teeth into my shoulder. Another burst of pain flooded through me, mixing with sheer desire. My cock hung heavy between my legs, and I shamelessly dripped pre-cum on the floor. Pinned like this against the wall, his fangs in my shoulder, his hand wrapped around my wrists in a bruising grip, my mind shut down.

He pulled back and thrust in again, and a whimper passed my lips. The intoxicating combination of shame and fear and pure, undeniable lust rushed through me. Cillian thrust forward with a snap of his hips, burying his thick girth inside me. The ridges, the thick as fuck base and middle of his cock drove into me, the pulse and heat of it making me wild. Cillian grunted, not letting up with his teeth as he rode me hard against the shelves. His groin collided with my ass with a smack, his balls slapping against me with each thrust.

A mixture of whimpers and whines exploded from my lips, and I tipped my head back, offering my neck in surrender.

The shelves creaked and groaned as he plowed into me, the books on them trembling. A few clattered to the ground on either side of me, only adding to the predicament. I sucked in a shallow breath, but he thrust back in hard, knocking it from my lungs. The pleasure grew overwhelming, the steady way he tagged my prostate over and over again.

Cillian let go of my shoulder, and the sudden ache there made my knees buckle. His grip on my hip kept me upright, those pinpricks of pain keeping me in the present. My whole body trembled as he fucked me with increasing force, like I was a mere toy at his disposal. Heat rushed through me, wild and fierce at the thought.

Cillian's tongue snaked over the bite mark he'd left, a mix of euphoria mingling with the ache.

"Little pet, you like this, don't you?" he murmured in my ear as he continued to fuck me relentlessly against the bookshelves. Another book toppled and crashed to the floor. "Getting pinned down and taken hard."

I whimpered, embarrassment flushing through me again. My cock was rigid and needy, my balls ready to explode, but I couldn't do a damn thing.

He continued to thrust inside me, the force sending my whole body forward each time. The powerful way he rocked into me, how he consumed me entirely, had me immolating. I panted like a bitch in heat, my legs spread, my hole stuffed so full I could scream. And still I craved more. I wanted him to knot me, to breed me, until I could no longer feel anything but him inside me.

Until he'd possessed me body and soul.

Cillian sank his teeth into my nape, and my whole body shuddered. I went limp, just like prey, as he bit down, continuing to thrust hard inside me. The ridges brushed against my prostate so many times my legs were going numb, my limbs quaking from the sheer force of the sensations rioting through me. Sweat burst on my forehead, dripping down, along with the drops coursing down my spine.

The sloppy sounds of his cock fucking into me filled the room, along with his grunts and growls that mingled with the growing whine in my throat. My whole body was oversensitive at this point, my nipples taut, my balls heavy and aching. My cock dribbled onto the floor as it swung back and forth each time he drove into me.

My thighs quaked, pleasure overriding anything else. Gods, I wanted him to consume me. To take me over. Neck bared, I surrendered to him in every way.

He'd brought each fantasy of mine to life.

"You're going to take my knot, pet," he commanded.

Another whimper left me, my palms sweating, my body on a razor's edge. I craved it more than my next breath.

Cillian let out a vicious growl that quaked through the room, and his cock pulsed inside me. Hot cum flooded my insides, and I gasped with relief at the sensation I'd been craving so badly. His knot began to expand, ballooning inside me until I was stretched so full I couldn't possibly pull away. He licked my neck again, the sting mixing with pleasure as my legs trembled. He was the only thing keeping me upright, as my limbs had ceased functioning.

"Do you need to come?" he asked, a mocking edge to his voice that I loved.

I bobbed my head.

He reached down and fondled my balls, which were so full they could burst. His touch against them was almost painful, and I tried to shift, but he gripped them so I couldn't. Another whimper escaped me.

Oh god, I needed to come so badly. Salt stung my eyes as sweat blurred them, but he kept my wrists pinned above me so I couldn't move.

"Rub yourself against my hand."

He placed his massive palm right in front of my cock, but instead of closing it around my aching length, he just offered the flat of it.

Heat rushed to my cheeks, but I bucked forward to brush my cock against his hot palm. The movement tugged at the knot inside me, and I sobbed from the pressure, from the combination of relief and torment.

"You've got the control here," he teased, a sadistic edge to his rich voice. I bucked forward again, running my cock along his palm, and the tug on my hole sent my knees quaking again.

"Fuck." I sucked in a breath as I tried the same motion again, the push-pull of blissful relief warring with the stretch around my hole. I could barely move forward, my movements restricted by the way I was tethered to him. Humiliation flooded through me at my desperation, and the next time I rubbed my cock against his palm, a pathetic mewl escaped me.

Fuck. I was so damn close. So on the edge of being able to find that relief, but I couldn't reach down to jerk myself off or rub vigorously, not with how I was pinned.

"Seeing you struggle is so hot, pet," Cillian murmured, his warm breath puffing against my ear.

I ground against his palm again, this time holding there a moment, even with the stretch against my hole growing painful. His knot was still firmly lodged inside me. I stayed there, rubbing again, the tension so extreme my whole body vibrated with it. Oh god. I was so close to coming.

I brushed against his open palm one more time, and that was all it took.

My balls drew up, and cum erupted from me. The orgasm crashed over me fast and fierce, like river rapids, and I got swept away with the raw power of it. My vision blanked, my limbs seized up, and a feral, wounded noise erupted from me. Pleasure rushed through me, the intensity enough that my teeth ached, and I succumbed to the waves of sensation as another spurt of cum rushed out of me.

Slowly, I came back down to earth, my breath escaping in sharp pants. Cillian was knotted inside my hole, and I relaxed against his hard, muscular body, sagging into his embrace.

He wrapped one of his arms around my waist, keeping me snug against him, our bodies covered in sweat and boiling hot. Then he lifted his cum-covered palm to my mouth.

"Clean it off."

Ngh. Fuck, he was so effortlessly commanding, and I'd been mellowed out from our play, no urge to push back remaining. I leaned forward and licked at his palm, slow, methodical movements. I lapped at him like a kitten, taking my time cleaning my cum from him.

When I finished, he rested the hand against my other hip and pressed a kiss over the bite mark on my shoulder. It still ached, the deep sort, from how hard he'd bitten, but the bit of sweetness sent my insides fluttering. I'd be clawed and marked all over after this, and I relished each and every one.

"Is that everything you hoped it would be?" he murmured against my neck.

"Yeah, it was," I responded, a shiver rolling through me. I'd held my fantasy secret within me for so long, the idea of getting chased down and pinned and fucked at my captor's mercy, and Cillian had filled the role perfectly.

I'd never met anyone who fulfilled me this way, not only with how he fucked and claimed me, but also...with more. The time with him today had confirmed how his presence set me at ease, and he coaxed my past from me with little effort. Around him, the loneliness wasn't as pervasive, as oppressive as it'd always been.

His knot began to deflate inside me, and he slipped out of my hole. The cum trickled down the inside of my thigh, and I savored the sensation.

I turned around to face him at last. Cillian snagged the tattered fabric of my clothes from the floor and slung them over his forearm. His slacks were unzipped and down around his thighs, his cock still out, but he wore the same button-down from earlier, just slightly more rumpled. The sight of him so put-together while I was stripped down and wrecked got me hot all over again.

"C'mere," he said as he approached. He tucked his cock back inside his slacks and zipped them up, then gestured me close. I took a few tentative steps forward, my legs wobbly, my whole body covered in marks, some soon to be bruises. Cillian scooped me up with ease, the way he often liked to after we fucked, and I didn't hesitate to rest my cheek against his chest. His heartbeat was strong, steady, and I found a bone-deep comfort there.

"Let's go back to my room," he said. "Might just keep you naked the rest of the night."

"How is that different from any other?" I asked, my voice slurred.

The exhaustion slammed into me hard, and my vision started to blur as my eyes grew heavier and it grew more difficult to keep them open.

Cillian stepped out of the library, carrying me in his firm grip, and as he strode down the hallway my lids shut, and I surrendered to the darkness.

CHAPTER 21

When I blinked my eyes open, I was in a bed.

It wasn't mine, but I recognized the silken sheets as Cillian's. Except he wasn't lying beside me like he usually did. I rolled over to my side, biting back a groan. The movement reminded me how much I'd been ravaged, and ungh. Tonight was everything I could ever have hoped for.

Cillian stood by the window, gazing out at the city. He cut a stark silhouette, even against the midnight landscape that lay beyond. There was something lonely about the way he lingered there, as if he carried an impossible burden. I'd been getting glimpses of the weight Cillian bore, evident in his loaded silences and obvious avoidance. And it was clearer today that he was tangled in something far deeper than he would speak of.

My heart ached. I wanted to reach out to him, offer him comfort, solace.

I pushed up to sit on the bed, and the creak of the mattress had him turning around.

"Awake at last?" he commented, a low, slow smile dawning on his features.

"Mmm, someone fucked me so good I could've slept straight through the night."

"Oh, who might that be?" he responded, his coy tone a joy. He strode over and settled on the bed next to me. "I'll need to look over your cuts."

"I'm not frail," I responded.

Cillian arched one of those dark, thick brows. "I'm well aware."

Heat rushed through me at the memory of how he hadn't held back with me. How he'd unleashed his inner beast and fucked me like he wanted to break me. Goddamn.

"I grabbed your phone and a set of clothes," he said, gesturing over to his dresser top where they lay. "As much as I want you naked in my room, I don't think the rest of the staff needs to see it."

I snorted and leaned back onto my elbows. "Who's to say they haven't already?"

A low growl escaped Cillian's lips. A thrill rushed through me at even a hint of jealousy from this man. He pushed up from his seat. "Let me go get you something to eat and the proper antiseptic."

With that, he strode out of the room, and my chest ached at his disappearance, even for a brief time. Somehow, I'd become intertwined with him without realizing. The desire to spend every waking second by his side beat at a steady thump inside me.

I pushed up from the mattress, even though my body was angry at the effort. My phone and clothes lay on the dresser, but I only bothered grabbing the phone before returning to bed. It blinked with an unread text, and since I didn't get many of those, I clicked it open.

Dad.

I'm worried about you. I've been asking around, trying to find a loophole, a way to get you back. I think I'm onto something.

My heart squeezed tight. The one person I missed from outside the Spires was him. And he hadn't forgotten about me. Yet how could I explain to him that I was coming to enjoy my time here, more than I ever realized I would? In my old life, I'd been replaced—at least at work—whereas here, I had purpose. I liked my PA work, I loved the library here, and the community I'd become a part of was something I'd craved for a long time.

And truth be told, here I had Cillian.

I shot him a message back.

I'm okay, Dad. I'll be fine.

Then I placed my phone on the nightstand and settled against the pillow. Cillian's booming footsteps alerted me he was about to return. My body hummed with readiness for his presence, whether the comfort he brought or the excitement. I was wholly addicted to both.

Cillian entered, looking the picture of sexiness with his tousled black hair, his button-down open and baring his chest. He carried with him a tray of food and a small kit in hand. I'd discovered that for as much as he loved to unleash with me, he also loved tending to me afterward. He was a creature of dualities, and the more I learned about him, the more enamored I became.

"Let me clean you up," he said, settling beside me again with the kit in hand. In a few deft motions, he had swabs doused in antiseptic, which would sting like a bitch. But this wasn't the first time he'd sunk his claws into me, and I hoped like hell it wouldn't be the last.

He swiped at the marks around my hip, and the sting made me wince, even if it faded fast. Cillian worked quickly, though, applying the antiseptic and then the salve afterward.

"You know, when I first met you, I never would've imagined you'd do this," I murmured.

He arched a brow. "Did you expect I'd toss you out after?"

"Well, truthfully, I didn't think you wanted to fuck me at all."

"From the moment you marched into my casino," Cillian said, his voice a low rumble. When I met his eyes, a shiver rolled down my spine at the intensity there. "Why do you think I came down in the first place? Your mettle had me intrigued from the start, as did the way you didn't hesitate to sacrifice yourself."

I'd expected him to comment on my looks, as that usually attracted most, but the fact that he hadn't sent a sharp spear of longing right through my heart. Fuck. Everything about Cillian had drawn my curiosity from the beginning as well, and now I was smitten.

Cillian shifted up farther on the bed and spread his legs. "Come here."

Clearly, he meant for me to sit between them, and I wasn't about to pass up the chance. I scooted up and leaned back. His arms wrapped around me, heavy but with a sense of safety I'd craved my whole life. He pressed a kiss to the top of my head, the sweetness of the motion coursing through me.

"The moment I saw you," he said. "I thought...maybe it could be you."

I waited for him to continue, but he trailed off, his quiet the sobering kind I didn't dare breach. Instead, I relaxed against him and soaked in the warmth he offered, heat rolling off him in waves.

"Why Olivia?" I asked, the question striking me.

A rumble vibrated deep in his chest. "Your curiosity is unending, isn't it, pet?"

"Is that all the answer you'll give me?" I asked.

Cillian stroked his claws along my thigh, the sensation sending a sinful shudder through me. "After you had to suffer through her presence, I at least owe you an answer. I've...not had the most successful dating history. My father always had business and wealth, and that offered a protection of sorts in this realm, despite us being demons. Ruthlessness was what he praised, and I was usually found wanting."

I didn't dare interrupt, his sensual, rich voice like a lullaby.

"Yet, I had my mother. She was kind, everything my father wasn't. She wanted to leave him, and I wanted to escape with her. Yet my father had been involved with some dangerous businessmen."

"Glacier Enterprises?" I asked, seeing the threads tie together.

He let out a low whistle. "Every time I think you couldn't be smarter, you prove me wrong. Them, exactly. My mother got caught in the crossfire—literally—and when she passed away, every bit of softness was beaten out of me. You asked why Olivia? Because even though I still mourned my mother, some twisted part of me tried to impress my father. And she was everything my father approved of. A go-getter who didn't hesitate when it came to underhandedness. Ambitious, cutting, strong. And yet those traits didn't end up saving my father either when Glacier Enterprises decided he was of no more use.

"When the company got passed on to me, I cut all ties with them, and I've been holding my ground ever since."

My heart ached at the loneliness in his tone, at how he clutched me a little tighter as he told his story. Somehow, Cillian had cemented himself in my heart, and the more I learned about him, the more claim he staked.

"And you managed to build yourself a community here," I murmured. "Color me jealous. Even out in the world, I barely had anyone I trusted, let alone wanted to spend time with for long."

"Bullshit," Cillian said. "You probably had boys lining up outside your door. Look at whats-his-fuck, the one we ran into."

"Guys interested in fucking me, yes," I responded. "But that only made me feel lonelier."

He squeezed a little harder, and I soaked in every ounce of the way that made me ache. As if he tried to cram my broken pieces back together. Somehow, he'd transformed from someone I loathed to someone I didn't want to be without.

"In a week, the Spires is hosting the National Dealer's Conference," Cillian said, changing the topic at whiplash speed.

"I'm aware, since I've been the one printing documents and coordinating with vendors for it," I murmured.

"Attend with me," he said.

My mind reeled, even though the immediate words jumped to my lips. "Fairly certain I'll be there working that night."

"No, by my side."

His words lingered in the air, a declaration that both excited me and terrified me in the same breath. What could that mean? It was one thing to declare our relationship in front of his friends, but another entirely to do so in front of his colleagues, in front of representatives of the city itself.

"Thorin will be there," Cillian murmured. "If he tries something with you while we're apart—" His grip around me tightened to the point that I struggled to get a breath in for a moment. But I didn't try to move him. The claim of his limbs warred with the fact he just wanted me there as a protection measure. It tangled up in my heart, which was already confused as hell.

"I'll go, but don't expect me to be like any of your high-profile exes. I'm a mere librarian, used to dusty bookshelves, not soirees for the rich and powerful."

"That sounds perfect to me." He reached past me and snagged a book from the pile on top of his nightstand—*The Death and Demise of Riordan James*. It was the biography of a significant figure during the Awakening, who had eventually been murdered in the chaos of the supernatural world melding with humanity's. He'd become a figurehead for the perseverance of monsters during that time, and yet my education was limited on him. Cillian had recommended the title earlier in the week, and since I'd spent most nights in his room, I'd begun to read it.

"What part are you at?" he asked, paging through to where I'd left the bookmark. "Ah, right around the unrest during the Awakening?"

"It's fascinating. There's so much I was unaware of," I murmured, the heat of shame rising to my cheeks again, that so many of my kind were so ignorant.

"Let's continue here," he said, cracking the book open a little further. To my surprise, he began to read from the page I was on, his low, sonorous voice lulling me into a deep, restful comfort.

One thing I'd learned this year was how much could change in the span of seconds. Tonight, I'd savor our date in the gardens and getting to fall asleep in his arms.

Tomorrow, I'd get ready for what guaranteed to be danger at the upcoming National Dealer's Conference.

CHAPTER 22

"Do I really need to wear this?" I asked Amelia, gesturing to the burnished gold tuxedo she'd provided. It was a finely tailored affair, and she had my size down pat. I'd never worn fitted clothing until I'd arrived here, and I couldn't say I hated it.

Amelia crossed her arms and leaned against the side of the open door. "You'll be on Cillian's arm tonight, so yes. Musty librarian chic won't cut it for this affair, since he's the host of this event."

"Rude," I responded as I closed the distance to snag the suit from her.

"I'm glad you're going," she murmured, her gaze softening. Getting those slips from Amelia was rare, and I froze mid-grab. "He's been...lighter recently. And I'm aware of what changed things."

I swallowed hard. "Maybe he's just out of his seasonal depression."

Amelia let out a sharp laugh. "Right. Do we call seven years of sulking seasonal depression now?"

"If it fits," I responded. "Do you have to don a fancy getup too? Some sort of ballgown?" Though the idea of Amelia in a ballgown broke my brain a bit.

She tossed her head back and laughed. "Security uniform for me. I'm on high alert tonight with the amount of threats lining up at our door. Someone has to keep Cillian safe, since he won't."

I swallowed hard, the weight of the comment sinking in deep. Cillian was immensely powerful, not just in size but in the way he strategized, how he thought ahead. Yet his recklessness, how he flirted with danger, how he showed up covered in gashes, only intensified the melancholy air that sometimes settled in around him. As if he were living moment by moment but knew he didn't have many left.

As if death had chased him for a while, gaining on him with every passing day.

"I'll try to keep him out of trouble," I commented.

Amelia lifted a brow. "Good luck with that."

"Hence the reason I said try," I commented. "Are you escorting me down once I'm ready?"

"Yes, so hurry up," she said. "I don't have hours to wait while you preen."

Thankfully I'd showered and done my hair, so the last thing I needed to do was put on the suit. I didn't bother to close the door on Amelia, simply swept into the private bathroom and shut myself in there. The air grew thick with residual steam, but I made quick work of peeling my clothes off and then slipping into the slacks and pressed button-down before wrangling the suit jacket on. The bow tie was last, and I stood in front of the mirror as I tied it in place.

Upon first glance, the tux had looked a bit too flashy for my taste, but it was more of a brown with burnished gold accents that caught the eye. It fit me as well as I'd hoped, the material comfortable, same with the way it clung to my body. My golden curls stood out even more in this suit, and the color made my blue eyes pop. I took the time to smooth down the fabric and tweak my curls, but all too soon, I was ready.

The person in front of me looked so different from the one who'd arrived in the Spires. I stood taller now, despite the danger I faced. I'd never liked my nose—found it a little too arrogant—but it fit me now in an unexpected way. I'd seen from Cillian that arrogance could be a weapon wielded in the right circles.

And tonight, I'd need everything in my arsenal.

I took a shaky breath in and then slipped on the socks and deep brown leather lace-ups provided. All of it offered armor tonight, especially if Olivia or Thorin were in the mix.

But I'd have the best protection in the world, because I'd be by Cillian's side the entire time.

When I emerged from the bathroom, Amelia let out a low whistle. "Not my type, but you're far too pretty, Beau Taylor."

I flushed. Amelia didn't give praise freely, so I'd accept the compliment from her.

"Let's get going," she said. "Cillian's waiting downstairs."

My heart thudded hard. I'd been busy helping with preparations, so now that the event was underway already, I'd be entering at the same time the other attendees were. Casinos from all over the world, not just Peregrine City, were congregating here tonight, bringing in their best dealers, their CEOs, their heads of marketing. We headed down the hallway and toward the elevator. The conference had been happening all day, but the gala was tonight, providing all the glitz Peregrine City had to offer, which was what everyone waited for.

We stepped onto the elevator, and Amelia pushed the second-floor button.

"Here," she said, passing me an elegant gold bracelet. "Put this on."

"What is it, a tracking device?" I joked.

Amelia gave me a level look back.

I slipped it onto my wrist. "Electronic or spelled?"

"Spelled by yours truly," she said, cracking me a grin. "With Thorin lurking down there, we aren't taking any chances."

"Thank you," I murmured, rubbing a thumb over the smooth surface. When I'd first arrived here, this would've felt like a shackle, but after experiencing the genuine threat of Thorin Glass and Glacier Industries, I'd rather Cillian be able to find me—no matter what.

Somehow, he'd become a safe place.

The elevator settled on the second floor, and the doors swept open.

"Come on," Amelia said. "Cillian's in the ballroom."

My throat dried as we swept through the second floor, which was already lavish and meticulously maintained. Now, even more delicate touches elevated it, from fresh bouquets of pink roses and sprays of assorted white flowers to the sweeping classical music that poured from the speakers. The closest I'd been to anything like this was a wedding, but my father and I hadn't been invited to many of those while I was growing up.

The chandeliers in the main area glittered, casting fragmented reflections onto the ground. Many people wandered by, in lavish dresses of every shade and tailored tuxes in browns and blacks. The beauty and wealth dripping off the people around me was unparalleled, but I'd spent a lifetime looking beyond the surface. I grew aware of the tight smiles, the lack of emotion in their eyes, as the guests engaged with each other. I was also aware of the variety of species represented here, a fair number of monsters among the throngs of people, from minotaurs to kraken, all equally well dressed. I didn't doubt a human-held event would have extended significantly fewer invitations to monsterkind.

As we headed closer to the ballroom, the noise grew louder from the volume of people sure to be congregating there. Sweat broke out on my palms. Who was I to be attending at Cillian's side? A random librarian who happened to be his personal assistant?

"Stay safe," Amelia murmured. "Don't leave Cillian."

I swallowed hard. "I won't."

I was here to avoid becoming a target or distraction, not because Cillian wanted to claim me as his in front of the city. As much as I'd begun to desire that, I needed to stay grounded.

We stepped through the doors into the magnificent ballroom of the Spires. The room was massive and held a dark elegance I expected from Cillian at this point. Black-and-white crystal chandeliers dangled down, casting their stunning beams and shadows onto the polished gray surface of the dance floor. The seats surrounding it were all black with rich blue accents, and the curtains were the same hue of blue. Azure flowers with lush petals decorated every table, matching the rest of the décor, and the flickering candles on every one added to the unique lighting in here.

Many people were seated, no one taking to the dance floor yet, but I spotted Cillian at once. He wore a black tux with a blue pocket square, the suit showcasing how massive he was. His horns were polished, his black hair tamed, and every inch of him appeared regal and stately. He was in the middle of a conversation by a table on the opposite side of the room, and we made a beeline in his direction. My nerves mounted.

We were only feet away when Cillian looked in our direction.

His gaze landed on me, and nothing else mattered.

Those rich golden eyes flared as he scanned me from head to toe, as if committing the visual to memory. A shiver ran through me at the intensity, at how the ballroom sparked degrees hotter when I was around him. As much as I'd worried about how the rest of the crowd would respond to me being at his side, I'd forgotten about the potency of his presence, how nothing else seemed to matter when his focus was on me.

"Your date for the evening," Amelia announced as she placed a hand on my lower back and shoved me forward.

I shot her a look, and she offered a secretive grin before making a disappearance.

Cillian's hand replaced hers on my lower back, and the touch ignited me at once. My whole body prickled with awareness. I'd experienced everything those capable hands could do, and the flood of memories, the claim in his gesture, sent a torrent of heat rolling through me. I could keep it together for a night, though, without climbing onto his lap and begging him to fuck me.

Even if those fantasies ran rampant through my mind.

"Beau, this is Frederick Highsayer," Cillian said, gesturing to the hulking man in front of me. Even though he appeared human, I clocked him as monster, particularly due to Cillian's comfort around him. Around human acquaintances, he tended to be on edge a bit more. The only exceptions were people like Gretel or Charles, who he knew well. Maybe this guy was a were like Theo?

"Pleased to meet you." I offered a hand, and Frederick shook, giving me a deliberate eye-scan.

"He's mine," Cillian said to the man firmly, a warning in his tone.

Frederick's brows rose. "Staking a claim? How unlike you, Ashmore."

The breath snagged in my throat. Given the reason I attended at his side, I hadn't expected Cillian to publicly claim me like this, but

I didn't mind the display in the slightest. Cillian's gaze met mine, the flash there the slightest bit feral.

"Are you going to be this insufferable with everyone we talk to tonight?" I asked, the words slipping from my lips.

A loud laugh escaped Frederick, and heat rushed to my cheeks. Shit, we had an audience. I'd gotten so used to our back and forth that I'd slipped into it naturally.

Cillian smiled, his fangs on clear display. "Absolutely. How else will people know not to flirt with you?"

I snorted, and thankfully Frederick seemed equally as amused.

Frederick glanced over at the door. "Looks like Mal and Ursuline are here. I'll give you two a moment to catch up." He strode away in the direction of the entrance, where I saw Ursuline's familiar face. The person beside them was unfamiliar, lanky and statuesque, with a long coat that swept the floor in an iridescent purple-and-green hue, and a black corset top that highlighted his slender frame. His gray skin with slight pebbling in some areas and tapered black horns marked him as supernatural.

"Is that the same Mal whose Slumbering Gardens we visited?" I asked.

"Yes," Cillian said. "I prefer to have my allies close in situations like this."

For as much as Cillian proclaimed to be a loner, I'd witnessed the depth of his relationships, how he had more than allies in these people—they were friends. Family, even. And after being included in that community, I realized how shallow my own relationships had been.

Cillian leaned in, his lips brushing against my ear. "You look delectable."

Fuck. My whole body immolated at his words.

"I'm tempted to just leave this whole soiree and find somewhere to take you—over and over again, until you're screaming."

I bit down on my lower lip to keep my moan back. "That's not playing fair, Cillian."

His wicked grin made me swoon. "Who ever said I played fair?"

A bit of extra noise came from the doorway, and Cillian glanced up. His hand stiffened on my back. I followed his gaze.

A man I hadn't seen since I'd run into him in the alley had arrived. However, I wasn't likely to soon forget his face. His tall stature was accentuated by his suit, his beard tamed and oiled today, but he wore the same ugly sneer as before. His gaze chilled me as he scanned through the room, clearly looking for one person. When Thorin stared at Cillian, for the first time I didn't feel the sense of safety that always enveloped me when by his side. Something violent and terrifying existed there.

I almost didn't register who his date was for tonight—Olivia. She wore a sweeping black gown that shimmered with her movements, and her crimson lips created a stark contrast even from here. She looked every inch the perfect arm candy, and given she was Cillian's ex, this had been a pointed choice.

"Looks like the trouble has arrived," Cillian said.

"Can we just petulantly ignore them all night?" I asked.

A sharp laugh escaped him. "Fuck, I'm glad you're here."

My heart squeezed tight. His honesty was a treasure he didn't offer everyone.

"Unfortunately, as the host I have to make a minimal effort," he said. "And I'd rather set the rules straight with him on this rare instance where he's in my territory."

"Are you concerned he'll try something?" My pulse sped a little at the thought of the danger we might face. I'd learned how unpredictable Thorin and his men could be.

"Not here," Cillian said. "He's dangerous, not stupid, and this conference is too public. We should get those introductions out of the way, though."

I sucked in a sharp breath, and Cillian leaned in again. He pressed a kiss to my temple, and the public PDA, the tender affection, sent a thrill through me. I still couldn't process the way he treated me in front of this many of his colleagues. It filled me with a helium-like buoyancy, and I craved this attention.

"I won't let him touch you," Cillian promised. "With me, you'll always be safe."

The deepness of his voice, the gravity there, cemented the promise deep in my soul. I'd always been wary before, cautious, but somehow I believed him. "Okay. I trust you."

Together, we strode across the ballroom in the direction of Thorin and Olivia. While we walked by the throngs of people, many stopped Cillian to offer a quick greeting, but he was an expert at staying on task. And his hand never left my lower back as he guided us forward. Tension crackled in the air the closer we got. This was the man who'd orchestrated deaths in Cillian's family, yet he still had to face him here. The reality made my gut sizzle.

Thorin's gaze traveled from Cillian to me, and a bone-chilling fear swept through me, yet I continued forward. I wouldn't abandon Cillian in this now.

We arrived in front of Thorin and Olivia, and the thickness of the tension couldn't be cleaved through with an ax.

"Well, you arrived," Cillian said, not bothering to mince words. "Keep your distance and respect this space, and we won't have a problem."

He stepped back, as if we were going to escape, but then Thorin spoke.

"Wait, Cillian. We've got something to discuss."

CHAPTER 23

C illian turned into a statue at Thorin's request, and I hated seeing him like this. As if my Beast was muzzled when he wanted to tear this man limb from limb.

Truth be told, I'd understand if he did.

Bloodthirstiness had never raged inside me like this before, but Thorin reminded me of every loathsome asshole I'd dealt with my entire life.

"What do you want?" Cillian snarled, his grasp on civility at its limits.

"You know what we want," Olivia said cryptically, a smug look on her lips I itched to punch off.

"Your time is running out," Thorin said, darkness simmering in his eyes.

Cillian's shoulders stiffened.

"Your attempt here won't work," Olivia said, casting an ugly stare in my direction. I restrained the urge to stomp on her foot. "The wheels are in motion, and they can't be stopped."

What was she referring to? I watched Cillian carefully, the hateful look in his eyes as he stared the pair of them down. How he could possibly be using me, I didn't know. After all, if he'd wanted to, I could have been cast away to the Pits, but instead he'd given me a position by his side. He'd offered me a community when I hadn't experienced that before. He'd offered safety and bliss and kindness.

"You're stating things I'm well aware of," he commented, and his hand slipped around my hip, drawing me to his side. "And Beau isn't an attempt. Leave him out of this."

The fierceness in his tone swept through me, expunging any doubts I had. Even though he held his secrets, I trusted him in a way I hadn't with many before.

"Tick tock," Thorin said. The cruel twist of his lips seared into me, and I hated how Cillian's muscles tightened, as if the man had something over him. As if the man could exterminate his life in the same manner he'd done with Cillian's parents. The idea of that—my soul chilled at the mere thought.

"Come on, Beau," Cillian said, guiding me away from them. "Let's go speak to people worthwhile."

I'd spent enough time by his side to notice when Cillian brimmed with that wild nature he often kept back, and Thorin brought it out effortlessly. However, he didn't have to face this alone.

I might not know what was going on between him and Thorin, but I did know Cillian. I reached for his hand on my hip and entwined my fingers through his. "Is that dance floor for show, or will there be actual dancing?"

Cillian cocked a brow. "I didn't think you were the dancing type."

"I'm not opposed," I said. "Just never made it much of a habit."

"And what makes you think I am?" he asked, a teasing note to his voice that I cherished.

"The way you move," I murmured, my throat dry with want. He was wildness and restraint in the same breath, and I craved him with everything in me.

"That's a very different sort of movement," he said with a low growl, as he let go of my hip and intertwined his fingers with mine again, holding my hand. "However, I'm happy to take the distraction you're offering."

Busted. My lips twitched with amusement, as did his. I'd never fallen in love before, no one had managed to get close enough to me, but with him I was dangerously close. He brought me over to the side of the ballroom where a man stood by a setup for handling the lighting and music. I recognized him because I'd done the coordination in the first place.

"Start the dance music now," Cillian said to him with the same politeness as always—which was none.

Yet the guy just grinned. "Sure thing, boss."

"Are you ready?" he asked.

I stared over at the empty dance floor and gulped. When I'd suggested the idea, I'd thought we'd wait until everyone flooded in and then mingle amid the crowd. Yet Cillian didn't seem to need crowds. He didn't mind standing out.

And I'd be right by his side through the whole night.

"Don't tell me you're getting cold feet now," Cillian said, the teasing edge in his voice the exact push I needed.

I shot him a look. "I'm the one who suggested it. Come on, lead the way."

A smug smile rose on his lips, one that made me want to kiss him.

Music poured through the speakers, louder, drawing the attention of the throngs of people who'd congregated for this gala. Based on some of the startled expressions, it would seem there was supposed to be more time for conversing before the music started, but Cillian was never one to follow the rules. I'd seen it in his board meetings, and I witnessed it here now.

He was a fighter, and I admired that about him more than anything. Anyone who'd been born into his life could easily have become corrupted. He could've become the carbon copy his father wanted him to be. But instead, he'd chosen to serve his community. To make space for others. To protect those in his circle with his resources and power.

Music poured from the speakers, an elegant classical piece that fit with the opulence of the gala.

"Is this where I admit I have no idea how to dance to this?" I murmured.

"Don't worry," he said, his rich voice setting me at ease. "Just follow my lead."

Cillian swept me out to the middle of the dance floor, and the press of eyes around us crept in, threatening to overwhelm me. Everyone stared at us, the casual conversation trailing to a trickle with the change in music and our appearance here.

And I didn't know how to dance. My only experience was the occasional foray at a club, and that sort of dancing wasn't the type to whip out here.

Yet Cillian gripped my hip with one hand and rested his other on my shoulder, and the way he casually possessed my body reminded me we'd already danced a dozen times over. He'd asked me to follow his lead, and I knew how to do that. The proximity of his body and the firm way he held me offered all the reminder I needed.

When Cillian took the first step, he swept me along with him, and I followed with ease.

Our bodies communicated even when our mouths couldn't. No matter the secrets that still brimmed between us, when we came together, everything else melted away. We were stripped down to all that mattered, and at the core of things, that raw truth was exactly why I trusted him.

Cillian swept me across the ballroom floor, a back and forth, back and forth sway to our steps that was easy to follow with the beat of the melody and how he telegraphed his movements. I'd surrendered to him over and over in bed, so this felt like an extension of that as I trusted him to guide me here.

So many stared at us, but as I focused on my dance with Cillian, the pressure diminished. As with any time we were close to each other, everything else faded away. Right now, it was just me and him dancing on the polished floor, the music cascading over us. He whirled me around with a smoothness that didn't surprise me but entranced me all the more. The tenderness in his expression struck me square in the heart. I never thought I'd witness it from a man I'd believed was formed from ice, but the more he melted for me, the more I craved him.

"You're doing well, pet," he murmured, his voice low enough only I'd hear. The praise trickled through me, filling me up with sunlight.

"You're the one taking a risk here, not me," I responded, unable to hide my snark. He grinned back at me, and the way his eyes crinkled made my heart reel. God, he'd ensnared me completely.

"Funny, because I'm not scared in the slightest." He swayed with me on the floor, our steps in tandem with the constant forward movement and retreat that was wholly us.

Out of the corner of my eye, I noticed another couple sweep onto the floor. Charles and Theo were dressed to the nines tonight, both in tailored tuxes, and they danced close to us.

"We couldn't let you two suffer alone," Charles called over.

"So you decided to add to my suffering," Cillian teased.

However, Theo and Charles had broken whatever invisible barrier had kept people from joining us, and other couples filtered onto the dance floor, swirling and turning around us. As much as a part of me had enjoyed taking the risk with Cillian, diving into the center of the ballroom with him, relief rushed through me that our movements were more obscured, that the spotlight was no longer solely on us.

We continued to circle around, this time to the next song that poured through the speakers, and I savored how Cillian guided me still, his movements fluid and graceful. I could feel the way his tension leached away, how our dance had accomplished what I'd hoped. His palm on my hip felt like a brand, and I loved how he staked his claim by both word and action.

"This wasn't a terrible idea," he said as we swirled around. "Normally I have to suffer through far more small talk."

"Perish the thought," I teased.

"Thankfully I only have to host one of these a year," he said. "And then I can go back to ignoring most of these people the rest of the time."

"You clearly hold them in such high esteem."

"Esteem is earned," he said, his tone taking on a more serious note. The way he stared at me, the intensity there, had me almost stumbling on the next movement. "You won mine early on."

Pride thrummed through me at the statement, even though I indulged in the urge to joke. "It was the constant reminders I was a librarian, wasn't it?"

Cillian snorted. "You're fearless when it matters, and I admire the hell out of that."

"Careful with all these compliments. They might go to my head," I warned as he swayed with me again. Here on the dance floor with him, I could feel how our souls connected, like sparks trying to find each other and merge.

I'd never experienced it before in my life, and I doubt I would again.

"Then I'll have to continue until you believe them," he said.

His words traveled straight to my heart and lived there.

***

We'd danced for a good hour on the floor before departing. Cillian ushered me over to the bar for drinks, and we made small talk with dozens of casino owners and their dates for the night. The sheer volume of people had doubled from when we'd first stepped in, and I'd long past hit my limit for socialization. Yet I was also aware of Olivia and Thorin's presence here the entire time.

I'd sipped enough expensive champagne to survive the night, though, even if I'd far rather be curled up in Cillian's bed. I'd barely been in my own room except to grab clothes as of late.

"Are they behaving?" I asked Cillian, glancing over to where Thorin rubbed elbows with a few of the other casino owners at one of the tables. Olivia had taken to the dance floor, mingling with a few others there. At least those who could spend time in her presence without getting frostbite.

"They won't try anything in public," he said. "Not where everyone else can see them. There's a reason he's never been caught before."

"Fuck, I hate that," I murmured.

"Me too." He slid his hand next to mine. "Want to go see the view of the gardens from the balcony?"

"You mean escape all the hellish superficial socialization? God, would I ever."

Cillian let out a loud laugh that drew a few eyes in our direction. Right, I'd forgotten he normally didn't show this side of himself around others. A thrill rose inside me again that I got to witness his amusement and laughs as freely as I did.

He gripped my hand and led me in the direction of the balcony, the double doors at the far end of the room more enticing than ever. We were stopped a few times along the way, but Cillian gave his quick nods of acknowledgement with a few words and moved on with an ease I envied. Since these people weren't wanting to talk to me, I just tuned out, keeping my gaze on the two problems in our sphere. For as much as I'd relaxed and enjoyed myself for parts of the night, I'd remained vigilant.

Cillian pushed the balcony door open, and the sweet nighttime breezes greeted me. We'd gone to the garden below countless times during the day. Once Cillian realized how cooped up I'd felt, he'd added the trip to our regular routine, a consideration I was well aware of. Flickering globes that emulated flame shone on either side of us, and I stepped out to the edge of the balcony, the combination of stone and wrought iron creating a stunning platform. I clutched onto the railing and stared out at the massive fountain down below, which was lit up. The combination was similar to inside, the interplay of light and dark everywhere here.

Sort of like the man behind it all.

Cillian leaned against the side of the balcony and drew in a deep breath. He stared out into the distance, but instead of wonder, a heavy reticence lingered in his demeanor, which I'd been cataloging more and more as of late. Less lonely and cold, and more...melancholy.

"Do you like it here?" he asked, the question seeming to come out of nowhere. "Not asking as the person holding a ten-year sentence over you."

I leaned against the railing too and drew in a slow breath. The heady perfume of the flowers combined with the crispness of the night air, and I let it swirl through me, lifting me higher.

"In the beginning, I hated it," I said slowly, letting myself mull over my feelings. "Everything reminded me that I'd had my life stolen out from under me, all because my father owed you a debt."

Cillian stayed silent. I half expected him to bring up the unknown details about my father as he'd attempted to do before, but the stone remained unturned. I was aware my father sometimes gambled, and my guess was that he'd taken things too far, got in too deep. That wouldn't have changed my decision.

"However, the more time I spent here, the more I realized how trapped I'd become out there. I'd cycled from work to home again and again, the brief interludes where I tried to connect with people barely scratching an itch. But the people you've surrounded yourself with here—they're wonderful."

"And...me?" he asked, his voice so low it was almost a whisper. "Do you think you could ever stay here with me?"

I swallowed hard. I didn't want to give him an impulsive response, even though my heart screamed yes. Because the truth was, when the ten years were up, I'd have my freedom, and I wasn't sure what my life would be like once I had the choice. "That's hard to answer because I'm not free to choose. Have I loved every night with you, though? I've never cherished anything more."

Cillian heaved a soul-weary sigh, one that lingered in the air, and the pain in his golden eyes made my heart break. I reached up and ran my thumb across his jaw, over his lower lip. Gods, this man would ruin me a thousand times over.

And the truth was, I wanted to let him.

"We've got years to figure it out, though," I murmured. "You'll most likely get sick of me far before that."

"I could never grow tired of you, pet," Cillian said, the scrape of his voice resonating deep in my bones. "You're sharper than anyone I've met, and around you, I've laughed more than I have in years."

Those words burrowed deep into my heart.

"If only we had more time," he murmured, the deep sorrow in those words pummeling me in the chest.

My brow furrowed. "What do you mean?"

Cillian offered me a sad smile, one that made me heartsick. "Nothing to worry about. We've got tonight, pet, and that's enough."

Worry trickled through me like cold river water, the iciness spreading through my veins. The comments he'd made weren't the first that had me wondering what the hell was going on here, but any time I pushed, I got tight-lipped responses and evasions.

"I'm glad you invited me here," I said, pushing up on my toes to press my lips to his. He let out a low groan and wrapped his hands around my waist as he claimed my mouth. His tongue dipped in and caressed mine before he kissed me hard enough that my mind reeled. The intoxicating taste of him, the silent thrill rising within me—I was addicted to him, and I never wanted to let him go.

This kiss melted away years, all the walls I'd built up over time until I was here with him, unguarded and whole. The world was cruel, capable of beating the softness out of anyone, and I hadn't realized how much I'd lost year after year. Yet here with Cillian, those pieces of me were reclaimed, even if it was only while I was here with him. And I wanted to fight for that with every ounce of my soul.

I surrendered to him, a soft moan escaping me as we kissed and kissed and kissed, until the stars fell, the moon succumbed to dawn, and the party beyond those doors faded away.

His question circled through my head on repeat.

Could I ever stay here with him of my own volition?

The truth was, deep down, if I had the choice, I'd say yes.

CHAPTER 24

"You're coming to game night?" Charles asked from the doorway on one of the rare instances I was in my room. Since the
ball, I'd even started moving my clothes over to Cillian's chambers.
Not like I had any particular attachment to the room I'd first settled
in anyway. The West Wing that had once been forbidden to me was
now as familiar as the rest of the Spires—apart from the locked room,
but I respected his privacy there.

However, this week, he'd started to grow quieter, a bit more with-
drawn, and the curiosity rose inside me again, the burning need to
know what was going on. Maybe someone would drop a hint at game
night. I wasn't sure what information he'd shared with his friends, but
every bit I could gather was valuable.

"Yeah. Are folks starting to arrive?" I asked, sliding my shoes on.

"It's a full crowd already," Charles said. "And Cillian's there." He
waggled his brows.

"I'm well aware." I rolled my eyes, even though a smile twitched at my lips. He loved to tease me about our relationship, but I'd rarely gotten this kind of lighthearted, comfortable ribbing from others in the past—because that would require deeper friendships.

"Figured with how attached at the hip you've been, you might want to be there too." Mischief danced in Charles's eyes. "Though you're not walking funny anymore, so maybe the honeymoon's over."

I snorted. It had taken me a little while to adjust to Charles's tendency to overshare, but now that I was used to him, I appreciated it. "Mmm, I wouldn't say that." Cillian had fucked me so good the other night my throat was raw from screaming. I craved him again now, just at the mere thought.

"Scandalous," Charles said. "I can only imagine Cillian's got an addictive cock. When Theo knots me—fuuuuck."

I smacked him in the shoulder. "Come on. I'd rather play games than hear about your boyfriend's cock."

"Your loss," he said with a shrug and a grin. "It's lovely."

We moseyed on down the hallway, a comfort and ease to walking with him that I appreciated. Amelia, Charles, and Theo had become closer friends than any I'd ever had before, and I even anticipated seeing more of the people I'd talked to at the last game night. Cillian surrounded himself with genuinely good companions, a reflection of who he was behind the reticence and cool demeanor.

"So are the two of you..." Charles asked, waiting for me to fill in the blanks. We'd been doing this for close to two months now, and I didn't have an answer for him. We were living day to day, and I knew I didn't want to be apart from him. Yet, at the root of it all, a part of me needed to be free to choose him, to choose this, but I wasn't.

I shrugged. "We're enjoying each other's company."

That was paltry compared to the depth of what I felt for him, how much he'd changed my entire life, but I didn't have any answers. Charles's bright smile slipped for a moment, a flash in his gaze I wasn't sure how to interpret. Maybe he thought I was toying with his friend.

"Cillian hasn't brought anything up, and neither have I, so until we have that discussion, I can't give you more of an answer," I clarified.

Charles nodded and let out a weary sigh. "He's stubborn to a fault."

That was the damn truth.

We turned down the corridor toward the dining hall, and voices traveled our way from the open room. My heart sped up. I wanted to delude myself into thinking it was nerves over who awaited us there, but the truth was, the second I heard Cillian's rich voice, my body and soul awakened for him. I'd known from the moment I met him that he inspired a reaction inside me, but I hadn't understood why the strength of it had been there from the start.

He and I could never have been anything casual.

We were destined for either a love foretold by the stars themselves or absolute ruin.

I still wasn't sure which.

When I stepped into view of the dining hall, I sought him out on instinct. He sat at the head of the long table they'd formed out of several pushed together, and he chatted with Sofia and Mal. Another woman was at the table, one I recognized from early on in my time here. The one who I'd also spotted in wolf form.

When Cillian's gaze landed on me, the slow smile that rose to his lips made my heart thump harder. I wandered his way instantly, my feet carrying me toward him. I slipped up beside him, and he reached out to drag me closer. When he tilted his chin up, I took the cue to lean down and kiss him, and my whole body sang from the contact, even though I'd seen him mere hours ago. However, the fact he didn't hesitate to claim me in front of his friends still vaulted me higher and higher. Having this man's esteem—that meant something.

"Sit here," he said, spreading his legs and patting his lap.

"Then I can't play," I countered.

Mal pushed up from his spot—I'd met him at the gala the other night—and found another open seat farther down. Even though he wasn't wearing the high drama outfit of the other night, his bright purple crop top matched his eyeshadow and nails. His dark curls were glossy and well taken care of, and his eyes were a hypnotic green with slits for pupils. "I'll move just to spare myself the show."

I accepted the proffered seat by Cillian's side.

"I wouldn't mind watching the show," Sofia teased, seated on the opposite side of me.

"Gretel keeps you plenty busy," the other woman muttered.

"Don't be jealous, Fae," Sofia teased. She glanced between her and me. "Have the two of you ever had an official introduction?"

"You were staying here for a spell, right?" I asked. Cillian coughed into his fist, and I locked in on Sofia. I'd begun piecing things together about why certain monsters resided in the empty rooms temporarily, but no one had given me a confirmation.

Sofia shook her head, an amused smile on her graceful lips. "Cillian, I don't understand why you're keeping it a secret from this boy."

"It's not a big deal," he grumbled, and I kicked him in the foot.

"Well, now I need to know." I crossed my arms and stared him down.

"He facilitates a safe space for monsters in need," Charles announced from the other end of the table. "When someone in the community is in trouble, these upper rooms in the Spires are a place where they can escape for a little or recover."

Theo snorted. "You're fearless."

"That's why you love me," Charles said, snuggling against Theo, their seats nudging together.

All of the goings-on up here clicked into place. How the dining hall had mysterious visitors, same as the ones who filled some of the rooms. A thrill rose inside me at the realization of what he'd been involved in all along.

"I was one of them not so long ago," Fae said. "Though I'm living in an apartment in the city now."

"Where did you come from?" I asked.

"A Human First commune out in the countryside of Arcosa," she murmured, her gaze darkening and head dipping.

Sofia let out a disgusted noise. A shudder ran through me at the mention of Human First, an order of humans who believed in expunging supernatural-kind. While I wondered what they'd been doing with a monster in their midst in the first place, I didn't ask. Clearly, it was a sensitive subject.

"So when she came to Haven, looking for somewhere to go, I sent her to Cillian's to recover," Sofia said. "We've worked out quite a system over the years."

"Are others involved?" I asked, my mind whirring at this point, my curiosity in overdrive.

"Many of us take on a role where we can," Mal said, a wan smile on his lips.

My gaze landed on Cillian, and my heart squeezed tight. Every secret exposed revealed a new layer to him, one that drew me closer. Despite him being the owner of the Spires, he truly had the heart of an architect. Except he wasn't just trying to create buildings, but communities as well.

And he'd created a magnificent one here. I'd never been prouder of him.

I reached under the table and threaded my fingers through his. He glanced my way, and the cockiness there dimmed with a vulnerability I found I liked far too much.

"So, it's a secret railroad for monsters," I clarified. "I adore that." My heart filled with pure sunlight. These people could've utilized their power and wealth for destruction, for terrible things, but instead they helped those who needed it the most. Fae's tumbles of black hair were pulled back into a ponytail, which revealed scars around her neck. Even the way she fidgeted with her hands revealed more scars around her wrists. Whatever had been done to her in that commune, she was clearly haunted by her time there.

"Are we going to gossip or actually game tonight?" Cillian asked, a slight gruffness to his tone, even though his hands never left mine.

"I don't know," Sofia said. "I think I want to enjoy a little more of your discomfort."

"Sadist," he muttered.

She arched a brow. "You're one to talk."

I choked on a laugh, earning a stern look from Cillian. One I happily met with challenge.

"Are we waiting for Amelia?" Charles asked.

"She's busy tonight," Cillian said. "Date."

"Ooooh." Charles's voice echoed through the dining hall.

"Jaffar will get here at some point, though we can play a few rounds of Bones while we're waiting," Theo said, bringing out a bag of bones with runes carved into them.

"And if I'm unfamiliar?" I asked.

"Then we'll teach you," Cillian said, squeezing my hand under the table. God, the casual care from him, the way he didn't hesitate to help—if there was anyone on this earth I could fall for, it'd be him.

And I was so close, freedom be damned.

"It's good to see you happy," Sofia commented, her voice low enough that only Cillian and I heard. A blush hit my cheeks at once. This wasn't the first time someone had said that, and the idea that I'd helped bring the change about blew my mind. She fixed her gaze on me. "Don't let him push you away, either."

"Like he'd listen," Cillian commented dryly.

I snorted. He wasn't wrong. Stubbornness had always been a foundation block of my personality.

"Bones?" Theo asked again.

"Stop offering everyone a bone," Charles teased.

"Is that supposed to be a wolf joke?" Fae asked, a wan smile on her lips.

"I mean, we all know how *I* was intending it, but both works." Charles grabbed the bag of bone tiles from Theo and began to pass them out. "Here, before my boyfriend expires on the spot. Let's get some gaming in."

"Did you order food yet?" Sofia asked Cillian.

He nodded. "Delivery will be here shortly." His thumb absently stroked my hand, our fingers intertwined beneath the table. The contact from him meant everything.

"I'll just distribute the pieces at this point," Theo said with a huff as he started to pass out the bone tiles. I reluctantly let go of Cillian's hand and gathered my pieces.

"Okay, explain what we do."

And so we got into the game.

We played a few hands of Bones, and then Jaffar arrived and we delved into a different game. Cillian had ordered sandwiches from a local place, and everyone tucked in. The laughter flowed freely, and I'd never felt lighter. Unlike a month ago, when I'd been worrying about Cillian, when the tension between us had been new and unexplored, our connection now added a richness to the interaction I hadn't realized I'd love so much.

He casually touched me and kissed me in a way that made me feel claimed, that made me feel like I belonged, not just here, but also to him. And I'd never reached those exultant highs before in my life.

Eventually, Mal decided to leave, then Fae. Jaffar and Charles were deep in a conversation at the table, and Cillian and Theo discussed the meal plan for the week. I sank back into my seat, happy to listen. I didn't need to yammer, and my well was full from our time around the table tonight.

My phone buzzed in my pocket, and I pulled it out. It was rare I got a message, enough that I usually checked them.

Dad had texted.

I'm in trouble. Deep trouble. This will be the last time you hear from me.

Fuck.

CHAPTER 25

"I've got to go," I said, rising from my seat and walking out of the dining hall. There was no way I could share the message with the table. My arms trembled as I excused myself from the room, and the moment I stepped out into the hallway, I dropped to my knees.

Fuck. Fuck. Fuck.

I'd traded ten years of my life so my father could survive. So he'd stand a chance.

Something was happening to him out there, and I couldn't go to him. I tried to call his number, and it rang. And rang and rang.

Voicemail picked up, his familiar voice making my chest crack open. My whole body trembled as I ended the call. I needed to go to his house, to find him in person, but I *couldn't*. I couldn't even leave the Spires without a chaperone. Yet my father roamed out there somewhere in Peregrine City, and he wasn't going to survive. There would be no reunion when I was released from here. No check-ins from him.

My only family out there, the only one who gave a damn if I lived or died, was in deep trouble.

Fuck.

Heavy footsteps approached, and a huge palm rested on my back. I didn't need to look up to know Cillian had come out to see what had happened. My eyes stung as I restrained the tears, not wanting to cry in front of him. Panic flared, loud and blaring in my mind as I tried to suck in a deep breath but continued to fail.

"What happened?" Cillian asked.

I sucked in another shallow breath. Fuck. How did I even explain this to him? He'd never let me go. He didn't trust my father. Didn't understand our connection or the loyalty I had to the one person who'd been a constant in my life.

Oh god, oh god, oh god. He was going to die, and I'd never even get to say goodbye. I'd leave the Spires after ten years to visit his grave. Bile rose in my throat, and the shakes descended over me.

Cillian scooped me up with the same ease he always did, and he clutched me tightly to his chest. "Let's go to my quarters and talk."

Normally, being in his arms offered all the comfort I needed—the hard muscle, the heat pouring off him. However, right now my body had turned to ice, and I couldn't seem to warm up. My breaths were still shallow, more like pants, and my mind kept reeling, reeling, reeling. Gods, what was going on? This was worse than when my father had disappeared.

At least then, I'd had hope.

The message he'd sent me now? That had been a goodbye.

My throat squeezed tight, and my eyes stung. What could I do? I'd never felt more trapped in my life, more helpless. Was he in immediate danger? Or was he heading toward an end that could arrive any day now?

The familiar surroundings of the West Wing flashed around us, and Cillian carried me into his room before depositing me on his silken sheets. I'd been here for weeks now, and it had become a place of comfort, but right now, all it did was serve as a reminder that I wasn't free.

A gilded cage was still a cage.

And I couldn't go find my father.

"I can't help you if you don't tell me what's going on," Cillian said, kneeling next to the bed. He grasped my hands in his, a pleading in his eyes that pierced through some of the panic.

"My father," I choked out. "He sent me a message...that he's in trouble."

Cillian heaved out a heavy sigh, and my chest caved in on itself. Of course. He hated my father. Didn't trust him in the slightest. There was no way he would let me go. My eyes burned again, and I gripped the sheets tightly in my fists, hard enough that my nails bit into skin.

"I know," I spat out. "I can't do a damn thing to help him."

Cillian stared at me unflinchingly, and he rested a palm over my fist. "This is killing you, isn't it?"

"What, being trapped and unable to help my father? Knowing when I'm free from here in a decade, that all I'll have to visit is a grave? He's the only parent I have left, my only support in the outside world." A tear slipped down my cheek as the words tumbled from me.

The silence reigned between us, thick and tense and impossible. This was the barrier keeping us apart, the one hurdle that remained preventing me from falling for him completely. The freedom to choose to remain by his side. The knowledge that at the end of the day, I was tied to him by a pact not by choice.

My throat tightened, and I met his gaze. His golden eyes held a mourning that pierced through me. Neither of us broke the quiet, as if something profound shifted between us, a transmutation of the relationship we'd held.

His palm tightened over my fist as he gripped hard. "Give me one more night."

I blinked. I couldn't have heard him correctly.

"Give me tonight, Beau," he said, his voice a low, gravelly scrape. "And tomorrow morning, you're free."

My heart thumped hard. "What about the time I'm supposed to serve?"

Cillian shook his head, the vulnerability in his gaze scoring me in the chest. "Mere months with you was worth a decade."

Oh.

I swallowed hard, my eyes glossing over. The immense emotion that swept over me was unlike any I'd ever experienced before. My heart soared and broke in the same breath, and fuck, this hurt. He was...letting me go.

Cillian was setting me free.

I free-fell for him in that moment, surrendered what little remained of my heart.

This man who pretended to be harsh, callous, and cruel had currents deeper than anyone I'd met. His actions spoke louder, the way he tried to better the world around him rather than bring it to ruin like so many others in his position.

"Can I return?" I asked, a tremble in my voice. "If I go to try and find my father, can I come back?"

Cillian nodded, even though he didn't voice the words at first. His eyes held a melancholy to them that made me ache, as if he didn't believe I would. "Always."

"What about Thorin?" I asked, the realization striking me. I wasn't safe out there in the world now, marked by Glass Industries.

"I'll keep him occupied while you search for your father," Cillian promised. "And if...you decide you don't want to return, I'll make it clear we no longer have an association."

I leaned in and rested my palm against his cheek. "That will *never* happen. I'm coming back, Cillian. I promise."

Before he could respond, I closed the distance between us and claimed his lips.

I kissed Cillian with a desperation that ached in my bones.

I kissed him with the yearning for a future where we would be reunited. Where this wouldn't be the end.

I kissed him because tonight, I would give him all of myself.

He tasted like brimstone and promise, like the long-sought hope that had begun to unfurl in me lately. Tomorrow, I would set out to try to find my father. But tonight, Cillian was the only thing on my mind. His lips claimed mine again and again, and I savored the moment before it slipped from my fingers. This was a man who'd transformed my entire world, and I didn't want to leave him.

I had to make sure my father was okay, but when I came back, I'd make sure Cillian understood I belonged to him.

I drew back from the kiss. "Tell me what you want tonight. Anything you want, and I'm yours. Tie me up, breed me, use me until you've got nothing left."

"I want your hands free tonight," Cillian said, the rumble to his tone returning. "You're going to be my good pet and take my cock as I fill you up again and again and again. I'm going to mark you, cover you in my cum so you don't forget that you're mine."

"Gods yes," I gasped out. "Can I...touch you?"

He nodded. "Wherever you want, pet."

"Are your horns sensitive?" I asked. It had been a curiosity of mine for a while, but when we fucked, Cillian often took me apart piece by piece rather than letting me return the favor. When he was feral and wild, he needed the control, and I was happy to hand it over, but tonight I wanted to feel all of him. I wanted him claiming me, taking me in every single way, but I wanted to bring him as much pleasure as I could too.

"They are. You can touch them while you ride me," he said, pushing to a stand. "Strip for me, gorgeous."

I licked my lips. "Can I suck your cock first?"

He ran fingers through my curls, his claws scraping against my scalp, and I shivered. "Get naked and on your knees."

Oh god. The way he commanded me made me lose my mind. I unbuttoned my shirt, shunted my pants and underwear off, socks and shoes ditched in the process. His room was comfortable, familiar, but a heaviness weighed in the air tonight, the realization that tomorrow I'd be leaving this place to find my father, and the uncertainty of the world outside it terrified me.

I lowered to my knees in front of him, the bite of the hard floor against them keeping me grounded. He loomed over me and tugged his shirt off first. Then he unzipped his slacks and dragged them down his thighs. My mouth watered as his cock sprang free, thick and ridged and bright red with a dark crimson head. His pre-cum glistened at the tip, and I leaned forward to lick it. The salty burst traveled through me, and I craved more, an addiction.

I hadn't tried to suck him down too often due to the sheer size of his cock, but I wanted to try to fit as much of him in as I could. He held the base of his cock in place, and I drew his tip to my mouth. The musky scent of him made me hard, the heat of his body so close to mine setting me on fire. I craved the weight of him in my mouth as I sucked him in a little deeper. His cock was velvety and smooth, and I ran my tongue along the bottom of his length, up and down, up and down.

Cillian let out a low groan as he carded his fingers through my curls and then gripped tight. The sting of his clutch combined with the ache of my knees on the floor, the edge of pain making me harder. My cock leaked between my legs, and I loved the sight of him looming over me, the reminder of how massive he was ever present.

I opened my jaw further and swallowed another few inches, the tip of his cock nudging against the back of my throat. I gagged a little around it, tears leaking down my cheeks even as I continued to suck through the motion. The weight of him there, how he filled me up, my jaw strained, turned me on beyond belief. Even though he kept his grip firm on my curls, he still circled the base of his cock with one hand, making it clear I wasn't close to taking all of him.

I started to bob up and down on his length, the tip bumping against the back of my throat over and over. Saliva poured from my lips, dripping onto my thighs and the floor, but I didn't stop. My eyes stung, blurred by the tears leaking from them as I choked on his cock again and again and again.

"You feel so good," Cillian purred, gentle compared to how he normally took me. I craved both, his wildness and tenderness in the same breath.

I drew air in through my nose as I continued to swallow him, his pre-cum trickling down my throat. He surrounded me like this, the musk of him, the feel of him, and I loved being on my knees for him. I'd offer my holes any time of day if he wanted, just to feel him inside me in some way.

The need to be filled by him grew to an ache, and goddamn, I wanted him to knot my hole so badly.

I sucked harder and reached up to touch his balls, a heavy weight in my palms. A shudder rolled through him at my touch, and I continued to tease them as I sucked. He started to shuttle his hand around his base, shifting his hips forward every time my mouth descended. My vision blurred, and the saliva continued to pour from me in a steady dribble. My thighs were drenched from it at this point.

"Fuck, I'm going to come," he groaned and pulled out of my mouth.

"On my face," I begged, closing my eyes.

A second later, his cum descended in a hot splatter on my forehead, my cheeks, dripping down my chin. A sinful shiver raced through me at the way he'd marked me. Fuck, I wanted his cum everywhere—across my body, on my tongue and in my belly, dripping from my hole. I rocked back on my heels and swiped at a glob of it then licked it off my finger. The salty taste delivered another shiver of satisfaction.

"You're gorgeous," Cillian murmured.

I swiped at my face, sucking more of his cum off my fingers. His shadow shifted above me, the creak of his steps retreating, and a second later, a cloth touched my face as he wiped the rest off.

"Why'd you take it away?" I asked, a slight pout to my lips.

Cillian's mouth twisted into a grin as he stripped out of his pants, socks, shoes, until he was completely bare. All those thick muscles on display had me wanting to drop to my knees again to worship him. "Because I have so much more I want to do with you tonight."

I'd take every last second I could get.

CHAPTER 26

C illian settled on the edge of the bed, those thick thighs clear and
spread. Fuck, I wanted to sink my teeth into them. I crawled
toward him on my hands and knees until I reached the edge of the bed,
and then pushed up until I was close enough to nuzzle at his cock,
which had deflated but was still heavy and long. I lapped at the tip
again, as if I could get more cum from it somehow.

"Greedy little thing," he said, his voice rich and melodic as he
gripped my chin, lifting me away from his cock. "Come sit on my lap."

I scrambled to obey, pushing up to climb onto those heavy thighs.
The feel of his skin against mine made me tingle, my body so aware
of his. Of the way he knew how to turn me into a puddle, into an
incoherent mess. He wrapped his arms around me, my rigid cock
sandwiched between our stomachs. His length was underneath me,
brushing against my taint, my piercing there, and the feel of his cock
stiffening below made me salivate. Fuck, I wanted to ride him something fierce.

"You wanted to touch my horns?" Cillian said, leaning back to press his palms into the mattress behind him, giving me free rein. "Go ahead."

A thrill raced through me. I was well aware of the gift he offered here, as he didn't hand over control, even minutely, to anyone. And yet, he was letting me worship him, bring him pleasure for once on my terms.

I reached up tentatively to what had been the objects of my curiosity for months now and stroked my fingertips along his horns. A strong shudder rolled through him, one I could feel with the way I sat perched on his lap. I brushed along them again and got the same response. His cock thickened beneath me, and he rubbed his length along my taint. The piercing there made it extra responsive, and I savored the sensation. A cry welled up in me at how sinful that felt, the velvet of his skin against the sensitive area.

I gripped his horns and twisted, and he roared, his grip on my hips giving a bite as those claws dug in. He rubbed his cock against me, and I continued to twist and tease at his horns, just to elicit the reactions from him.

He panted. "Careful, pet. I'll slide right in." Cillian reached over to snag the lube he'd sat nearby and slicked up his cock. I vibrated with the need to feel him, to have him claim me.

"What will you do if I play with these while you fuck me?" I asked, running my hands along his horns again.

He let out a low growl. "I'll fuck you so many times your hole will be sore for weeks."

I swallowed hard. "As long as I can feel you until I return."

The playfulness faded away as a sobering air swept in, a reminder that come morning I'd be leaving the Spires. I'd be leaving his comforting embrace.

Cillian's gaze darkened, his feral nature returning in full force with another growl. I gripped his horns hard, and he lifted me up by my hips. The tip of his cock nudged against my hole, and then he thrust inside, splitting me open. If I hadn't been taking his length for weeks and weeks now, it would've ripped me apart, but my body had adjusted to accommodate him.

The thickness around the center stole a moan from me, and when he settled all the way inside, this position only enhanced the way he filled me to the brim, to the point I couldn't possibly take any more. I kneeled into the bed on either side of him as he let go, and I sank my weight down. His cock was thick and long, and I panted from the way he made me feel claimed and taken.

"Please," I gasped out.

He'd ridden me hard for over a month now, and it wasn't nearly enough. I needed him with a desperation I was unused to, like our very cells were trying to mesh together, as if our souls attempted to merge.

Cillian leaned up and kissed me, the sensual brush of his lips sending a thrill through me. And then he began to move. He shifted his hips forward, the casual buck shuttling his cock deep inside me. He brushed against my prostate with the movement, and my vision whited out from the sheer pleasure that traveled through my limbs.

"So good for me, pet," he murmured as he wrapped his palms around my ass cheeks, keeping a tight grip on me. He thrust in harder, the slick and steady movements sending wave after wave of bliss through me. My thighs trembled, and my arms buzzed as I clutched his horns. He grunted and let out a groan each time we shifted, each time I adjusted my grasp on his horns. The feedback loop was intoxicating, and I lost myself in it, the way I rode up and down on his length, bringing my hands along his horns in the same motion.

Watching Cillian's lashes flutter, his heavy exhales escape, his intoxicating golden gaze drill into me, was everything I'd hoped for. The air between us sizzled with tension, with pressure, with everything unspoken that burned between us brighter than the sun.

Together like this, we were pure starlight, volatile and unreachable and so pristinely beautiful it made my soul ache.

Cillian fucked into me harder as I descended on his length, loving how he speared me open. Loving how his ridges caressed my insides. Power coiled in his muscles, evident by the flex of them, in the effortless way he held me up while he thrust into me again and again. He'd unloaded on my face earlier, the slightly sticky residue still there, but I craved his cum again. I wanted it flooding inside me, his knot stretching me until we were connected on a deeper level than I believed possible.

His black hair was tousled, his jawline sharp, and his eyebrows wicked. I memorized every detail of him as I sank down on his length, bliss radiating through me again. His scent wrapped around me, the brimstone and musk that had lured me in from the start. Cillian's hot breath puffed against me as he took me hard and fast, with an increasing desperation that lit through the air between us.

As if we were chasing eternity, knowing it was quickly slipping out of our grasp.

"Fuck, I'm not going to last long," Cillian groaned out, and I gave another pump to his horns. He shivered again and thrust deep inside my hole.

"Do it," I dared him. "Fill me up. Take me as many times as you need to tonight."

I wanted to feel him everywhere, permeating every cell of my body.

As if a thread snapped, whatever had held Cillian back loosened. He let out a guttural roar and fucked me harder. Sweat dripped down my forehead as I tried to keep pace, my thighs burning as I dropped onto his length over and over again. Yet he thrust into me like a man possessed, fast enough I couldn't keep up. His grip on my cheeks kept me aloft, and he took me with a brutality that overwhelmed me. The sheer pleasure that hit hard and fast stole my breath away until I was gasping, just writhing in his lap, my grip on his horns more an anchor than anything. My balls ached, my cock straining with the need to come, but I didn't care. I wanted to ride him until he knotted me. I didn't want to release until he told me to.

Cillian's loud, long moan pierced the air, and a second later, his hot cum rushed inside me. His knot began to inflate in me, and he released the hold on my cheeks so I sank right down on him as the knot stretched me with the delicious sting I'd become addicted to. No one, absolutely no one, fucked like Cillian Ashmore.

His head tipped back, the cords of his neck on clear display, and those fangs glistened in the low light of his room. My cock throbbed, and I reveled in the delicious combination of satiation and need. His cum was plugged inside me like this, and I loved being connected to him on this level. Fuck.

"Damn," Cillian swore as his breaths came out heavy. Slowly, he fluttered his lashes open. His sinful smile stole my heart as he looked me over with a hunger that hadn't extinguished in the slightest. "Someone feeling desperate?"

A whimper escaped me, and his smile widened.

He ran his palms along my thighs, and I loved how I was knotted facing him, bolstered by his lap. Cillian tipped his head down, and his long tongue slipped out. He wrapped it around my nipple, and fuck—that felt too damn good. I writhed, but I couldn't go anywhere, not while I was knotted to him like this. He lapped at my nipple, caressing it with his tongue in a circular motion that shot lust right through my system. My cock gushed more pre-cum.

He switched to the other nipple, beginning to toy and lap at it with his tongue. The onslaught made my whole body light up, and I wriggled in place again, but the tug of his knot against my hole reminded me I was stuck in place. He continued to toy with the tip of my nipple, gliding against it over and over again. I heated up from the inside out, as if I were about to burst and go supernova. Yet he continued to toy with me, ignoring my desperate cock.

Cillian ran his palms down my sides, along my hips, my thighs, his warm, callused skin activating everywhere he touched. All while he continued his assault on my nipples, alternating one at a time until the feeling grew so intense the almost ticklish burst of pleasure made me squirm. He seemed to revel in it, touching and teasing me until I panted for him, my breaths coming out ragged. I was growing so hot inside, I thought I would immolate, and yet all I could think of was being fucked by him again.

Even with him still inside me.

I could never get enough of this man.

And I didn't want to leave him.

I leaned in and pressed my lips against his elegant neck, tasting the salt of his sweat. He stopped toying with my nipples and looked up, those golden eyes shining with a depth of emotion that terrified me. Yet it was all I'd wanted for a lifetime.

Cillian kissed me then, and the power behind it made me melt. No words were exchanged in this moment, but they weren't needed. The desperation between us rose with every passing minute, as we both understood this could be our last. That once we left the sanctity of tonight, we might no longer be able to reclaim any of this.

His knot began to deflate inside me at last, and he pulled out.

His cum started to flood out, some of it trickling down the inside of my thigh, but Cillian pressed his fingers against my gaping hole, stopping the flow.

"You need more of my cum inside you," he murmured, rubbing his fingers against my wet and sloppy hole. "I want it leaking down your thighs for days."

Ngh. I panted, the throb in my balls unbearable. I would explode if I didn't come, and yet I didn't want to either. I wanted him to fuck me and toy with me for as long as possible.

"Flip over. On the bed on your stomach," he said, giving my hole a light spank. The squelching sound it made sent a flush of heat and embarrassment through me. I loved it so much. Slowly, I rose on my knees, my thighs trembling, and then I extricated myself from Cillian's lap to flop in the middle of the bed, stomach first. His cum gushed from my hole, making a mess between my thighs.

Cillian settled behind me with a creak, then a schlick, schlick sound. I glanced back to see him stroking his cock with the glisten of more lube. Even after fucking and knotting me, he looked harder than I believed possible. A demon's refractory period was much shorter than a human's, and for that I was grateful. His black hair was tousled and messy from how hard he'd fucked me, and a sheen of sweat slicked over his muscles, making them glisten in the low light.

"Mark me," I begged. "As much as you can."

"You want me to unleash on you, pet?"

"You know I can take it," I challenged.

His golden eyes flared with a fierceness that turned me on beyond belief. He swallowed hard and ran his palm against my cheek. "No one can take me like you do."

My throat grew tight, and my eyes burned. The melancholy tinge to his words, they sounded too much like a goodbye.

He settled behind me again, and I slumped forward into the bed. My erection dug into the mattress, and I gave a slight shift of my hips, just to feel the silken sheets against it. A shudder rippled through me, and Cillian squeezed my cheek tight.

"You can come on my cock or not at all," he said, and then he nudged the tip of his cock against my hole.

There was no resistance as he slid right back in where he belonged. His cock was thick and perfect, and feeling it inside me again offered such staggering relief it came as a surprise. Even though I'd be sore in the morning, I wanted the ache for as long as possible. My moan echoed through the room as I gripped the bedsheets tight.

Instead of riding me the way he normally did, he blanketed my body with his. Cillian's hands wrapped over my fists, his legs bracketing mine and his heavy weight over the top of me as he crushed me into the bed. I died a little in that moment, knowing I'd never find heaven like this again. His body crushed mine into the mattress, making me feel small, vulnerable...and protected. My throat grew tight as I shifted my hips, trying to get him to move.

Cillian nipped at my ear. "No, pet. I'm in control here."

A shudder ran through me, and I surrendered to him. He ran his fangs down my neck, across my shoulder, the sensations making my cock leak. I writhed beneath him to feel how his big body kept me trapped. I wouldn't want to be trapped by anyone else.

Cillian pulled his hips back at last, his cock withdrawing to the tip—then he slammed into me again. A torrent of bliss thundered through me from the way he nailed my prostate, from how the shift dragged my oversensitive cock along the silken sheets. "Good pet," he murmured, his grip around my fists tightening. I swallowed hard, those words warming me from the inside out.

He thrust inside me again, finding a flow, an inexorable push-pull that had me panting. Flare after flare of pleasure rolled through me as he rocked my body against the mattress, my prostate so sensitive at this point I could scream. My balls ached to the point of pain, and each shift of his hips dragged my length along the sheets, the friction *almost* enough, but not quite.

Cillian's grunts behind me, the powerful flex of his muscles around me, had me drifting higher and higher. Sweat slicked our skin between us, the fiery inferno uncontained. I drank in the scent of cum, of sweat, of *him*. All of it turned me on even more. He fucked into me with a slow, sensual deliberation that would be my undoing. Each glide made my limbs tremble, but there was nowhere I could go, trapped under his body.

"You're mine," he murmured as he thrust in, the ridges of his cock sparking bliss all over again. "*Mine.*"

I was his. Body and soul.

The inexorable glide of his cock inside me was addicting, and my cock was so close to shooting off, but I needed more.

I let out a whimper, unable to form words.

Cillian growled, and he fucked in hard, right as his teeth descended into my shoulder. My whole body went limp from the way he claimed me, and I fully surrendered, my mind going blank. The sting of the bite offered the pain I craved, and the endorphins shot through me just as my cock rubbed against the silken sheets.

That was all it took.

My balls drew up, and my orgasm exploded. My spunk shot into the mattress, and white-hot bliss flooded through me. Breath halted, vision stuttered, everything shut down in the wake of such a powerful force. I soared to heights I'd never reach again, not without Cillian taking me there, to a space where I drifted in pure pleasure and nothing else mattered.

Everything else faded except for us.

Cillian continued to thrust into me until his muscles tightened around me, and he let out a muffled roar, his fangs buried in my shoulder. His cum flooded through me again for the second time tonight, and his knot began to expand inside me. The stretch stung even more this time, my hole oversensitive and overworked, but I still craved the fullness inside me, knowing we were locked together.

I didn't budge underneath him, dead to the world. His weight rested on me, but I savored the heavy feel of him, how he covered my body entirely. I slowly came back to earth, but I was in the best damn place possible. He unlatched from my shoulder, and an ache bloomed on it afterward. Cillian took his time licking at the marks he'd left, ones I needed to bear.

Fuck. I couldn't imagine not having his marks on me, of leaving this place.

My eyes burned, and I was relieved I faced away from him. The drops leaked onto the sheets instead. The yearning to stay in this place, in this moment, grew so overwhelming I found it difficult to breathe.

Cillian nuzzled into the crook of my shoulder, pressing an idle kiss there. His cock was buried in me, his knot keeping us tethered, and I wanted that forever. Somehow, in such a short span of time, he'd branded himself on my very soul.

"When you leave in the morning, don't say goodbye," Cillian murmured.

"What?" I asked, his words driving a dagger through my heart.

"I can't stand the idea of saying goodbye to you."

My throat grew tight, and more hot tears leaked from my eyes, soaking into the sheets. Because truth be told, I couldn't either. "I'm coming back."

"Don't make promises you can't keep," he warned, his muscles stiffening around me.

"I'll always find a way back to you," I said, a thread of pleading in my voice. I needed him to understand that this wasn't the end. That we weren't over. I would find my father, and then I would return to this man who'd awakened a hope inside me I'd thought impossible.

That I could find someone to belong to, who belonged to me in return.

Cillian's grip tightened over my hands, and he pressed another kiss against my neck in response.

Maybe it was better we weren't facing each other right now. He was still buried inside me, and I knew he could feel the tremble of my limbs, hear it in my voice, but I didn't want him to see me break. Just like I didn't want to see the melancholic sadness in his eyes, a knowing there, as if he believed this truly was the end.

For tonight, I'd hold onto any remaining moments I could claim with him.

But in offering me my freedom, Cillian had claimed the final piece of my heart.

I belonged to him.

I would *always* return.

CHAPTER 27

When I woke up in the morning, the bed was empty.

Cillian was nowhere to be found.

My chest caved in. He'd made himself scarce so he didn't have to face the goodbye, and I couldn't blame him. If I tried, I wasn't sure I'd be able to walk away either. However, I also wouldn't be able to live with myself if I didn't attempt to find my father. His messages were all that had kept me afloat during my early days here, and fuck...I just needed to know he was okay.

I pulled on my clothes from yesterday and slipped on my shoes. All the movements made a little of his cum leak out of me, and it dripped down the inside of my thigh. His scent lingered in the room, the brimstone and deep plum I craved. I made it to the doorframe but paused there. His bed was rumpled, from us. After his knot had deflated, he still hadn't pulled out, but he'd held me the entire night, his grip a little tighter than normal.

My heart ached, a visceral thing in my chest. I'd never experienced this sense of longing before, and I knew deep down, I'd never find a connection like this again.

"I'm coming back." I whispered the promise, the reminder.

Then I stepped out into the hall.

It was quieter today, filled with an emptiness that hadn't been there before as I strode in the direction of my room. The idea that I was headed out into the world again made my skin crawl, like a nakedness I had grown unaccustomed to in Cillian's presence. This was what I'd initially fought for, and the irony hadn't escaped me that now, when I was finally granted my freedom, I no longer wanted it.

I walked into my room and got changed into something simple—sweats, a T-shirt. Not like I could go to my old apartment either. I'd been evicted from there. My belongings, my life was here now, and the reality settled me a little bit. I snapped on a bracelet, a few rings, slipped my phone and my wallet into my pockets, but my skin still crawled at the idea of heading out into the world now after so long in this safe haven.

A cough sounded from the doorway. Amelia leaned there, and the lines on her face were deeper, a grim expression.

"I was told I'm to escort you out today?"

I ran fingers through my hair. "I'm coming back. I promise. My father's in trouble, and I'm...I'm all he has."

"Haven't you done enough for him?" she asked, her tone sharp. Her judgement was clear, and my shoulders tightened.

I heaved out a breath. "I was supposed to be here for a ten-year sentence, and then what? Released out into the world? My father's the only person I have out there."

Amelia's gaze softened. "Cillian's a fool to let you go. I..." She let out a low curse. "I was hoping you'd be the one."

I swallowed hard, not quite able to discern her meaning.

"Come on," she said, tilting her head toward the hallway. "Let's set you free, Beau Taylor."

My chest squeezed tight as I headed for the doorway.

When we began our trek down the hall, my footsteps echoed louder, and each one fell heavier. The thread connecting Cillian and me grew tighter and tighter until I feared it would snap. When I stepped out of the Spires, would he forget me?

Amelia entered the elevator first, and I followed. The ride down held an ominous silence that was reminiscent of my first ride up here, so different from the casual conversation we normally engaged in, and my heart ached.

"Is there any way I can convince you to stay?" Amelia asked, a note of urgency in her tone.

"I'm coming back," I promised again. Maybe if I said the words enough, they'd become binding, a message out to the universe.

Amelia's silence was an answer, a darkness in her expression that twisted my insides.

The elevator settled on the ground floor, and with a *ding*, the doors opened. We stepped out, and the sense of violation, of something wrong, rippled through me all over again. As if leaving here today would end in ruin and despair. Fear bubbled up inside me, turning my limbs leaden as we strode through the opulent casino floor, heading in the direction of the door I'd first come through.

The symmetry of the moment wasn't lost on me, and it felt far too much like an ending.

We stopped at one of the many doors lining the front, and Amelia grabbed my hand. "Beau, give me your phone. I'm putting my number in it." I handed it over, and she quickly typed it in and set it to call to confirm, her phone jangling in response before she shut it off.

Then Amelia passed my phone back. "If you need help, call me. Don't hesitate. Even if you decide you don't want to return here, the offer still stands."

I shook my head, my eyes stinging again. I'd never made friendships like these before, people who'd stand by me during tough times. "Thank you."

"Charles is going to be mad you didn't say goodbye," she said with a half smile.

"I'm not saying goodbye because I'm not leaving for good," I said. "You act like I'm going to vanish, when who knows? I could be back here tonight."

Amelia's eyes downturned, a sadness in them that made me uneasy. "If only life worked that way. Stay safe, okay?" She patted me on the shoulder, turned on her heel, and with that, she marched off.

Leaving me to exit the way I'd arrived—by myself.

I stepped out of the Spires, but unlike the last time when I went to the city with Cillian, now I felt exposed. A sense of wrongness mounted within me as I strode down the sidewalk, a free man. Except, now that I was free to choose, all I wanted to do was return.

I'd fallen completely and utterly in love with Cillian, and I needed to tell him.

I *would* tell him.

The Casino District looked so different in the daytime, not the seedy underbelly of the city that it transformed into at night with stumbling passersby and flashing neons. However, my back prickled as I walked in the direction of the subway. I wouldn't be taking it to my apartment, though. No, I'd head straight to my father's. The pit in my stomach grew and not because I hadn't eaten. I couldn't stomach food if I tried.

I glanced at the Spires, how the majestic building carved a stark mark on the skyline. How it'd carved a permanent mark on my heart. I pressed my fingers to the bruised bite mark Cillian had left on my shoulder last night, the ache there mirroring the one in my chest.

Walking out here amid the public made me feel invisible, as if I were just a specter floating through. Yet at any point, if Thorin's men pinpointed my location, I could be in trouble. Cillian had said he'd handle Thorin, but the awareness was imprinted in my bones now after witnessing firsthand the sort of danger that existed from being in his crosshairs.

I patted my pockets, as if a weapon would magically burst free. But I was no witch, no monster. I had no abilities to protect myself if Thorin decided to deploy his men. Just Amelia's number.

I quickened my steps toward the subway and stepped down the stairway to join the others waiting on the station's platform. The lights flickered, a contrast to the overly cheery sunshine up above. It felt more fitting to my mood now.

The subway train screeched to a halt in front of us, all metal and chaos, and I sucked in a sharp breath and stepped aboard. The pervasive sense of wrongness clung to me like plastic wrap, and I couldn't seem to detach from it, as if I was leaving everything good in my life behind. The subway creaked and swayed as it set off deeper into the city, and my heart matched the same unsteadiness.

Loyalty was a foundational piece of my being. If someone couldn't stand up for you when it mattered, they weren't worth keeping around. And my father had stood up for me my entire life. Stepping in at school when I'd been bullied, supporting me all through my childhood, and even moving us to the city so I could pursue becoming a librarian like I'd always dreamed.

Even after I'd gone to the Spires, he'd checked in with me regularly—called me, emailed me.

He'd been trying to find a way to free me.

I needed to find him.

The station closest to my father's apartment flashed into view on the overhead screen, and I made my way to the exit. The subway screeched to a halt, the doors opened, and I stepped off.

I jostled with a few elbows upon exiting, mingling with strangers an unfamiliar feeling at this point after my freedom and space in the Spires. Many would have hated the seclusion, but I'd loved it, as I'd had more companionship than I'd ever experienced out here in the city.

The air smelled like exhaust as I stepped onto the platform and headed up the steps, back into the searing sunlight. I squinted, trying to let my eyes adjust as I walked onto the crowded sidewalk, dozens of buildings looming in every direction. Around here, they were a little more rundown, but this was an active part of the city, even if it didn't have as much glitz and glamour as other sections.

I scratched at my light jacket, wishing I'd brought a messenger bag or something. The visceral feeling, like I was exposed, hadn't left since I'd walked out of the Spires. I glanced behind me, but none of the passersby seemed to pay me any mind. No one lurking around any of the buildings or peering out at me from windows either.

My father's apartment building lay at the end of the block, a tall, teetering one crammed with tenants on every floor. I'd spent plenty of time over here for dinner and a chat, something we'd tried to arrange regularly. The familiar sight of the chipped concrete steps and the twisted black railing quieted something inside me, knowing that at least everything hadn't entirely flipped on its head in the months away from my old life.

Except I didn't know what I'd find when I entered, and the *thump*, *thump*, *thump* of my heart grew so loud it drowned out the honks and the thrum of engines from the streets.

I strode up the steps and used my key to enter the building, which felt foreign at this point. A quiet filtered through the place, probably because most of the tenants would be out at work. Sweat broke out on my palms as I ascended to the second floor, a trek I'd made often. They still hadn't repaired the dent in the wall or the flickering overhead light.

When I stepped in front of my father's apartment, I rested my hand on the doorknob. Would it be locked or open? Would he be waiting inside, or would I have to start my search for him all over again?

This time, he wouldn't be held at the Spires, but we were overdue for the discussion of why he'd been there in the first place.

I was ready for the truth, whatever it ended up being.

I turned the knob and was able to push the door open. Unlocked. It creaked, announcing my entrance, and I peered inside. The living area didn't appear abandoned—no film of dust coating everything. My father had never been neat, and his normal stacks of books were piled high on the coffee table.

A thump came from the kitchen, and I stepped into view. "Dad, are you there?"

He sat at the kitchen table, hunched over, and papers were scattered over the table's surface in a messy array. His skin had taken on a pallor as though he was ill, his curls were in disarray, and the hand holding his mug trembled. Yet he was still my dad. He was still alive.

The relief bubbled up my throat, not quite released into the world yet.

"What's going on?" I asked, glancing around the room, as if it would offer me some idea of why he'd sent the message. Of what had happened. He wouldn't look up at me, just continued to stare at the liquid in his mug. His ragged breaths indicated he was alive, but his lack of response unnerved me.

My senses were screaming.

What was going on?

Self-preservation kicked in, and I reached into my pocket for my phone. I quickly swiped the screen and hit the call button to dial the last call it had made—to Amelia. The slightly tinny sound of the phone call picking up registered, but before I could respond, Dad looked up at me. The expression on his face aged him fifty years. His eyes were red-rimmed, the lines on his face haggard.

"Beau, I'm so sorry."

My stomach dropped. The look in his eyes, the sense of unease, all of it clicked into place.

His bedroom door opened at the far end of the apartment, and the last person I wanted to see stepped in.

Thorin Glass.

CHAPTER 28

I was going to be sick.

Thorin strode in, his footsteps echoing through the room. His dark hair was slicked back, his noxious presence taking over the entire place. His grin chilled me to the bone, a triumph there that terrified me. The man had the same imposing presence as when I'd first met him, a malevolence in his stare, a deadness there birthed from pure evil.

He was flanked by three guys outfitted in black, with guns strapped at their sides. They moved with the fluidity of experience, with not only competence in their job but the understanding of coordination.

This had all been planned.

I'd walked straight into danger, and my father had been complicit. Had he been threatened? Had...

When I looked at him, the bowed posture, the tremors rocking through him, the way he refused to meet my eyes told me everything I needed to know.

No, he'd sold me out.

My stomach rolled. Oh fuck.

My throat squeezed tight, and I backed up a step, farther away from him.

"I'm sorry, Beau," he begged, staring into his mug as if it might absolve him somehow. "I was out of options."

Fuck. Disgust roiled through me. How could he? How *could* he? Rage thrummed through me, and sheer despair tugged on its heels. This was my father. I'd sacrificed *everything* for him—twice. The conversations we'd had since I'd entered the Spires, the check-ins, all the concern he'd levied my way with message after message—had it been fabricated? My mind spun at a dizzying force as the weight of this descended.

My own father.

The person who'd raised me, who'd taken care of me as a kid, who *loved* me.

Yet he'd sold me out.

To Thorin fucking Glass.

"I'm surprised Cillian let you go," Thorin said, his cruel voice slicing through the air. "He's really shown his weakness."

"Fuck you," I snarled.

Thorin simply smirked. This apartment seemed to shrink in size, and yet the door and my escape lay interminably far away. A dizzying distance, even though it had felt like nothing when I'd walked in. I glanced at the only avenue out, then back to him, and he shook his head. "We're all armed, and you won't get far."

He lifted the pistol from the holster at his side, making his threat clear. The sight of it caused the breath to snag in my throat. The barrel was exposed, its lethality making the deadliness of the situation crystal clear. Thorin wasn't fucking around.

Except, then he aimed the gun in the direction of my father.

"You're no longer of use."

One moment, my father sat at the kitchen table clutching his mug tight.

The next, the porcelain shattered on the floor, dark liquid flying everywhere. Time slowed as my father tumbled from his chair with a heavy thud, one that resounded through the room. Red liquid and chunks splattered across every available surface. Several flecks hit my cheeks, hot and wet.

I froze in silent horror.

I only looked at where my father landed once, but the sight of him would be emblazoned in my mind forever.

The man I'd known, the one who'd raised me, was splayed out on the floor, his head...fuck, there was so much blood. Rivers of blood. Pools. Pieces of pinkish-gray brain matter strewn across the floor. Splinters of his skull like a scattered jigsaw puzzle. His arms and legs splayed out, unnatural, unmoving.

His head wasn't intact anymore. My father was no longer recognizable. And his body had stopped moving. The body that had wrapped me in so many soul-squeezing hugs over the years. The one that had held me when I cried over bullies and breakups. The one that had lifted me onto his shoulders as a child so I could pretend to be taller than the trees.

Completely still.

Bile rose in my throat, and I lowered to my knees as I vomited on the floor. Oh god.

Horror grabbed me by the throat, making breathing difficult.

Oh god, he was gone.

Gone.

I averted my gaze, unable to look at the body on the floor mere feet from me. My insides iced over.

No. This had to be some terrible nightmare.

"Get up," Thorin growled. "We're getting out of here."

My mind blurred, barely registering his demand. Rough hands grabbed me instead, tugging me up, and one of the guys in black yanked at my pocket. I felt out of body, numb, as if I didn't belong in it anymore but instead stared down on all this happening to someone else.

"Boss, he has his phone on," the guy said.

"Break it. By the time whoever he called gets here, we'll be long gone." Thorin stood in front of me, and my body rioted at his proximity. The stench of his cologne, his oppressive aura, the gun dangling in his hand.

The gun that shot my father. The man who shot my father.

A crunch sounded beside me, and bile rose in my throat again. Any chance of Amelia finding me now was dashed. Numbness settled over me like a blanket. I should be resisting, should be trying to push or shove or run away. Yet Thorin Glass had just murdered my father in cold blood. Hadn't even blinked or shown any remorse.

My father was dead.

He was dead.

I'd left Cillian to try to save him, and it turned out there had been nothing to save after all.

He'd sold me out, and for what, I didn't even know. And even after all that, he hadn't survived.

My fingers were numb, same as my feet. Hands yanked me away from my father's body, away from his apartment, and I didn't even fight back. I swallowed the golf ball in my throat, trying not to break down. Static hummed in my mind. I couldn't process what had just happened or I'd scream and scream and scream. My whole body trembled as the soles of my shoes scraped against the asphalt.

If only I'd pushed my father a little more for answers of why he'd gotten in trouble in the first place.

If only I'd asked Cillian what my father had done.

If only I had stayed at the Spires.

"Get him in," Thorin commanded. The guys bracketing me on either side managed to shove me over to an open car door. I teetered to the side, but they hopped in with me, an uncomfortable fit in the back. The guards kept their grip tight on my arms, but my body felt like it had iced over, too numb. One or both of them reeked of sweat and cigarettes, and bile rose in my throat. Thorin stepped into the driver's seat and turned on the engine. Once we left here, no one would find me.

No one would save me.

My father had been my one connection to the outside world, and he'd sold me out.

Fuck. Anguish bloomed in my chest all over again.

"What did you have on him?" I croaked out.

Thorin's gaze was locked forward on the road as he coasted down one street after another. "Did you not even ask what he did to run afoul of Cillian? I'm shocked your lover never told you."

I swallowed hard. He tried, and then I'd asked not to know. I'd willfully remained blind, a choice I had already come to regret.

The vision of my father splattered across the floor flashed in my mind, and my throat burned. I choked back the spew, the acidity coating my mouth.

Thorin let out a bark of a laugh. "Your father decided to negotiate a bad deal on behalf of his company...with Cillian. Your father made an offer for Jove Enterprises to handle assets for the Spires, one the company hadn't authorized. The plan had clearly been to weasel his way in, convince his company to follow through, and then skim from the top. However, Jove Enterprises wouldn't play ball, and when the lawyers at the Spires scrutinized the final contracts, they caught onto your father's plan. Cillian doesn't look fondly on those who go back on their word, and so your father was going to be held accountable."

Until I had stepped in. Fuck. My stomach spasmed, but there wasn't anything to puke up. I thought he'd had a gambling problem, as it had come up before in the past, something that could be fixed.

Not that he'd sold his morals.

"So, after you pulled your naïve and noble switch, and I saw Cillian's interest in you, I approached your father. No one would hire him after he'd pulled what he did, so he offered to help lure you out in return for a higher-level position in my company." Thorin laughed again. "You never make deals when you're desperate, though."

He truly had sold me out.

My stomach dropped. How much of my past was a lie? When had he grown this amoral? Not that he'd been a champion of justice growing up, but he'd been kind to me. He'd loved my mom. He'd never talked about work much at home, but I knew it had sawed away at him sometimes. However, I never would have thought he'd sell me out. Never. It was like the man I'd known my entire life had been bodysnatched, and now I'd never get the answer as to why, because he was dead.

The two men on either side of me jostled elbows often enough to remind me they were there, and my breath snagged. Their proximity made my skin crawl. Their grip on my arms ensured I wouldn't be able to bolt away, even though we were in the middle of a moving car.

"We got lucky you took the bait, though," Thorin said. "Our window with Cillian was closing, but it looks like we'll get everything we want. He's run out of time."

"What does that mean?" I asked as Thorin wheeled into a vacant warehouse parking lot. The huge building was tucked out of sight, surrounded by larger ones that cast deep shadows over the lot. I'd expected him to drag me off to Spectacle Casino at first, but that would've been a lot harder to conceal in the middle of the day. Enough people streamed in and out of Casino Alley that someone would've noticed armed men smuggling me inside. Guaranteed he planned to move me elsewhere once nightfall hit, though.

Thorin never answered my question, simply pulled to a park and then hopped out of the car. The guy on my right opened the door, since clearly we'd be moving at any moment. My mind hummed, just maintaining the static, and my body felt like it belonged to someone else. Thorin walked up to the other guard, who'd been sitting in the passenger seat. "Keep him here for the time being. I'll call when we're ready for the transport."

He then strode to the driver's seat, all while my guards jostled me out of the back. They dragged me from the car, and I didn't resist, because right now I'd rather be with them than alone with Thorin Glass.

Bang.

The sound of the gun going off echoed in my memory, even though I'd barely registered it at the time. Over and over and over again it played. A sound that would haunt me in my nightmares to come. If I even survived this.

Thorin hadn't been affected in the slightest.

"This way," one of the guys said, giving my arm a tug. I was too lost in my spiral to even register, and my feet moved on automatic. Thorin's car roared to life again, and he zipped out of the parking lot.

I wished I could warn Cillian. Find a way to tell Amelia more. I hoped she'd heard enough of what had been said while the phone was on that at least she could try to protect him. The idea that my naivete might have hurt Cillian made my stomach spasm again.

My father had sold me out.

The concept was unthinkable, and the situation had unfolded so fast I barely had a moment for the reality to settle in. Yet if I survived this, the betrayal would haunt me for a lifetime.

I should've questioned him more instead of blindly trusting. I'd gotten myself into this situation, and I had to live with the repercussions. Shame rolled through me. And now Cillian faced trouble because of it too. After he'd set me free, this was how I repaid him.

My stomach churned.

The warehouse smelled like must and sawdust, and one of the guards flicked a light on, the stacks of pallets making it appear like any other warehouse in the city, rather than my temporary holding cell. They guided me over to a small office, switched on the light, and shoved me in.

The guard who led the way turned toward me and pulled out zip ties. He let out a grunt, grabbed my wrists, and bound them together, then crouched to do the same with my ankles. The squeeze of them made me itch, made me want to scream, but the sight of the gun in the holster at his side kept me still. Kept me silent. I'd seen the result of that firing earlier today.

"I'd sit if I were you," he said, giving an up nod in the direction of a chair beside the desk. "It'll be a long wait."

The guard to my right grabbed the chair and pulled it underneath me, and I lowered myself onto the seat. It squeaked from the sudden weight, but my legs were shaky enough that I didn't want to try to stand again. Once I settled, the three guards left the room and shut the door behind me.

Leaving me in utter silence.

The room was simple and small, clearly an office that didn't get used too often. A chipped wooden desk sat beside me, the walls the sort of paste white that made reminded me of glue, and the floor an unremarkable gray. My skin crawled at the lack of distraction—my mind was the last place I wanted to be.

My mind just kept screaming the same loop on repeat, one I needed—desperately needed—to silence.

A few muffled sounds of what could be conversation sounded outside the room, but then they tapered off. I skimmed the desk for anything that might loosen the zip ties, but they'd put me in a spartan sort of holding cell. Which made sense, but I cursed their preparedness.

I settled back in the seat and stared up at the ceiling. This morning, I'd woken up in the bed of the man I loved after a night with him that I'd remember for the rest of my life.

Then I'd left the Spires, and it had all gone downhill from there.

The one thing that had been awaiting me on the outside was my father. And he'd sold me out to Thorin fucking Glass. Had his resistance when I first offered to take his place been feigned? Hot liquid stung my eyes, but I didn't bother to restrain the tears. They streamed down my face, and I couldn't even wipe them away. No one was here to see them anyway. It had been him and me against the world for so long, and I struggled to wrap my head around what had happened in those brief moments in his apartment. That ultimately, he'd valued his own comfort before mine.

Enough to turn me over to Thorin Glass.

The sight of him on the floor flashed in my head, and my stomach convulsed again, but there was nothing left to vomit up. I was starving at this point, my whole body feeling weak from lack of sustenance and sheer exhaustion after the adrenaline crash, but there was nothing I could do in here.

Blood. So much blood. The scent invaded my nostrils, reminding me I probably had flecks of it on my skin. I reached up with my zip-tied hands and tried to swipe at my cheeks. A few red streaks came off on my fingers, which meant I'd just made it worse. The coppery stench was everywhere, though, as if I'd never be able to scrub it off.

Why had my father trusted a man like Thorin Glass?

Why had he betrayed me?

My heart ached. I'd never get the answers—not the real ones from the man himself. Because he'd bet on the wrong person, and Thorin had murdered him in cold blood once he'd outlived his usefulness.

The zip ties dug into my wrists and ankles, and my whole body ached as if someone had smacked me repeatedly with a two by four. I had no idea how much time had passed, but the silence out there made it feel like it had been hours. It was just me in here with my thoughts, which was the worst place to be.

And I had no idea when Thorin would return or demand my retrieval. Once I was sent to Spectacle, or wherever in Glacier Industries he planned to keep me, I was beyond fucked. Yet, what could I do? I'd left the people who would've defended me, and I'd placed my trust in the wrong person. Cillian seemed to have his own hornet's nest that this had inspired.

My heart ached. I just wanted him to be okay.

The pale white of the wall swirled before me, and I stared up at it until my eyes ached, until I let them flutter shut. The moment I did, my eyelids turned to granite, and trying to open them again became impossible.

My breathing evened, and a dizzying swirl of darkness claimed me. Ugh.

I blinked my eyes open, an ache behind them, my mouth dry like I'd slept for hours. The room around me was the same pale white office as before. My stomach sank. It hadn't all been some terrible nightmare. Heaviness weighed down my body, even though I'd clearly fallen asleep. I had no idea how much time had passed, but I was relieved to have spent it unaware rather than conscious.

A thump sounded beyond the door, and I straightened up, rousing to attention.

Someone else was here.

The doorknob rattled.

CHAPTER 29

I braced my shoulders for whoever was about to enter.

As much as I'd been defeated and beaten today, I could fight here and now. Because if they managed to drag me off to another location, I'd be doomed.

My body was tensed. I'd launch my weight at whoever entered the second they got close enough.

The doorknob rattled again, and a second later, it flew open.

Two people I worried I'd never see again stood in the doorway. Amelia was dressed in all black, her silver-threaded hair pulled into a tight bun, and her features bled with a different sort of seriousness than normal—battle ready. And Theo stood by her side, similarly attired in all black. A little bit of his wolf had crept into his features, his fangs poking down, his claws extended, and his ginger hair trailing onto his cheeks.

The relief punched me so hard in the chest that I sagged forward.

I thought I'd never see any of them again, yet Amelia had been as good as her word.

At least someone had.

Bitterness at what I'd lost corroded inside me, clashing with the gasp of necessary air that their presence delivered.

"How?" I asked as they stepped in. "Wait, there are guards in the warehouse."

Amelia snorted. "They were the furthest from professional. I've fought harder foes in my sleep." Relief thundered through me. How had she and Theo dispatched them while I'd slept? The lethality they employed only confirmed how dangerous both of them were. She fixed her gaze on me. "You're the reason we found you."

My brows drew together, and I followed her stare, which was locked on the golden bracelet around my wrist.

The one she'd given me for protection at the gala.

Understanding crashed in.

"I wasn't sure if its use had worn off," I murmured.

"What sort of witch do you take me for?" she scoffed. Simply being able to talk to her made my chest squeeze tight. God. I'd only left this morning, and I already missed the entire crew at the Spires so damn much.

And Cillian. I wanted to see him most of all. Being apart from him had caused a deep, unabating ache in my chest, one that only grew by the second.

Theo knelt next to me and sliced through the zip ties around my ankles with his claws, then tackled the ones around my wrists. The second I was freed, I moved my wrists and ankles around. The freedom rushed me, and for a moment I wasn't sure if I'd be able to move with the dizzying wave that went straight to my head.

"What happened to the guards?" I asked, not sure I wanted the answer.

"Currently trapped in a nightmare, so I'm a bit zapped for juice. We've got a limited window to escape." Amelia tilted her head toward the door. "You coming?"

Damn, curse witches were scary. I bobbed my head and tried to surge forward. My legs wobbled, nearly buckling beneath me. Fuck. I was weak as a kitten from having barely any sustenance, an adrenaline drop, and puking my guts up. "Not going to be winning any fights like this."

"Luckily you've got muscle now," Theo said, crouching. "Climb onto my back."

I didn't argue, as I didn't want to cause us any trouble in getting out of here, I just climbed onto Theo's broad back and slumped there. My eyes stung from the relief that ached through my marrow. I'd expected to have to fight for my life later, to resist in any way at getting dragged to Thorin's. Yet the friends I'd made in the Spires were the sort of loyal I'd shown but apparently hadn't received in return.

"We've got to get to Cillian, before it's too late," Amelia said, taking the first steps out.

"What happened?"

The words "too late" played on repeat in my mind, but all I could focus on was getting out of this place.

"I'll explain in the car," she said as she led us through the warehouse, footsteps echoing to the tall ceilings. Theo followed quickly on her heels, and I clung to him. My whole body sagged against his weight, and my vision blurred slightly.

The three guards sat slumped forward along the side wall, close to the exit point. All of them seemed to be deep in slumber. My shoulders tensed. Were they truly sleeping, or...

"They're hard out, but we don't want to wait around for when they wake up," Theo reassured me, as if he'd sensed my concern.

Theo and Amelia's footsteps echoed through the warehouse, and a second later, we burst out into the fading sunlight.

"Car's over here," Theo said as we quick-walked over to a black SUV. I clutched onto him, exhaustion pummeling me after everything that had occurred today. I could still barely believe any of it had happened. Part of me still expected to wake up back in the warehouse office—or even worse, back in my father's apartment.

Amelia hopped into the driver's seat, and Theo helped me off his shoulders and into the back seat. I slumped against the interior of the car, face pressed against the window. He slid in beside me and brought the door shut. Unlike the last time I'd been loaded into a van, though, the people with me now were safe.

They were protecting me.

"Why did you come for me?" I asked, my voice hoarse. My chest twisted tight at the reality that the people who'd shown up for me were the ones I'd walked away from.

"I made you a promise," Amelia said. "I keep my promises."

She might be one of the few who did.

She started the car and took off with a screech of tires.

Those words sank deep into my bones. These were the sorts of people worth my loyalty. Not the person I'd given all of it to before. My stomach roiled again.

"And Cillian?" I asked, needing to know he was okay.

Amelia's pause made my stomach drop. "There's a secret we've been keeping from you—because honestly, we weren't sure it would work if there was interference."

"What?" I asked. Tension roiled in the car, the sensation that whatever she was about to tell me now could change everything. There had always been a secret lurking in the Spires—I'd sensed it the entire time I'd been there—but every time I'd tried to find the answer, it had only seemed farther away.

Amelia let out a heavy, loaded sigh. "Cillian's under a powerful curse, cast by his ex, Olivia, and a technomancer, Henrik. Sponsored of course by Glacier fucking Industries."

A million melancholic glances slammed into me at once. The cryptic way everyone talked about him, how he stared off into the distance as if he'd become petals waiting to get swept away by the breeze.

Oh no.

"What kind of curse?" I asked, my whole body locking up. Because deep down, the answer settled in place.

"A death curse," Amelia said grimly. "The Rose Protocol."

His tattoo. His fucking tattoo. I swallowed hard, my mind spinning faster and faster.

Death curse.

"Curse witches use emotion to cast, like channeling your own hopes and fears, converting that to adrenaline, and then powering it that way. The mark of her curse looks like a tattoo on the skin. Death curses are highly illegal, but since he's not dead yet, no one has come after Olivia and Henrik. Guaranteed Thorin has a plan in place to protect them. Olivia could never have pulled off a timed death curse like this, something so heinous, on her own. But Henrik used his technomancy to transfer the curse to binary—a code laid out into the tattoo on his skin that's tied to a countdown on his computer."

The one on the screen in the locked room.

The truth socked me in the gut. It had been around me this whole while, the realization that Cillian was running out of time.

Fuck. Fuck. Fuck.

"There has to be some way around it, though, right? Isn't there some sort of exchange in casting curses, some energy needed? Witches can't go around dropping death curses with no penalties, no loopholes," I said. I was certain I'd learned about curses years ago in a few of my books on monsterkind, and there were stipulations for casting certain types without alerting the authorities. Plus, the casting of said curses cost the user as well—but maybe Olivia's connection to him had allowed her to cast in the first place. We whizzed through the city at top speed, narrowly zipping through yellow lights and swerving around car after car.

"Cillian had to fall in love and be loved in return," Amelia said, a twist of bitterness in her tone. "Something Olivia believed to be impossible. I told you, us curse witches have a penchant for the dramatic."

My stomach bottomed out.

Amelia's gaze met mine through the rearview mirror. The understanding there smashed into me. She'd known I was the key to Cillian's continued existence, yet she'd let me leave today without saying a word.

Cillian had let me leave, knowing I carried his last chance of survival with me.

Oh god.

A sob made my throat spasm. "There's still time, isn't there?"

"Not much," she murmured. "The clock is counting down to the end tonight."

"No." I clapped a hand over my mouth, my shoulders shaking.

We needed to get to him. We needed to get to the Spires.

"If I'd known, I never would've..." I gasped out.

"You had to be free to make the choice," Theo said beside me. "None of us fault you for leaving."

"Fat lot of good that did," I muttered darkly. Silence rang through the car. Amelia had been on the phone, which meant she'd heard everything. She knew of my father's betrayal, and of his death.

"All we can do is try to get to him now," Amelia said. "Before the vultures pick him apart."

My throat tightened. "Thorin?"

"No. Olivia," Theo said. "She called to set up one more meeting. They've been trying to convince him to sign the company over to them in exchange for lifting the curse. Cillian has refused. He's a stubborn shit."

"Money's not worth his life," I spat back. "Why not just hand it over?"

"Because the good he does for all of us is worth protecting." Amelia's voice rang out harsh and clear.

Fuck. She was right. The system he'd created here to protect monsters in need, everything he'd built—in Thorin's hands, it would crumple to dust. The reality of that socked me in the gut.

Yet a deeply selfish part of me didn't care.

I wanted him.

No one else. Just him.

"We need to get to Cillian." My heart thundered, like it was about to march right out of my chest.

"Doing the best I can," Amelia said, tires screeching again as she veered into the right lane.

I peered out the windows. Up ahead lay the familiar towers of the Spires. My mind still raced with everything I'd just learned. Spinning, spinning, spinning. The information slammed into me, peak overload, as I'd been wandering in the dark for so long, blinded and reaching out for answers.

Yet all the clues had been there. The mournful look in Cillian's eyes last night settled deep in my chest, moments which felt like a lifetime ago.

Because he knew once I walked away, he truly would never see me again.

I was the only one who hadn't been aware.

Acid rose in my throat, even though there was nothing left to vomit up, and my heart thumped so hard I swore it would revolt out of my chest. I balled my hands into fists, my nails biting into my palms. Fuck.

I'd told him I'd come back to him. Cillian...fuck, he needed to be alive. I couldn't imagine a world without him, where I wasn't safely tucked in his arms. Where we weren't verbally sparring or spending time walking through gardens or reading together in our spare moments. Where I wasn't in his bed every single night.

My insides ached with a deep sorrow, something as vast and consuming as staring at a starry sky and knowing it'd be the last one you'd ever see.

Our night together had been Cillian's final one, and he'd spent it with me.

A desperate tremor rolled through me again, anguish keener than the edge of a knife. I sucked in a shallow breath, trying to restrain the scream, the sob, that grew inside me with every ensuing realization.

We couldn't get there fast enough.

Because I was worried we *wouldn't* get there fast enough.

"Almost," Theo murmured at my side, his gaze locked front and forward on the road. The car brewed with tension, the truth out in the open at last.

And yet all of us were clearly worried, because if we didn't make it in time...Cillian's life was on the line.

My heart was lodged in my throat. All I wanted was to see his face. To tell him the truth that had brewed in me for a while now, waiting to be set free.

That I loved him. Truly loved him in a way I'd never before experienced with another soul.

Cillian Ashmore made me believe in fate.

That somehow, no matter what happened, our paths would've aligned. That we would've found each other, fumbling through the dark until we discovered light.

Except now that I'd found him, I couldn't fathom losing him.

The world would be a terrible place without The Beast of the Spires.

"Any other secrets you've been keeping from me?" I asked, needing to distract myself somehow. Otherwise I'd break.

"We've all got our personal skeletons in the closet," Amelia said. "But I'm not giving away any of those unless you get me drunk."

"Which is impossible," Theo warned. "I've seen her drink for an entire night and walk out unaffected."

"Witch's tolerance," she said, a sharp edge to her words, even as she joked.

We walked on this razor's edge together, and that alone kept me from falling apart.

Amelia made a sharp right, sending both Theo and me tilting to the side. I chewed on the inside of my cheek hard enough I tasted blood, but I kept my focus front and forward too. The Spires was so close. So fucking close. My whole body hummed with readiness, even though I was still shaky and barely functional.

It didn't matter. I'd run the whole staircase up the Spires if I had to, if it meant getting to Cillian in time.

Amelia slowed down and slipped into a side alley. A second later, she drove us into a small garage, the darkness closing around us.

"Private entrance to the Spires," she clarified, clearly for my sake.

"Out, now," Theo said, but I didn't need the prompting. Before Amelia had even shut off the engine, I pushed the car door open and hopped out. My feet hit the ground, my legs shaky, but I strode forward regardless. A dim light on the other side of the garage signaled an elevator, my guess to the main floor.

Amelia walked in line with me, and Theo outpaced us fast. I had the feeling she would've been up there with him already but was making sure I didn't faint or pass out along the way. Which was fair. I had no idea how much time had passed, and my whole body felt shaky and weak.

Theo pressed the button, and the elevator doors slid open.

I quickened my pace to close the distance as he stepped inside and held the doors open for us. Amelia followed me in, and then we shot up.

Once we hit the first floor, the doors opened onto the familiar main floor of the Spires. Slot machines jangled, lights flashed, and the rich carpeting was immaculate. The crisp scent of cleaner greeted my nose.

The moment I stepped inside, relief cascaded over me. This had somehow become more of a home to me than my own had ever been. We burst out onto the floor, our hurried steps echoing with their thumps.

"We've got to get to the upper floors," Theo said. "Charles said Cillian's doing something stupid."

My chest twisted, but I didn't stop walking. "Of course he is."

The elevator that had become engraved on my soul lay to the right, past the reception area, where employees chatted with customers, unaware of what was going on. The elevator I'd first used to travel up to a place I'd never expected to feel like a home. And yet, it had.

From across the room, I caught sight of those golden doors opening.

That could only be two people.

And two figures strode out.

Except they weren't Cillian and Charles.

A familiar middle-aged man stepped onto the floor, well dressed in a suit, as if he'd just come from a meeting. My gut clenched. I recognized him—not just from pictures online but from the day Thorin had almost captured me outside the Spires. Henrik.

And Olivia.

Her gaze landed on me, and her crimson lips twisted into a triumphant smirk. The pair closed the distance between us, even as we marched forward to get to the elevator.

Olivia shook her head, and when her eyes glittered with that unfathomable cruelty, I knew the words that would come before she spoke them.

"You're too late."

CHAPTER 30

Too late.

The words echoed in my mind over and over.

I rushed past Olivia, not even bothering to acknowledge her. The elevator lay within reach, and any second wasted was precious.

We couldn't be too late. I couldn't fathom a world without him in it. My system was flush with jittery energy, like I'd downed too much coffee. Theo and Amelia were right by my side as we reached the elevator, and Amelia pressed the button. A second later, the doors slid open.

All three of us stepped inside, and Amelia used her key card first, imprinted her thumb on the panel, and then pressed the button for the upper floors.

The elevator *whooshed* up, but my heart lodged in my throat. The *ding*, *ding*, *ding* rang through the silence between us, none of us willing to speak, as if by breaking the silence we would acknowledge what Olivia had said.

My mind whirled. Had Cillian given in to Thorin and signed over his company? Or had he refused, and she'd meant it was too late for Cillian's life?

Selfishly, I only cared about his survival.

Anything else could be rebuilt, but a world without him in it looked far darker than I could fathom.

The doors slid open, and we stepped into the hallway. It was so familiar my bones ached, this walk I'd done a thousand times over in the past few months. But now we headed toward the West Wing. I didn't question that if he'd be anywhere, it would be the locked room.

We reached the end of the hallway and made the turn, all of us quickening our paces. The corridor ached with a quiet that unnerved me, and our footsteps echoed, echoed, echoed. An emptiness existed, as if the powerful presence that had consumed the space up here was now gone.

When the platform to the West Wing appeared in sight, I didn't attempt a walk anymore.

I broke into a flat run.

My body was weak, and I was running on an adrenaline deficit, but I needed to find him.

The beat of my heart matched the frantic thump of my footsteps.

I vaulted over the step up to the platform and bypassed his room, even though the sight of it sent a shard right through my heart.

I never should've left.

I never should've abandoned the demon I loved.

The locked door lay open.

I burst through it and skidded to a halt.

The big monitor that had the countdown displayed on it flashed 0:00.

Charles knelt in the middle of the room.

Beside him lay Cillian, crumpled to the ground. His massive body was carelessly slumped there, not like he'd lain down but had collapsed. His head tilted to the side, his arms out, legs askew. His eyes were shut, his mouth partially open. And he was as still as the grave.

Oh no. No, no, no.

My feet carried me forward, even though my soul had left the building. Charles was pale and somber, the only time I'd ever seen him without a smile or glimmer in his eyes. He clutched his thighs in a white-knuckled grip, and his mouth formed a thin line.

I didn't stop until I reached Cillian and dropped to my knees.

"Cillian." I gasped his name out like a prayer, casting a desperate wish into the universe. That he was okay. That what I saw with my eyes wasn't real. His body wasn't moving. There was no rise and fall of breaths, no spark of life.

Instead, the man whose presence had drawn my attention from the first second we'd met lay still. Devoid of anything that had once dwelled within him.

My throat spasmed, and a broken sob escaped. I clapped a hand over my mouth, the sound far too loud in the quiet room.

"He wouldn't save himself," Charles said, his voice broken. "Even in the end. He signed the contract with Thorin—in order to protect you."

Oh god. Another sob exploded out of me, and my eyes burned with hot tears. Cillian Ashmore was the noblest man I'd ever met, who deserved far more than the cards he'd been dealt.

He couldn't be gone.

I threw myself over his chest, the tears flowing freely now. "Come back to me," I begged, clutching him tight. Except he remained still, unmoving.

Every moment flashed before my eyes.

From the earliest days, when I'd loathed him, when his comments had felt casual and cruel, and yet I'd been drawn to his presence regardless. When he'd left me books by my bedside, and when he'd stolen me out to the gardens at work because he understood what I needed. And those nights. Those glorious nights that I'd wished wouldn't end. Where he'd fucked me senseless, where he'd shared secrets from his past. Where I'd opened up to him too, and we'd built a trust I'd never believed possible.

And last night, his anguish had been just as intense as mine, yet he'd made love to me the whole night long.

Cillian had loved me so deeply he'd set me free.

He might not be free with his words, but he was a man of action, and I understood in my bones what that had meant. From the moment we met, we'd been magnets drawn together, again and again. I'd believed fate had propelled us together for a reason...except I'd been too blind to see.

Until it was too late.

I sobbed harder, my whole body shaking, as I pressed my cheek to his chest, desperate to hear the beat of his heart—anything. Only stillness remained. His unmoving and silent form, so different from the magnitude of his presence before. My soul was being torn apart by the second, entirely unmade. I'd never fallen in love like this before, as incandescent as starlight and burning just as hot. Yet with Cillian, I'd never stood a chance. My tears soaked into his shirt, but they poured from me unceasingly.

My chest spasmed, my insides tearing apart piece by piece.

"Come back to me, dammit," I begged. "I love you, Cillian Ashmore. I love you with every ounce of my soul."

The tears wouldn't end, wetness imprinting on my cheeks, soaking into his shirt. I clutched him hard, waiting, wishing for a response yet knowing there wouldn't be one. I had walked out when he needed me most, and that truth would haunt me for the rest of my life.

A hand rested on my back, warm, heavy, and reassuring.

A gasp sounded from behind me, and I sat up. The hand slid down my back but remained pressed against me.

Cillian stared at me. Those magnetic golden eyes were open.

I choked on a breath. "Are you...?"

His hand drifted up and down my back, and a riot of emotions welled inside me. The feel of his palm against me, the sheer electricity of his touch confirmed this was real. This wasn't in my imagination.

"You came back," he murmured, his beautiful eyes softening.

"I promised I would." The words came out raw, my cheeks wet with tears. "Fuck, why didn't you tell me? I never would've left if I'd known..."

"You love me?" he asked, his tone low and gravelly and hesitant.

"More than I believed possible," I responded. I gripped his shirt, meeting his gaze head-on. He was here. He was here and talking to me, and I wouldn't waste another second. "And I'll continue to love you for as long as you'll have me." He stroked my back, even though he didn't move from his spot—most likely too weak.

His lips twisted in a wry smile. "What about forever?"

My heart squeezed tight. "You'll get sick of me."

"Never," he responded. "In case it wasn't clear, I've been in love with you for a damn while now. And I didn't think that was possible for me."

Those words offered a balm to my soul I hadn't realized I needed. While our relationship had been tumultuous and full of fireworks from the start, this confession settled in like a spring breeze. It carried the same scent of early blooms and promise, a fragility and hope there that I clasped tightly to me.

A cough sounded behind us. "As toothache-sweet as this reunion is, holy fuck, Cillian," Amelia said, dropping to the ground beside me. I didn't let go of him, not for a second, but I understood they were worried about him as well.

"I thought you were dead," Charles said, his voice hauntingly quiet. "How....?"

"Do you need help up?" Theo asked. "Or are you planning on lying around down there for the next century?"

I shook my head and wiped my tear-blurred eyes on my sleeve. I hadn't let go of Cillian's shirt, and I wasn't planning on it. He was lying here in front of me talking, moving, smiling at me. Telling me he loved me. The ache inside me transmuted to something different, yet consuming all the same. Not the agony of loss, but the depth of a love I'd never tapped into before.

More powerful than anything I'd experienced in this life.

"If you want to give me a hand..." Cillian said. "Can't get upright on my own."

"I'm waiting on an explanation," Charles said. "So how about you conserve your energy for that."

Theo snorted and settled behind Cillian, and I gripped Cillian's arms as together we got him upright. Once he was stable, I slid my hands down until they were interlinked with his, mine feeling small in his massive clutch. I wasn't moving an inch away from him. Part of me was terrified that if I looked away, he'd vanish before my eyes.

Cillian heaved out a weary sigh. "Truthfully, my best guess is that you managed to get to me in time. I've studied the curse a dozen different ways, searching for a loophole or anything I could do to combat it. Once activated, it worked as a life drain, which would explain why I'm so weak right now."

"So you weren't quite dead?" Charles said, disbelief ringing in his voice.

"If he was entirely dead, he wouldn't have been able to come back," Amelia confirmed. "I do know a thing or two about those types of curses."

"Is the rose tattoo still on you?" I asked, checking his forearm. Where once there'd been the intricate black rose tattoo, only smooth red skin remained. Relief rushed through me in a fierce sweep.

"Yet now Thorin gets your company," Charles said. "I watched you sign it over to Olivia and Henrick."

Cillian's crooked smile sent a pang through my heart. Even though today had been hell and my mind, body, and soul had been through the wringer, I understood a bit about how he operated.

"Upon your death, I presume."

Cillian shook his head at me, an unguarded wonder in his eyes. My heart soared. "I've never met anyone cleverer in my life."

"Rude," Amelia said, collapsing onto the floor with the rest of us. "Though, I'm glad you'll be able to nullify that contract posthaste."

"What about Thorin, though?" Charles asked. "What's to stop him from causing another problem like this?"

Amelia lifted a finger. "Mm, so, several things. First off, the curse itself required a personal element Thorin doesn't have. Olivia was Cillian's ex, which gave her a foothold, but that isn't the sort of moxie you can tap into more than once."

"You're terrifying, the lot of you," Charles said pointedly. I snorted. He wasn't wrong.

"But secondly, I wouldn't worry about Thorin for much longer," Amelia said. A wicked grin played on her lips, and Cillian's smile grew.

My brows drew together. They'd figured something out, but I was unclear as to what. Truthfully, right now I didn't care. I had Cillian with me, and that was all that mattered.

"The moment you rang, Beau, Cillian sent us after you," Amelia said. "However, I recorded the entire call, up until I presume they destroyed your phone."

My pulse sped. The puzzle pieces slotted quickly together in my mind.

"And with that, we've got proof of Thorin Glass committing murder," Cillian said gravely. He squeezed my hands, still intertwined with his, sympathy shining in his eyes.

My heart twisted. The thought of my father formed a screaming blank void in my mind right now, a nest of hornets I didn't dare touch. Better I kept that in a locked box for now.

"Will it be enough to nail him?" I asked.

"The recording is too damning," she said. "There's no way he can evade the evidence we have on him."

"All thanks to your call," Cillian said. "Smart move, pet."

"I was just trying to share my location," I said, a hiss of a sigh escaping me. Relief fluttered through me on tentative wings. After the extreme highs and lows of the day, I was beyond wiped out. Drained beyond measure. "I'm glad we can salvage something from this mess, though."

Because I hadn't dragged anything else from it. My view of my past was shattered, my father gone, and broken bits resided inside me that would be slow to heal. Cillian's hands clutching mine were the only things keeping me from spinning into oblivion. As much loss as I'd experienced today, I hadn't lost him.

And that meant everything.

"What about Olivia and Henrik?" I asked. "Them escaping scot-free seems like bullshit."

"Thorin's protection kept them safe—he has too many ties in with law enforcement. However, if he's out of the way, I kept a long and detailed record of my curse and their involvement," Cillian reassured me. "They won't roam free for long."

"Why don't we get you to your bed?" Amelia suggested to Cillian, a hand on her hip even while she crouched on the floor. "You were drained and need to rest."

"Will you come with me?" Cillian asked me, a seriousness in his tone that held me captive.

"Like you need to ask," I said, squeezing his hand tight. "I'm yours, Cillian Ashmore. For the rest of our lives."

The truth lay starkly between us at last, and as terrifying as it seemed, admitting it was also freeing. Cillian had proved his love in every way, and free to make the choice, I'd choose him every time.

"Come on," Theo said, offering an arm to Cillian. I grabbed his other one and looped it around my shoulders, even though Theo did the heavy lifting in helping him upright. My legs were shaky, and I was close to passing out at this point, from hunger or the adrenaline crash, who knew.

"Both of you need to rest," Amelia said. "I doubt Thorin fed you anything while he kept you prisoner. We'll grab some soup and bread from the kitchen."

Charles and Amelia set off ahead of us down the corridor, clearly making their way to the kitchen, while Theo and I directed Cillian to his bedroom. When we entered, the last remaining taut string in my chest loosened.

Home.

I was home.

We lowered him onto the bed, and he wrapped his arms around my waist, the weight of him causing me to topple forward.

"If I'm stuck here, then so are you," he said, a genuine smile on his lips. I used what remaining energy I had and readjusted myself on the bed beside him, one I'd slept in many a night.

Theo snorted. "I'll leave you two lovebirds to it. Lia and Charles will bring some food in when you're ready for it." He paused. "I'm glad you're alive. Both of you. This place wouldn't be the same without you."

With that, Theo turned on his heel and headed out of Cillian's room.

Quiet descended between us, the enormity of everything that had happened starting to settle in. Cillian managed to loop his arm around me, and I rested my cheek to his chest, just to hear the steady *thump, thump, thump* of his heart. Savoring the fact that he was here. He was alive.

"I should've told you why I didn't trust your father," Cillian murmured. "I regret not speaking up."

"I wouldn't have let you," I said. "I didn't want to hear it."

His body was warm beneath mine, and even weak and depleted as he was, I felt safe here. Protected. I gripped onto his shirt. I'd protect him too, in whatever way I could. If anyone tried to come between us again, I'd tear their heart out. The exhaustion swept over me, and my eyes felt heavier by the minute. Cillian's breaths were even, as if he careened toward sleep, and I didn't want to keep him up, not after everything he'd gone through today as well. Yet I had one more question.

"Why didn't you tell me?" I asked. "About the curse. About all of it."

"You had to love me of your own volition. If those feelings weren't wholly true, but were just because you felt guilty or didn't want me to die, the curse would never have been lifted anyway," Cillian said, the rumble in his chest lulling me closer to sleep.

"Curses are stupid," I muttered, letting my eyes fall shut.

"Luckily you're smart enough to thwart them," Cillian responded. "Rest, pet. I'll be here when you wake up."

That knowledge was all I needed.

I closed my eyes and careened toward oblivion.

CHAPTER 31

W hen I cracked my eyes open, I felt like I'd been bludgeoned by a billy club over and over again.

A heavy weight surrounded me, the scent of musk and plum and brimstone, and I recognized it as Cillian. I let myself bask for a moment there in the warmth, the comfort of having him draped around me.

Then the events I'd tried to shut out slammed back in.

Of my father's betrayal.

His murder.

Cillian almost dying.

My throat tightened, and Cillian squeezed me a little harder.

"You're awake," he said, letting go of me and pushing upright in the bed.

I followed suit, even though my muscles were belligerent, and the scent of tomato and spice caught my attention. Two bowls filled with soup and plates of bread and butter lay on the nightstand, courtesy of Charles and Amelia.

"How long have we been out?" I asked, my stomach rumbling.

"Food first, then we can discuss further," Cillian said, gesturing for a bowl. I passed him one with the bread, then balanced my own in my lap. It was lukewarm at this point, but I didn't care as I took the first sip. The rich tomato broth offset that gnawing hunger at once. Damn, I was starving. I gulped down the soup as fast as humanly possible, then started tearing into the bread. I barely had a second to savor it with how quickly I consumed the food. Cillian did the same, the silence between us broken up by slurps and chewing.

When I finally polished it off, I placed the empty bowl on the nightstand and then sat back in the bed again. I heaved a huge, relieved sigh.

"Let's head to the bathroom next," he said as he leaned past me to place his bowl down too. "I'm sure after the day you had, you could use a shower."

I grimaced. Based on the stiff spot on my cheeks, blood had probably dried there, and I hadn't gotten a chance to clean it off. My father's blood. My stomach rolled. "Please."

I pushed up out of bed and headed into Cillian's bathroom first to take a piss, my bladder aching. The room was luxurious, a place I'd spent far too much time in over the last month. He stepped in a few moments later, his presence looming and steady, as I tugged off my shirt, my pants and briefs, my socks, letting them fall to the ground. Part of me wanted to burn them.

Cillian had somehow stripped down even faster, and he bent over the tub, completely naked. If I hadn't been exhausted and heartsick, I'd be turned on, as his physique held a constant allure for me, a strength and sturdiness there that I craved. Yet I let him turn the shower on and usher me into it. He pulled the curtain to shut us in afterward.

The hot water cascaded down on me, offering absolution, and I basked in the steam that rose around me as it washed my body of the day, even if it couldn't erase the memories. Cillian stepped behind me, and he wrapped his arms around my body, holding me tight.

"I'm sorry," he murmured in my ear, the sound almost drowned out by the roar of the water. "About your father."

A lump formed in my throat. Even after my father had betrayed me, even after he'd disappointed me beyond compare, my mind still tangled with the memories of what was. Of what we'd had before he'd sold me out to Thorin.

And what was worse? I was left with all these questions. Ones that would never get answered, because they required the man himself.

Of why he'd betrayed me. Of why he'd tried to scam the Spires. Of whatever had fueled him to keep so many secrets from me.

My heart ached, and the first sob erupted from my throat. My whole body shook with them as Cillian held me steady in the shower, the water washing my tears down the drain. There was no escaping that this event would color my entire existence from here on out, and yet...I still had something to hold onto.

The very person who clutched me tight like he was afraid I'd vanish.

My tears began to subside, and I turned around, encircled by Cillian's arms. My mouth met his.

This wasn't just a kiss—no, it was a reclamation. It was our souls meeting together again in a reunion that almost brought me to my knees. Cillian slipped his tongue into my mouth, claiming me hungrily with a desperation that reminded me of all we'd nearly lost.

I melted to his touch, to his hands on my hips, to his lips on mine. A deep, guttural groan escaped him, vibrating against my mouth, and I basked in the taste of him, the feel of his hard, muscular body against mine. In the safety I felt in this demon's presence, which was unparalleled.

His kiss offered a balm to my soul when I needed it the most, and the water washed away the rest of my grief, my terror, if only in the moment. Right now, all that existed was the two of us.

His firm grip on my hips kept me upright as I kissed him with everything I had in me, trying to convey the depths of how he'd changed me. How his love had transformed my entire life.

Cillian let out a low growl and nipped at my lower lip. He pulled back to tip his forehead against mine. "Beau, I almost lost you."

"I think that's my line," I responded. Water sluiced down our bodies, but I reveled in the heat and comfort it brought. "I can't imagine a future without you."

"You won't have to," he said. "But you're no longer a prisoner here. You're free to come and go as you please."

I swallowed hard. "Like Charles, Theo, and Amelia? I can still live here?"

He clutched my hips a little tighter. "You'll be lucky to escape this room most times, because I'm going to defile you daily. I want you with me, pet. In my bed, in my home, in my life."

"Can I still work as your personal assistant?" I asked, unsure what lay ahead with our situation shifting.

"Yes, thank fuck," he said, his fangs poking out with his grin. "I would never be able to find anyone as meticulous as you." He poured some bodywash into his hand and began to rub me down with it. I surrendered to his callused, competent palms, his care not to nick me with his claws.

"I will miss being a librarian, though," I said as I washed the suds off. "There's something addictive in being able to curate all that knowledge." I squeezed some bodywash into my own palm. "Your turn."

Cillian let me coat him in suds, and I took my time enjoying the glide over his massive pecs, his thick thighs. God, he was magnificent. And he was all mine.

He let out a low hum that vibrated through the air. "What if you still had those responsibilities?"

"I'm listening."

"The books I have...the collection continues to grow, and I need to expand it. I'm thinking one of the rooms down in the casino. While most are here to gamble, having a library here where anyone can come and spend some time reading would add to the draw of the Spires." The sheer tenderness in those golden eyes would unmake me.

My heart squeezed tight. "I love you, Cillian."

He brushed his thumb against my jawline. "And I love you, pet. You're the best thing that's ever walked into my casino, and I never want to let you go again. I don't think I'd survive."

"If I have any say in it, you won't have to." Gravity descended on me, a reminder we'd almost lost all this today.

"Let's get out of the shower," Cillian said as he reached over and turned the spray off. "Want to take a walk?"

My brows drew together as I stepped out of the tub, grabbing a towel to rub down. "Where are you thinking?"

"Just the garden," he said. "We'll catch it before nightfall."

"Sure." I headed over to his drawers and snagged a T-shirt and sweats I'd stowed in one of them. I'd started to accumulate clothes in there throughout the weeks spent in his bed. Even though I'd cleaned up and changed into new clothes, the bloodstains lingered in my mind, a slight tug at my psyche I couldn't escape.

Cillian threw on a Henley and slacks, then slipped on his shoes. He extended a hand. "Come on."

I slipped my hand into his, and we made quick strides down the hall.

Voices sounded from the dining hall, but we left them be. Tonight, we needed a moment together before we shared time with the others. Cillian had almost died. I hadn't been sure I'd ever make it back here.

I wanted to bask in what we'd salvaged, and what we had to look forward to in the future.

When we stepped onto the elevator, I leaned in against him. He wrapped an arm around my shoulders, and I sagged into his hold. Even after he'd been drained, he still radiated a strength that drew me in. I didn't think I'd ever get enough.

The elevator doors opened to the main floor, and we stepped out. While both of us were normally dressed in business attire, here, tonight, we were casual. We'd walked through brimstone and fire today.

Cillian rested his hand on my lower back and guided us through the floor. All the sounds of the machines and gamblers faded around me, my focus solely on our destination. I'd thought my father had a problem like many here, gambling his life away. That might have been forgivable.

However, no, he'd sold me out for opportunity. And that was far worse.

I concentrated on the heat of Cillian's palm on my back. How it spread through me. How he gave me respite when I needed it most.

We strode through the corridor leading to the gardens, and Cillian pushed the door open before guiding us outside.

The soothing sound of moving water greeted me first, followed by the perfume of the sweet flowers that still bloomed in these manicured gardens. My heart's heavy burden grew lighter for the first time today.

I would always remember my first visit here with Cillian, discovering a glimpse behind the mask. The first crack in my armor against him.

He led me to the same bench, and my heart careened all over again.

I sat down, and he joined me, wrapping an arm around my shoulders, and I leaned my head against him, nestled in the crook of his arm. The steady rise and fall of his breaths soothed me as much as the sparkling fountain in front of us catching the fading light.

"Thank you," Cillian murmured.

"For what?" My brows drew together.

"For saving me."

A deeper resonance dwelled in those words, and I understood at once. Because Cillian had been suffering under the same loneliness I had. The weight had grown heavier and deadlier by the day.

"You saved me too."

I interlaced my fingers through his and stared out at the horizon beyond. The golds and reds and magentas streaked across the sky in a magnificent display. A sweetness lingered in the air, intensified by the sharpness the burgeoning night brought. The light and darkness intersected here, like a liminal space where all was possible, where the rules no longer existed.

I soaked in the glory of the colors bursting across the sky, and the way the slight chill of the breeze contrasted with the heat radiating between Cillian and me. On the surface, we couldn't have been more different, and when I'd first arrived at the Spires, I never could've imagined falling for "The Beast" here.

Yet Cillian had integrity imprinted on his bones, and he cared, truly cared in a way I thought people had forgotten. He was the protector I'd always wished for when I was a kid, the one who'd swoop in and keep me safe. Yet he inspired me to stand strong in turn. To defend him with everything I had.

And I'd continue doing so for the rest of my life.

The sun might be setting on this day, but we had the rest of our lives to chase this beautiful dream together.

EPILOGUE

Haven Diner stood out amid the landscape of Peregrine City, its neon lights beckoning the wayward traveler.

A lifetime had passed since I'd first stumbled through the door in search of information about my father.

Now I arrived on the arm of the love of my life...as well as one of the monsters who'd helped Sofia establish the place. The more I learned about their organization, the more I loved Cillian for his involvement. The majority of his closest friends were involved in some way in keeping the vulnerable monsters in the city safe. In helping people get on their feet again. In using their resources to help all monsterkind advance forward.

They were so different from the Human First organizations that were prevalent outside of the cities, where hatred flourished. Last I'd heard, Damian had joined up with them, which didn't surprise me in the slightest. I was relieved not only to be far away from him but that I'd surrounded myself with better people, ones I admired.

"We're running late," Cillian said, quickening his pace.

"I'm fairly certain that was your fault," I commented, a wry grin rising to my lips. When we'd been getting ready, Cillian had bent me over, taken me until I screamed, and knotted me. I still felt the tingle from the rough way he'd ridden me, but I hadn't complained. Even if it had set us back in getting ready.

"Shush," he murmured as he guided us toward the entrance of Haven. The glass windows showcased a variety of customers inside, from all different walks of life. We were there to see Sofia and Gretel, as well as a few of our friends, in celebration. Months had passed since Cillian's curse had been lifted, but the case of Thorin's murder of my father had dragged out a bit.

However, the verdict was finally in. Guilty.

Thorin wouldn't be our problem any longer. Within days of signing the contract with Olivia, Cillian had contacted his lawyer and had it nullified. Olivia had no mojo left to use against Cillian, as the death curse wasn't something that could be repeated, and Amelia was already bringing the information Cillian had collected on Olivia and Henrik to the Council, the supernatural authorities. And none of Thorin's other lackeys had caused any more issues, even though that didn't stop Amelia, Charles, and Theo from remaining vigilant.

I stepped into the diner, and the rush of memories dizzied me for a moment. Of being petrified and talking to my father's contact. Of trying to protect a man who never deserved it. My gut churned at the realization that everything I'd done for him hadn't mattered in the end.

Yet it had led me to Cillian, so I couldn't regret it all.

A ruckus sounded to the right, and a smile rolled to my lips. Already I recognized some of the voices. The scent of cinnamon and allspice wafted through the place, adding to the warmth. One of the larger side booths was cram packed with people, and we were about to join them. Charles and Theo were squished on one side, Mal and Ursuline in the middle, and Amelia hung on the end with Gretel.

"Go. They'll make space," Sofia said, swooping up beside us. "You'll scare my customers away."

I snorted. "Like anyone here's going to be scared of a little noise."

She grinned at me and glanced between us. "I'm glad you found him, Cillian. You complement each other perfectly."

My throat tightened with emotion. She was too right. Even though push and pull still existed between us—times I reminded Cillian about manners or when we bickered—overall, we made each other better. And that was what I'd been searching for from a relationship my entire life. One where we learned and grew in each other's presence, like flowers slowly blooming toward the sun.

"Maury mentioned you owed him some information," Sofia said, her eyes twinkling. "He might be visiting the Spires soon to claim it."

My eyes widened, and Cillian passed me a look. However, I hadn't promised anything outside my capacity as a librarian, and that I'd happily employ. "We'll discuss it later," I said. "Nothing to worry about."

"Look who finally stopped fucking to show up," Charles called over, and I rolled my eyes. I'd long since gotten used to his level of crass, and I found it refreshing after spending the day in meetings with Cillian, dealing with the businessmen he had to navigate through.

"You're welcome," Cillian responded as he slid into the small space at the end of the booth and nudged at Charles's shoulder. "Make some space."

"Would a please kill you?" I asked as I lifted my brow.

"Pretty sure it would," Charles responded as he and Theo nudged over as much as possible. I sat down on the scrap of seat left, and

Cillian's arm wrapped around my shoulders as he drew me in close to him. I didn't protest the PDA at all. In fact, I reveled in it.

"You're out in public again," Mal said with a gasp, bringing his hand over his mouth. "I never thought I'd see the day."

"I'm also not getting stalked and harassed every time," Cillian said. "It didn't make excursions enjoyable."

"May Thorin Glass get everything karma has in store for him," Ursuline said, lifting their cup of coffee with one tentacle.

"Well put," Amelia said, her grin sharp and her gaze lethal. After learning a bit more about her, I'd come to understand she was truly the scariest thing in the Spires, and I had undying respect for the woman. Especially after she'd come to my rescue.

"What are you ordering?" Cillian asked me.

"Last time I came here I was so nervous I just choked down some coffee," I said, shaking my head. "Get me whatever you think is good."

"Right." Cillian didn't bother with the menu, and when Sofia slipped over with coffees for the both of us, he placed an order for roast beef sandwiches. I'd grown so used to eating and ordering at the Spires that I was a bit spoiled by Theo's meals.

"Riordan shit in the main hall again," Charles complained to me.

"Take that up with him." I shrugged. "I clean his litterbox on the daily."

"How you got him to agree to a cat is beyond me," Theo said. "Mr. Brooding for Breakfast never allowed pets before."

"My father never let me have a pet," Cillian said. "I just didn't see the purpose."

"And now he's smitten with Riordan," I teased. It was true, though. I hadn't even been the one to mention a cat to Cillian. He'd remembered an earlier conversation and brought it up, knowing I'd always wanted to get one.

Those little details, they proved his love with a steadfastness I'd craved. And I wouldn't stop falling for him either.

Every single day, I woke up and fell in love with him all over again.

His eyes met mine, a tenderness gleaming in the golden depths that soaked through me. I wasn't sure how I'd survived without him in my life before, but I couldn't any longer. Laughter came from Gretel and Amelia, and Charles began to bicker with Ursuline over the last game night. Their voices sounded all around me, filling me with a warmth and comfort I didn't think would ever be accessible.

Cillian's arm tightened around me, and I leaned in against him, basking in the safety his presence brought. I'd never be lonely again, and it was all thanks to him.

When I'd first come to the doors of the Spires, I'd believed my life was ending, when in truth it had only just begun. I'd thought Cillian was my captor, but he'd been the one to set me free.

And even if I lived a thousand lives, I'd choose him every time.

Afterword

Thank you for reading Beau and Cillian's book, the launch of the Monstrous Cravings series!

I'm so thrilled to finally get to write this series, and it's been a welcome return to paranormal romance, as well as an exciting start to stepping into monster romance terrain. Despite the differences though, the series ended up embracing my trademark trope of found family, and I've been thoroughly loving it. Plus, Beauty and the Beast is my favorite fairytale, so I had to start with it. While Beau falls for the Beast, one of the good guys in the fairytale, the rest of the series will feature our leads falling for the villains—and I'm so excited.

The next fairytale we're diving into is the Little Mermaid, and I'm so enthralled with this universe and how it's unfolding. Each book brings the monster community closer together, and I can't wait to see where we'll be further down the line. There are so many fairytales I want to play with, and a lot of the leads have already appeared in this first book.

Haven Diner is my latest favorite safe space, and this little band of found family rebels has my whole heart. I hope you fall in love with this world just as much as I have!

If you enjoyed the book, leave a review. Kind words are what us authors survive on, and I can tell you personally I treasure each and every one.

Have you checked out the start of the Monstrous Cravings series, the origin of Gretel and Sofia's relationship? Check out the Lure of the Witch for free!

Want the latest updates on my books? Best way is to join my reader group, Katherine McIntyre's Mayhem, or my newsletter!

ALSO BY

Ready for the next Monstrous Cravings book? The Little Mermaid
Retelling, the Beacon and the Brine, is coming...

**A desperate human dreamer. A sea monster bound by contract.
A forbidden romance that could set them free...or end in destruction.**

After one mistake too many, Eric's family is marrying him off.

Arielle Triton is his future bride-to-be, gorgeous, eligible, and from a
wealthy family with connections to New Atlantis...who also hides the
fact they're merfolk. Except there's no spark toward Arielle, none of
the soul-searing romance Eric dreamed of.

Yet, Ursuline, the serious cecalia who's their family lawyer? From the
moment he meets them, he's drowning in their sharp gaze, living for
their low chuckles, their dry wit. But Ursuline is bound to the Triton
family, just as Eric is bound to marry someone he doesn't love. And
as those feelings grow stronger for Ursuline, the tug-of-war between
duty and desire become unbearable.

As the truth behind the Triton family wealth surfaces, Eric can no longer ignore the weighted whispers or disappearances from the staff. However, learning too many secrets in the Triton household is deadly, and if he and Ursuline stand a chance of survival, he's clutching onto one hope.

Some contracts are destined to be broken.

ALSO BY

Want hurt/comfort romances featuring a geeky, queer found family?
Read across the rainbow with the Dungeons and Dating series!

Strength Check (Dungeons and Dating #1)
Wisdom Check (Dungeons and Dating #2)
Intelligence Check (Dungeons and Dating #3)
Constitution Check (Dungeons and Dating #4)
Dexterity Check (Dungeons and Dating #5)
Charisma Check (Dungeons and Dating #6)

Or if you want your hurt/comfort romances kinkier, check out the
Leather and Lattes series!

Immersion Play (Leather and Lattes #1)
Extraction Play (Leather and Lattes #2)
Percolation Play (Leather and Lattes #3)
Filtration Play (Leather and Lattes #4)
Concentration Play (Leather and Lattes #5)

ALSO BY

If you're looking for light kink, high heat, and low angst, dip your toes into my other universe...Hot Under the Collar, filled with geeks, bears, and blue collar workers.

Sweat Connection (Hot Under the Collar #1)
Hot Conduit (Hot Under the Collar #2)
Joint Penetration (Hot Under the Collar #3)

And if you enjoyed the folks in Hot Under the Collar, then you'll love the spinoff into Ollie's family with The Brannon Boys!

Heat Transfer (Brannon Boys #1)
Bond Strength (Brannon Boys #2)
Direct Nailing (Brannon Boys #3)

ABOUT THE AUTHOR

Katherine McIntyre is a feisty chick with a big attitude despite her short stature. She writes stories featuring snarky women, ragtag crews, and men with bad attitudes—high chance for a passionate speech thrown into the mix. As a genderqueer geek who's always stepped to her own beat, she's made it her mission to write stories that represent the broad spectrum of people out there. Easily distracted by cats and sugar.